TAKE THE SHOT

A PHILADELPHIA BULLDOGS NOVEL

DANICA FLYNN

Content Warning: This book deals with the death of a previous partner, past miscarriage of a character and infertility.

Take The Shot
Copyright © 2019 Danica Flynn

This is a work of fiction. Names, characters, businesses, places, events and incidents are either products of the author's imagination or used in a fictitious manner. Any resemblance to actual persons, living or dead, or actual events is purely coincidental.

All rights reserved.

No part of this publication may be reproduced in any form, or by any means, electronic or mechanical, including photocopying, recording, or any information browsing, storage, or retrieval system, without permission in writing from Danica Flynn.

ISBN: 978-1-7342012-1-5

Cover Photography: Halay Alex/Shutterstock
Cover Design: Emily's World of Design

Copy Editor: Melinda Utendorf

For my partner, J, thank you for always believing in me, even when I didn't.

CHAPTER ONE

DINAH

The bass thumped against the wall, shaking me from my concentration as I tried to write. As if on cue, my phone vibrated against my desk lighting up with 'Mom' across the screen. I silenced it, dodging yet another call from my mother wherein she tried to persuade me to go out on a date with another 'nice Italian boy from the old neighborhood.' See also: balding, divorced dads. Not that there was anything wrong with that, but I was only thirty and she kept trying to set me up with guys closer to my dad's age. My family meant well, but they just didn't understand what it was like to be a widow at my age. Or what it was like to endure a dangerous miscarriage that almost killed me.

Not that I'd ever told them that last part.

I put my headphones on and tried to drown out the sounds of my neighbors having another party. I didn't really mind the noise, it was a Friday night after all. I was always invited to their shindigs, but tonight I had to get some writing done. I stared at the screen blankly, trying to figure out how to dig myself out of this plot hole. Working a full-time job in marketing sucked when all I wanted to do was write my novels.

I cranked up the volume of my own music. I drummed my fingers on the tabletop as if it would will the words out of me. When I heard the thumping bass through the wall again, I knew tonight just wasn't my night. Not that I was going to blame the hockey players next door, this was on me.

I lived in a kind of swanky condo next door to two pasty Canadian hockey players for The Philadelphia Bulldogs. TJ was a lovable douche, but friendly enough. His roommate, Noah though, was a tall, lanky hottie with long hair who said 'eh' a lot. Even when I had a husband, I had to admit he was cute.

When Jason died suddenly in a car crash two years ago, Noah had sent flowers and came to the funeral. He handled all the hockey questions my dad and three older brothers threw at him, even though it had been wildly inappropriate. My family were loud-mouth Italians from South Philly, so it hadn't really been all that shocking that they razzed my friend, the hockey player, at the funeral for my husband.

The Mezzanettis did not give a single fuck about anything.

Like ever.

My phone buzzed on the desk and I tried not to smile when I saw it was from Noah. Speak of the devil.

NOAH: *Is the music too loud?*

I smiled at his question. He was such a good old Canadian boy. I could barely stand it. It definitely made it harder for me to not think about just banging one out with him, just one time. I couldn't do that, no matter how much I wanted to, that would have made things *too* complicated.

Plus, I was pretty sure he was just really nice because he was Canadian and was not into me like that. He was a sweetheart, and it wasn't like he ever had fantasies about me.

ME: *Kinda. I'm on deadline.*
NOAH: *Sorry. I'll ask them to turn it down.*
ME: *It's fine!*
NOAH: *Come over!*
ME: *What part of deadline, did you not understand?*
NOAH: *Please?*

A smile curled up onto my lips. I couldn't help it when it came to Noah. He may have been a total hockey hottie, but he was also my best friend. It was sweet that he cared enough to ask if the music was too loud. That was Noah, he always was putting others before himself. I think deep down I knew that it was one of the reasons I couldn't stop myself from fantasizing about what his big hands could do to me every time he smiled at me. Or how when he looked at me with amusement in his azure eyes it sent shivers all the way down my spine. Half the time, I didn't know how I kept my composure when I was around him. Maybe it was because I knew I was one hundred percent not his type. Besides, at the fresh age of twenty-two, he was a bit too young for me.

I couldn't focus tonight, but it was crunch time, and I was coming up on the deadline to get my first draft to my editor. It was fine, I would just spew garbage and fix it later. I turned up the volume on my music and poured out all my sorrows into my laptop. I still had a plot hole, but I didn't know what to do about it right now. I didn't think it was something I was going to resolve tonight. I had to look at this with fresh eyes, not eyes that were lingering on my phone.

I closed my laptop and proceeded to melt into my couch

listening to *My Morning Jacket*, even though it reminded me of Jason. And then I felt even guiltier for thinking of Jason and Noah within the same sentence.

My phone buzzed against my thigh. I rolled my eyes at TJ now hitting me up to come party with the dudebros.

TJ: *Girl, come over!*

ME: *On deadline!*

TJ: *Come over anyway! Noah would be happy to see you.*

ME: *He's SO not into me. I'm too old for either of you fuckers.*

TJ: *hahaha. Yeah...okay....*

ME: *What does that mean???*

TJ: *come over!!!!*

Ugh, TJ was insufferable. I loved that guy, but also I hated him because he saw right through me and he knew if things were different I was down to clown with his roommate. He had been encouraging it, and I didn't understand why.

I met my husband in college, and I never imagined being with anyone else. It also didn't mean I needed to be alone forever. I didn't exactly think fucking my next-door neighbor, no matter how cute he was, was a particularly good idea. Not that I hadn't thought about it, multiple times and when alcohol had been involved. That's how TJ found out that I had the hots for his best bud. We went out drinking together last year when Noah had been dating this pretty blonde. I had let it slip that I thought Noah was hot, and TJ had been holding it over my head since then.

It had been two years since Jason's death and since Noah found me passed out in the stairwell. Immediately he had jumped into action, took me to the hospital and probably saved my life. Then held me while I cried after the doctors told me that the scarring when they did the D & C meant it would be harder to bring another pregnancy to term. I never really wanted kids before, but learning that it was unlikely for me, straight gutted me for months.

I never told anyone about the miscarriage, so naturally everyone just assumed the dark depression I went into afterwards was solely because of my dead husband. That was only partly true. The only one who knew and kept my secret was Noah. Noah, the gentle giant who let me soak his t-shirt while he stroked my hair and told me everything was going to be okay. Even when I felt pretty fucking far from okay.

Noah was a good friend. The kind who held my hand while I cried myself to sleep in that hospital bed. The kind who missed a practice and got benched for a couple games, because he cared more about his friend than playing a fucking hockey game. Even if it could have cost him his career. Which was why nothing could ever happen between us. I couldn't bear to lose his friendship.

I was trying to make a decision on if I should attempt to figure out my plot hole some more, or if I should go next-door, when my phone buzzed again. This time it was my oldest brother Frankie.

FRANKIE: *Can you please just tell Ma you're okay?*

I groaned and typed away back to him.

ME: *I'm FINE! Just tired of her trying to set me up with old men.*

FRANKIE: *Sorry, Dee-Dee.*

FRANKIE: *I'd tell her to back off, but you know how she is.*

ME: *I thought it would get BETTER when her and Dad moved to Florida.*

FRANKIE: *You're cute!*

I groaned again. I loved my family, but they could be

nosy as fuck. And blunt as shit. Two days, TWO WHOLE DAYS, after Jason was in the ground, my mom started asking if I was seeing anyone. Like, lady, let me mourn a bit! Of course it was because my mom was expecting grandchildren. Even though she already had one from Frankie and his wife, and honestly my meathead brother Tony probably had some running around he didn't know about. I didn't have the heart to tell her that I couldn't have kids. I wasn't ready to pour a pound of salt into that wound.

I sighed, and dropped my phone back onto the couch. Now I was frustrated, and I really needed a drink. I urged my body off the couch and decided to say fuck it and go next-door. Maybe the shitty beer TJ drank would mellow me out.

TJ opened the door and screeched mere seconds after I had knocked, "You came!"

I laughed when he bent down to my five-foot-two frame and laid a sloppy drunken kiss on my cheek. A lovable douche indeed. He must have been really into it tonight, because if there was one thing I discovered about the Desjardins, it was that they could put it away. His twin sister was somehow worse, if that could be believed. His pale face was red from all the beer and his short cropped dark hair was hidden by his backwards baseball cap. What was it with hockey boys and wearing hats backwards?

"Not in two years," I joked.

TJ broke out into a hyena laugh, that I was concerned he was going to fall on the floor and start rolling around on it. He wiped the tears from his eyes. "Seriously?"

"Seriously," I deadpanned.

"What about that guy last month you met at one of our games?"

I rolled my eyes. The last Bulldogs game I went to, I

ended up chatting up the guy next to me. He was nice enough, and I figured it was time to get back on the horse. It was the wrong horse. Like so bad, I had to tell him to stop before we even had sex. I came over here after he left, laid on the floor in their living room and asked Noah to put me out of my misery.

I put my hands over my face in mortification. "Please don't remind me."

TJ handed me a beer. "Come on girl, we need to find you a man soon!"

I scoffed at him but took the beer.

TJ was smirking at me now. "I think I know one perfect for you."

My eyes slid over to Noah sitting on their couch with a beer in hand. "T, he's not into me. Plus, the age difference would be weird."

"We're not *that* young! What's eight years? That's nothing!"

CHAPTER TWO

NOAH

I sat staring at my phone wondering if Dinah was going to text me back, but she was on deadline for her next book, so I knew she wouldn't. She wouldn't let me read this one yet, even though I told her I really liked the first one. She had been surprised that a dumb jock like me wanted to read a cute romance story. Like men didn't want to have a happy ending too or some other bullshit. I ran a hand through my shaggy hair and took a long sip of my beer.

TJ slumped on the couch beside me. He glanced at my phone in my hand and rolled his eyes. "Dude, are you still pining?" he asked with a groan.

I shoved my phone in my pocket. "What?" I played dumb and took another huge gulp of my beer.

TJ raised a black eyebrow at me. "Come on, D has no idea you're into her. You got to tell her."

I shook my head.

I guess my subtle ways of telling Dinah I was interested hadn't really worked. TJ was my teammate, roommate, and good bud, but Dinah was the first person in my life that I thought was my best friend. The first woman who looked at me not as Noah the hockey player, but Noah the person. When we first moved here, I was heartbroken when I found out she had a husband. Then he died tragically and she broke apart. I had sent her flowers, and tried to be a good friend to her. I even endured her insane family who instead of consoling their daughter and sister, told me to stop turning over the puck so much. Philly fans were something else.

She would only ever see me as her good bud and kid brother. Definitely not someone that she would ever wrap her arms or even her legs around if I was being honest with my fantasies.

TJ cocked a grin. "If she comes over, you have to finally make a move. You're both single, it's time, bro!"

I chewed my bottom lip.

TJ nudged me when he heard a knock on the door. He jumped up and answered it, before I could argue with him further.

He greeted Dinah with a wet sloppy kiss on the cheek. A stab of jealousy struck through my heart at the sight of it. She laughed at him and walked to the kitchen island in our open-concept condo and struck up a conversation with our teammate Benny. Which was hilarious because Benny at six-foot-four and her at five-foot-two, looked like the opposite ends of the height extremes in the room. I chugged more of my beer and amped myself up. This was it, I had to finally make a move on her, if not, she would never know and I would regret it for the rest of my life.

Probably.

Dinah was sitting on our kitchen counter, drink in hand and laughing hard at whatever TJ and our other teammate

Hallsy was saying to her. Benny was no longer hanging in the kitchen, which I was kind of grateful.

Women loved Benny, and he was the kind of guy women could seriously fall in love with. He was a good guy, not the asshole playboy the media tried to paint him as. Ever since some racist-ass gossip columnist painted him as the "Latin Lover" he had developed a reputation as a playboy. One that couldn't be further from the truth, especially since he was the only player I knew that didn't do one-night stands. Like ever. Being a pasty white guy from Winnipeg, I was never going to understand what my teammates, Hallsy, Mac, and Benny went through being players of color, but I knew there needed to be a culture change in our sport. Especially after shit like that got published in the media about one of my best buds.

Hallsy's girlfriend Mia was just shaking her head at all of them. Dinah looked up at me when I walked in, and I mean really looked up, because with my six-foot-two frame I tended to dominate every room I walked into. Her dark brown hair was pulled up into a messy bun, and she wore black leggings and an old-school Patrick O'Sullivan jersey.

Uh oh, she must have writer's block if she finally came over tonight. She should have looked sloppy, but she looked comfortable, at home, and gorgeous as hell. I shouldn't have been into it, but I so was.

She smiled at me, her green eyes looked like they sparkled underneath the lights of our kitchen. Damnit, I didn't think I could tell her how I felt now. I finished my beer and took another out of the fridge, getting a second one for her. She laughed when I handed it to her and I bent over to hug her in greeting.

"Hey," I whispered into her ear, trying to be all calm and cool. When really I was a ball of nerves.

She wrapped her small arms around my back as I hunched over to meet her small frame. "Hey," she said back.

I pulled away and TJ was making this annoyed face at me. It wasn't like I was going to make a move on her with everyone standing around watching. Mia was looking between me and Dinah carefully, and cocked her blonde head in question. I ignored it.

"What's so funny?" I asked, trying to cut the tension in the room.

TJ's eyes sparkled and I knew I was in trouble. "I asked D for relationship advice."

A smile tugged at my lips. When we became friends, I had complained to her that girls were so complicated, but she explained it was pretty simple. I thought about her answer a lot. A LOT. Also maybe when I was horny and in the shower too. And maybe she was the star in those images I conjured in my head.

"Yeah? What's that?" I asked, nervously pushing my brown hair behind my ear.

I turned to Dinah and she was chugging her new beer to keep from repeating it.

"Come on, tell him!" TJ egged on.

She gave him the finger, but sighed. "It's really simple. Don't cheat, eat pussy."

Mia laughed a little too loudly. She cocked her head and eyed Hallsy. "You know, she's not wrong!"

I laughed too, but it was that nervous laughter when I didn't want people to notice that I was blushing so hard. Hearing that word out of her lips made me think things I didn't want to. Things that made my cock thicken against my leg. It made me imagine what it would be like to have my face in-between her thighs giving her what she wanted. You weren't supposed to think about your best friend that way. I felt a tightening in my pants, and shifted position to lean up against the fridge and hoped no one noticed. TJ was giving me the eye and nodded his head over at Dinah.

Mia was laughing a little too hard and Hallsy was shaking with laughter, his black corkscrew coiled hair bouncing around at the motion. I must have missed it. Dinah was laughing again.

"That's it! It's really not that hard. Just give her what she wants." She took a sip of her beer again.

"That can't be it," TJ scoffed.

She sighed at him. "Or just go read a romance book and figure it out yourself."

"A romance book?" Hallsy asked. He stroked his dark-skinned hand across his clean-shaven face as if in thought. His dark brown eyes twinkled with mirth at the thought.

Mia and Dinah shared a look. "Yes, because women always get what they want in romance books," Dinah explained.

"And what's that?" Hallsy asked.

"For you to touch her clit or eat her out!" Dinah exclaimed with another laugh.

TJ roared with laughter. He pointed at her. "Come on, you up for beer pong? Riley wants a rematch."

She shook her head. "Nah. You know I'm bad at it."

TJ grinned at her. "That's why I wanted you to play on Riley's team."

She laughed some more. "It's not like he isn't going to team up with Benny. Man, their bromance is ridiculous."

Hallsy had his arm around Mia, but he nodded to TJ. "We'll play." Hallsy and TJ shared a look, and Mia smiled at me. Oh no, I think they were all making an excuse to go back into the other room with the rest of the party to leave me alone with her. Seeing her here now, I wasn't sure I could make the move.

They all filtered out of the room and Mia gave me a thumbs up. I internally groaned, was I so obvious to everyone? Except to the person who mattered?

I moved closer to Dinah, but she was staring into space now. I called this her 'story plotting' face, and I had a feeling that was what she was calculating in her head right now. Her talent to pull characters and stories from out of her imagination always astounded me. Riley said he had a friend from back home in St. Paul, who was also a writer, and he asked her once how she came up with it. She had just shrugged and said, "It's a gift." I knew it was the same thing for the small woman in front of me, who was spacing out and not paying attention to the heated gaze I was throwing at her.

"Hey," I nudged her with my shoulder. "You finish it yet?"

She pulled away from whatever dream-like state she had been in and looked up at me with a smile and twinkle in her green eyes. "Yeah...but I don't think it's ready yet. I think I have a plot hole."

I put a hand on her leg and squeezed her knee. She giggled, I knew she was ticklish there. God her laugh was like music to my ears. "Can I read it?" I begged.

She shook her head. "It's a kissing book!"

I laughed and pushed my hair behind my ear again. "So? I read your first book, I liked it."

She gave me a quizzical look. "Really? You did?" she asked in a small voice.

I had definitely told her this already, but maybe she didn't believe me the first time.

My hand roamed up her thigh, resting on her waist

while my thumb absent-mindedly stroked across her hipbone. She had to know I was trying to make a move, but she wasn't trying to stop me.

Why wasn't she trying to stop me?

"Yeah, it was really good. You really know how to write a good love story," I complimented her and it wasn't a lie.

She put her hands over her face and looked at me in-between her fingers, but didn't try to move my hand away. I kind of wondered if she noticed it at all. I moved so I was standing directly in front of her now, my legs squeezing in-between her spread thighs. I just wanted to scoop her up in my arms and take her to my bedroom, but I never would have done that without her consent. I wanted her to want me. I wanted to see her tipping back her head and moaning my name in pleasure, but I wanted it to happen because *she* wanted it to happen. Because she *wanted* me.

"You really liked it?" she asked again and pulled her hands away from her face.

I grinned at her. "Yes! Is this one about the best friend in the first one?"

She nodded. "He's the love interest in this one, it's about another girl." She stared up at me for a moment and then she sat up straighter. "Oh my god!"

"What?" I asked.

She pushed me away and hopped down from off the counter. "I figured it out! I need to go fix something."

"You just got here," I whined.

She frowned. "Sorry, I'm chained to the muse! Give me like an hour and I'll be back. Or just come over and get me. Okay?"

I smiled and nodded. I hunched down to hug her again and then she was off. I chugged the rest of my beer. I didn't think I was ever going to be able to make a move on her.

God, I wanted her to see me as an object of her desire, but she was always going to see me as just a friend. I didn't believe in that crap about the Friend Zone. I mean, yeah I guess it existed, but women didn't owe you anything just because you were nice to them.

When I looked up, TJ was standing in the kitchen. He had a frown on his face. "Dude, did you just blow it?"

I shrugged. "I don't know yet."

TJ groaned at me. "You're hopeless! I love you man, but you either ask her out or you move on. I know something happened between you two already."

Oh.

No.

After Dinah's husband died, she was a wreck, and I tried to be a shoulder for her to cry on. I tried to be there for her as a friend. Then one night I came home early, while TJ went home with some girl he met at the bar, and I found her in the stairwell passed out. I ended up taking her to the hospital. I missed practice the next morning, because making sure my friend was okay when she needed me was more important than playing some game. I ended up getting benched a couple games, but I never told anyone what happened.

I had held her in my arms that night and let her cry onto my t-shirt over the baby she had lost. My heart snapped in half for all the bad luck she had to endure that year. I've never known the loss of a partner or a child, but I do know how my heart wrenched in my chest when I saw the pain and anguish etched across the face of my friend.

Riley and Benny walked into the kitchen with grins on their faces. "Was that the girl that you got benched a few games for?" Benny asked with a huge grin across his face.

"You're still not hitting it?" Riley asked. He ran a hand through his blonde hair in frustration.

TJ laughed and pulled out a bottle of vodka to pour us shots. I glared at Riley. I didn't like him talking about her like that. Like she was some conquest and not a person with thoughts and feelings of her own. None of those jerks deserved her, and none of them understood that woman like I did.

"It wasn't like that," I said through gritted teeth, balling my hands into fists.

Benny's grin faltered when he saw my expression. His dark brown eyes bored into me with a question, but I wasn't biting.

"Then what happened? Why did you miss that practice?" TJ asked.

"Did she tell you?" I asked.

He shrugged. "She just said that you helped her with something."

He handed me a shot glass and the four of us knocked one back together. "Then, it's not my secret to tell."

Riley asked me cautiously, "So you won't care if I ask her out?"

I nearly choked on air. "What?"

TJ pointed at me. "If you don't make a move on her soon, Riley's gonna ask her out."

I poured myself another shot and clinked glasses with Benny who had gotten awfully quiet. He gave me a small sad smile of pity. I guess Benny knew all about unrequited love. He was practically in love with TJ's sister. Too bad she hated his guts.

CHAPTER THREE

DINAH

Noah was going to kiss me. Noah, my cute neighbor, had been trying to put the moves on me. Maybe he was just drunk. He was kind of cuddly when he was drunk. There have been a couple times when we have gotten loaded at his place and he ended up with his arm around me, clutching me to his side. I had never minded or protested, because it felt good to be held by Noah, even if it was just as friends. I sat there sitting on top of his kitchen counter while his hand slid up my thigh. Of course then I figured out what I needed to change in my book. Thanks, Muse, for being such a cockblock. I've been burned in the past by The Muse, so I knew I couldn't let it go and I had to go back to writing or I'd lose it for good.

I sat down at my keyboard, and my fingers flew across the keys as the words poured out of my head. I finally felt good about this book, like all the words were clicking together in my head. Satisfied, I sent it over to my editor and closed my laptop. I finished the beer Noah had given me and started on another one from my own supply when I heard the knock on my door.

I glanced at the clock, it was already midnight, maybe I should have gone to sleep, but I wanted to look Noah in the eyes again and see if what I saw next-door was true. That he wanted me. That he saw me as more than just a friend.

"Come in," I called.

He opened the door, the top of his large frame nearly hitting the doorway. He pointedly locked my front door and glared at me. "You really should lock your door."

I shrugged and walked into my living room to hand him a cold beer. He took it from my hands and I said, "I knew it was you."

He shook his head at me, cracked open the beer, and took a sip. "I just worry."

I rolled my eyes. "Oh, honey, I'm a big girl."

I slunk down on my couch and he joined me, lifting my feet up and letting me rest them across his lap. We always felt comfortable with each other, but the way he was looking at me made my breath hitch in my throat. Had he always looked at me that way? Or was I just imagining it?

I cleared my throat. "Hey! You never told me about your date with Ashley!"

He groaned and took a huge chug of beer.

I laughed. "Oh, honey!"

He ran a hand through his longish brown hair and gave me a grimace.

"Was it that bad?" I asked.

"I felt like she just saw dollar signs in my eyes when she looked at me," he confessed with a sigh.

"Aw, Noah. I'm sorry!"

And I really was. It was no secret that Noah made lot of money. Hell, I only lived in this fancy condo because Jason had a trust fund from his grandmother that we found out about when she died. If the condo wasn't paid for already, I probably wouldn't have lived here. Some people lived to chase the fame and fortune that came with pro-athletes. Noah was a sensitive guy and I knew it got to him that a lot of girls he went out with didn't really *see* him for who he was. The ones who did, ended up not being able to handle having a boyfriend who was on the road for most of the year.

He smiled at me and it went to his eyes making his blue eyes twinkle. I looked down and drank some more of my beer. I shouldn't have been thinking about Noah like this. Then again, earlier, when his hand had been roaming up my leg, it felt like tiny fires were licking across my skin. It had left me anticipating for more and wondering if his hands would dare wander elsewhere. Like the juncture of my thighs, and maybe his tongue would wander there too.

"Why are you blushing?" he asked amused.

"Nothing! What? I'm not blushing! It's the beer."

He smirked at me. "Are you okay?"

I nodded. "Fine." I heard cheering from next door. "Did you want to go back over?"

He shook his head. "Nah. Sometimes TJ and the boys are too much. Unless you want to?"

I sighed in relief, because I was so tired. Figuring out my book had taken this weight off my shoulders, but now I was just exhausted. So we talked instead for a little, him filling me in on their latest road stretch, even though I watched every game I could. Then he started begging me to let him read my book.

"It's too early!" I protested.

"Come on," he whined and gave me that pouty puppy dog face. Ugh, he was too cute. "Let me read it."

"Fine," I huffed.

I must have been imagining it earlier, because now we just felt back to normal. Just Noah and Dinah, two friends low-key hanging out on a Friday night.

"You look tired," he observed.

"I am," I agreed. "Should you head to bed?"

"Are you kicking me out?"

"No!" I protested. "I just thought you had a game tomorrow."

"Yeah, but it's later. Will you come?"

I cocked an eyebrow at him. "You want me to come?"

"I always want you to come."

I barked out a long laugh, and his pale face turned beet red. "I didn't mean it like that!" he explained but put a hand on his face and laughed behind it.

I leaned back on the couch and watched him squirm in embarrassment. Why did he have to be so cute when he was embarrassed? "Noah, I'm sorry, but you know what it sounded like," I said in-between laughs. I rolled my shoulder trying to get a knot out of it.

He must have noticed, because he pushed my legs off his lap. "C'mere," he said in this husky voice I had never heard him use before. I felt a tightening in my lower stomach.

"What?" I choked out.

He sat up and pulled me over to him, so my back was against his chest and I was sitting in between his legs. His big hands rubbed over my tense shoulders and up my neck. My heart kept thinking, *go lower*, but I tried to shake it off. "You're really tense," he whispered in my ear.

His breath was hot in my ear, and I felt a shiver run down my spine. A moan escaped my lips involuntarily as he rubbed the tension out of me. "Why are you so tense?" he asked.

I sighed. "Work on top of working on this book is super stressful."

His hands continued to get the knots out of my back. How did he know how to do this? "Is this okay?" he asked and ever so gently placed a kiss on my neck.

HOLY FUCKING SHIT.

That...

No...

No way!

"Y-yes..." I stammered and bit my lip to keep another moan from escaping.

Seriously if that was his move, it was a damn good one. His big meaty hands kneading the knots in my back was putting my feelings into overdrive. His hands worked me over, while his lips pressed feather-light kisses across the skin where my neck and shoulder met. I was afraid if I closed my eyes I was going to wake up from this dream.

I leaned back against him, and he wrapped his arms around my waist. He didn't kiss me again, so I was unsure if it had actually happened or if I had just imagined it. I was really tired, and his strong arms wrapped around me made me relax. I was really tense and stressed out, and him rubbing my shoulders made me melt.

We ended up lying on my couch together for a bit with his chest pressed up against my back and his face nuzzling my neck. I still wasn't quite sure what was happening. Noah did get really cuddly when he was drunk, maybe that was all this was. When I felt Noah's breathing get steady, I slipped out of his arms and went into my bedroom. Had that really happened? My hand touched the spot on my neck where he had kissed me, and I felt like I was on fire. I needed to get a shower and scrub the dirty thoughts in my head away.

I changed into pajamas after my shower and towel-dried my hair. I glanced at the clock, it was really late, but I planned on doing nothing but working on outlining book number three tomorrow, so it was fine. I always had a hard time sleeping, it was kind of why I became a writer. When I couldn't sleep, I wrote my stories. I sat on my bed and was startled when I heard footsteps in the other room. A dark, tall shadow came over the door, and I jumped at it, until Noah's form stepped over the threshold into my bedroom.

He had a sheepish look on his face and he pushed his hair behind his ear. He always did that when he was nervous. Why was he nervous? It was just me. "Sorry," he said when he saw me jump.

I rolled my eyes. "You Canadians and your apologizing."

He grinned, but when we locked eyes, I knew then that what had happened earlier had not been my imagination. He sat on the bed beside me, and his hand cupped the back of my head. I froze at his touch and his eyes scanned my face questioningly. "Is this okay?" he asked.

"Noah..." I trailed off dreamily.

"Yeah?" he whispered in a small voice.

"Noah...just fucking kiss me already."

He laughed and leaned over to actually listen to me for once. He pressed his lips to mine, soft at first, ghosting across mine as if he was afraid to push too hard. His hand gripped the back of my neck, and I was melting into his gentle caresses. His tongue slid over my bottom lip, and I opened to him. Letting him explore that part of me I had kept locked away for so long. His kisses matched his personality — gentle and kind. When he pulled away it felt like a moment too soon, and I saw that my hands were gripping the front of his shirt hard trying to pull him towards me down onto my bed. His eyes shot up in surprise, and I gingerly pulled away and looked down at the floor.

His finger gently lifted my chin up to look him in the eye. "Was that...okay?"

Oh my god, he was too freaking cute.

"Was it okay?" I asked confused. "The kiss?"

"That I did that."

"Oh honey, yes..." I whispered huskily.

He grinned at me, and I think it was the biggest smile I had ever seen him wear. I wanted to make him feel that way all the time. To have that badge of honor that I was the reason his eyes twinkled brightly when he smiled.

"It's late, you should probably get to bed," he commented.

"Uh huh," I agreed, but I was little drunk off his kisses and not really paying attention. I also was trying to see if he was going to kiss me again. Couldn't he tell that I wanted him to kiss me like that all tender and tentative again? And then rip all my clothes off? Why weren't we naked yet?

"D?" he asked.

"Hmm?"

"You okay?"

I nodded. "Fine. Just tired."

"You should get some sleep."

I shrugged. "I don't really sleep."

"Since when?" he asked.

"Forever? I've never been a good sleeper. You probably want to go back to your own bed, you've got a game tomorrow."

He nodded and he bit his nail. "Come on girl, let's get you to bed."

I laughed. "Are you going to tuck me in or something?"

He pulled back the comforter and did exactly that, but then he got in next to me. He wrapped his arm around me from behind and stroked my hair. My back pressed against his chest as he held me close against his long frame. It felt good to be held, but I was still half convinced that I was dreaming. There was no way that Noah freaking Kennedy, superstar hockey player, had kissed me tonight and was now in my bed not trying to have sex with me.

Why wasn't he trying to have sex with me?

I would have shed my clothes and let him have me any way he desired. I would have unraveled myself and let my guard down for this man who knew all my secrets. I would have let him break me down if he just pressed his gentle lips to mine again. But this was Noah, and instead his hands stroked my hair soothingly until I drifted off to sleep.

CHAPTER FOUR

NOAH

I had psyched myself up so much over that kiss, that I couldn't bring myself to go any further than that. I couldn't believe Dinah had kissed me back. She hadn't pulled away or said, 'Oh, honey...' in that condescending tone that I secretly loved. She had kissed me back, hungrily, like she wanted me to rip her clothes off and make all my fantasies come true. But we had both been drinking, and if she really wanted to cross that line with me, I wanted her to be sure about it.

It was super late, but I stayed with her until I heard the soft pattern of her breathing. Of course I finally made a move right before a road trip. I wasn't sure I would even get to talk to her and tell her how I really felt for another week. God, was I an idiot for doing that? Her kisses were demanding and hungry, but the rational part of my brain couldn't give myself over to that yet. Not like this.

I slid out of bed and planted a kiss on her forehead before letting myself out and back to my own condo next-door. I had a key to her place, so I made sure it was locked before I left. I slunk into my room, hoping to avoid TJ, who luckily was passed out already. I collapsed onto my own bed, and noticed I was still harboring a stiffy. Dinah Lace was going to be the death of me. But despite the uncomfortable hardness in my pants, I fell asleep with a smile on my face.

"You coming to morning skate or what?" I heard TJ yelling what must have been two hours later.

I bolted out of bed with a start. "Shit! I forgot to set my alarm."

TJ rolled his eyes at me. "Come on, let's go, I'll drive over. It's game day."

I rushed around getting dressed for morning skate.

In the car TJ was smirking at me. I side-eyed him. "What?"

"I noticed someone didn't come home last night," he said in a sing-song voice.

"I did, it was just really late."

TJ got into the exit lane to get us to the arena in South Philly. "Uh huh," was his unconvinced reply.

"TJ," I warned.

"Did you finally get it in?"

"What? No!"

He looked hurt. "Did you at least tell her how you feel?"

"She knows."

"How does she know?"

I studied my nails. "I don't kiss and tell!"

"But you didn't take her to Bone Town?"

I scoffed at him, "No."

"Buddy! You really like her, don't you?"

"Yeah, I do. I don't—it's D, you know?"

He punched me in the arm. "Oh man, you're like in a

puddle on the floor right now. That girl's gonna be the death of you."

He laughed and he parked the car at the arena. He shook his head at me while we walked into the arena and to the dressing room. I knew he would not stop razzing me about this. I got dressed for morning skate, and texted one of the sales people asking if I could get an extra ticket for tonight. The cute blonde who used to be an intern, Maxine, could probably help me out. I still wanted Dinah to come to the game, even if we were hopping on a plane for Detroit right after. Maxine came in clutch and hooked me up with an extra ticket, so I texted Dinah. Max was cool like that, she was quiet and reserved, but was always willing to help out.

ME: *Come to the game tonight?*
DINAH: *You want me to?*
ME: *YESSSS!!!*
DINAH: *Ok.*

I felt a towel hit me in the face and I looked up from my phone to see TJ and Riley looking at me with grins on their faces. "Did you ask her out?" Riley asked. "If you don't, I will. That wasn't an empty threat."

I shook my head. "You're not her type."

Riley cocked a blond eyebrow. "What do you mean?"

I pulled the practice jersey over my head and laced up my skates. "She doesn't like fuckboys."

TJ, Benny, and Hallsy all roared with laughter. Our captain, Girard looked at me curiously. "Who are you talking about?" he asked.

Marc-Andre Girard was the blonde-haired French-Canadian who had been on this team for the past eight years. When the last captain had a career-ending injury, the organization gave him the "C". He was a good guy, and a good player, but sometimes I wondered if he actually liked me. Dinah should have been interested in a guy like him, around her age, and not a young kid like me.

TJ nudged me in the ribs, but when I didn't say he explained, "You remember our neighbor, D?"

"Your neighbor whose husband died? The one you missed a practice for?" he asked.

They were never going to let me live that down. My fist clenched as I stood up to get out on the ice and to end this conversation. "That's the one," was all I would admit to.

Girard narrowed his eyes. "Why *did* you miss that practice?"

"Not that it's any of your business," I started and stared pointedly at TJ. I guess I might as well tell everyone so they would get off my back. I just hoped Dinah would forgive me for telling them her secret. "I had to take her to the hospital, she almost died."

TJ's face fell. "Wait, what? Dude, you never told me that."

I put on my helmet and skated off on the ice to start in on the shooting drills. TJ and Riley shared a look of concern, but I had my head down and was focusing on running through plays. I had to compartmentalize so I could play well in tonight's game. Even though my heart kept on thrumming thinking about Dinah.

TJ skated up beside me and started shooting drills with me. "Kens, why didn't you tell me?"

I shook my head. "Not my secret to tell."

He scratched his face underneath his eye shield. "You know, she begged me for coach's number so she could explain. That's why he put you back in the lineup."

"She did?"

He nodded. "You two are both hopeless. So how did she almost die?"

I shook my head.

"Will you just tell me? I won't say anything."

I wristed a puck into the net, and tried to ignore him. TJ was a scrapper on the ice, so he knew how to get into someone's head to be a nuisance. It was great for our opponents, not so great if he was your friend.

"She had a miscarriage," I finally said. "Don't tell anyone I told you."

His eyes were wide with shock. "What? Her husband's?"

I pointed a finger in his face. "Not a word, T!"

He held up his hands. "No, obviously. Fuck, losing her husband and then her baby...fuck, that must have been hard on her."

I nodded. There were many nights when I wasn't off playing hockey that I was her shoulder to cry on or her friend to talk to.

"Is that why it's taken you two years to finally make a move on her?"

I nodded again sadly.

What was I going to do, swoop in after her husband died and ask her out? That was just low. She had been hurting and then to find out she had a part of him with her, but it all went to shit? I couldn't have done that to her. I was the good friend and the shoulder to cry on. I just didn't want to be that anymore, and I hoped she figured that out by now. Last night, she had demanded I kiss her, and then she kissed me back hungrily, like she wanted more. Like she wanted the thing I had fantasied about for so long. That had to count for something. I wasn't a complete idiot by finally making a move. Right?

TJ thumped me on the back. "You're a better man than me. That's probably why she likes you."

I smirked at him. "You're everyone's annoying kid brother."

"Hey now!"

"Even to your sister and you guys are twins!"

I laughed and skated off away from him over to the bench to take a drink of water. Girard skated over to me. "Hey," he said.

"Hey, Cap. What's up?" I asked.

He eyed me cautiously. "Coach told me what actually happened, said your girl called him. That's rough. You know me and Brianna, we went through that."

I paused. Brianna was Girard's wife and she had recently gone through losing a child.

He shrugged. "Anyway, good on you for helping her out."

"She's my best friend, I had to help her."

He nodded. "Look, the age difference between you will be complicated, but if you really like this girl you should go for it."

I looked at him surprised. "Oh…okay."

He clapped me on the back. "Plus, she doesn't basically suck your dick like all the other girls you've dated, so I like her."

He smirked and skated off. Still had no idea if that guy actually liked me or not.

❄

I hadn't been sure if Dinah was actually going to come to the game. Dinah was a hardcore fan of the team. She was Philly born and raised. She usually watched, and would buy her own ticket if she wanted to come to the game. She didn't like the idea of me paying for her to come to the game. I was more than surprised when she caved tonight.

When I stepped out on the ice for warm-ups, I was in the zone. Unfortunately, in the first period we played like absolute garbage. It didn't help that I got pretty much boarded right in the numbers. My head had been throbbing, but I seemed okay. Daniels, the guy who did it was a pretty good dude, but all bets were off when you skated out onto the ice. He got a five-minute penalty, even though the team was calling for him to get kicked out. I seemed okay, but I took a bit to get up onto my skates and I hunched over with my stick on my knees. TJ helped me skate over to the bench so the doctors could get a look at me.

"Kennedy, you okay?" Coach LaVoie asked when I returned to the bench. Coach had trouble with concussions back in his day, so he was super conscious about any signs of head injuries.

I nodded, but I wasn't sure if I really was or not.

The first period had been a shit-show. We barely got any shots on goal, and the other team already had two goals. Coach tore us a new asshole during the intermission. I didn't normally check my phone during games because it distracted me, but I wanted to know if Dinah came. There were a couple texts from her.

DINAH: *FINE, I came.*

DINAH: *You're playing like garbage, you fuck.*

DINAH: *Am I not allowed to say that to you now?*

DINAH: *NOAH! Is your head okay?!?*

DINAH: *That was such fucking bullshit, rep missed a few calls there.*

DINAH: *OMG, I just realized I am very annoying with these texts. SORRY!*

I couldn't help the smile from creeping up on my lips. Benny leaned over to see what I was looking at. "Is that really what gets you going? 'You're playing like garbage, you fuck'?" he asked with a laugh. "If so, you should really talk to TJ's sister, because that girl HATES me!"

I shoved my phone back into my cubby. "Rox hates you because you asked her if her tits were fake. Who does that?"

Benny frowned at me. "I said I was sorry! I didn't mean to blurt out what I was thinking!"

TJ was snickering. "She's never going to forgive you. Also, stop staring at my sister's tits! Gross!"

"I can't help it if your sister's hot!" Benny argued.

"Dude!" TJ whined. "Off-limits."

Benny scoffed. "Yeah, that's never gonna happen."

I ignored their bickering and thought about Dinah's texts. She was right, we were playing like garbage. Now I was just kicking myself that I would be on the road for the next week, and wouldn't get to see her or really talk about what happened last night.

CHAPTER FIVE

DINAH

"Hey..." Brianna Girard trailed off looking pointedly at my phone. I stopped texting Noah like the annoying hockey fan I was, and turned to her.

"What's up?" I asked.

"You and Noah, how did that happen?" she asked.

I bit my lip. "Um, we're just friends."

She laughed. "What do you mean? You rarely come to games and when you do, you don't sit with the rest of us. Something definitely happened."

The boys were coming back on the ice, so I pretended to watch the starting line-up on the ice. Number 13, Kennedy was back on the ice. He seemed okay, but that check into the boards had been ROUGH. That was a bad boarding call, and I couldn't believe Daniels wasn't ejected from the game for it. Hitting a guy in the numbers was a big no-no in hockey. I was really worried about Noah's head. I lived through the bad concussions that the current head coach Claude LaVoie went through. It had been a bad era in hockey. Not that today was any better, concussions in this sport I loved were still really bad. I couldn't help wondering if Noah was just doing that tough hockey guy thing and playing through the pain. I worried about that gentle giant.

I watched Girard win the face-off and take the puck up the offensive zone, he passed it to Noah, who one-timed it into the net. I cheered with the rest of them and drank a little more of my beer.

During the TV time out, I noticed Brianna had her hand on her stomach and looked upset. "Hey, you okay?" I asked

She shook her head. "It's just hard. I'm sure you heard."

"Noah and TJ told me. I'm sorry."

She waved me off with a hand. "I don't think you understand what it's like."

I sighed and took a sip of my beer, even though my hands were shaking. I took her hand in mine and looked her in the eyes. "No one will understand what the pain, both physical and emotional will feel like."

She gave me a confused look.

I sighed. I really didn't like to talk about this. "Right after my husband died, I found out I was pregnant, and then I miscarried."

She gripped my hand. "Oh, Dinah. I had no idea."

I shrugged. "Not something I like to think about, but yeah it sucks. I—"

"What?"

I blinked back tears. "Noah was the one who found me. I almost died and I can't have kids now."

"Oh my god, Dinah! I'm so sorry!"

I waved her off. I didn't know what had possessed me to reveal that secret. "So I understand how you feel, you're allowed to be upset about it."

TAKE THE SHOT

She smiled sadly at me and her gaze returned back to the ice. The game was on, so I settled in and watched my favorite team racing across the ice after the puck. The second period had gone way better than the first, but I was worried about Noah. In his last shift he looked injured, he was hunched over and was bracing his stick across his knees. Mia was sitting next to me now and sent a worried glance my way.

"Do you think Noah's okay?" she asked.

I shook my head. "He seems hurt. He always plays through the pain. He feels like he has to prove himself or some shit."

Mia laughed. I was sure she understood, Hallsy had a lot of injuries last season. "So what did you two get up to last night?" she asked.

I blushed and tried to hide it behind my beer. She just laughed harder and now Brianna was interested in what was so funny. I just shook my head. "Nothing!"

Mia was smirking. "Not even to move forward with your advice?"

I nearly choked on my beer. "No."

"Hallsy actually listened to it," she murmured with a wicked grin.

"No shit!" I exclaimed. I gave her a high-five. "Get it, girl!"

Mia laughed. "You're so inappropriate."

I shrugged.

Mia laughed again. "I wish I could be as blunt as you. Is that why you and Roxanne Desjardins get along so well?"

TJ's sister was almost more blunt than I was. She also was a woman who didn't give a fuck. I missed that lady. I just wished her and Benny wouldn't fight so much every time she visited. I didn't understand those two. They should just save us all the trouble and finally bone.

Brianna raised her eyebrow at me. "Okay, now you have to spill."

I groaned. "I just enlightened TJ, Noah, and Hallsy on what women really want. Don't make me say it."

"What's that?" Brianna asked amused.

"To not cheat and to go down on your lady," Mia told her. "She's not wrong, Bri."

Brianna started laughing. "You did NOT say that."

I shrugged again and waved them off, watching the play on the ice below. I didn't want to say that Noah had kissed me last night, because I wasn't sure what to make of it. That kiss he gave me was so sexually charged, I was surprised he hadn't pressed me into my mattress and had his way with me. Nope, not Noah Kennedy, he tucked me into bed and held me until I fell asleep. I swear, he was created by women in a factory. When I woke up this morning and he was gone, I convinced myself that it had just been a dream. There was no way that my cute younger neighbor was actually into me.

I felt even more confused when he texted me asking me to come to the game this morning. I liked coming to the games, but I felt weird coming to them and sitting in the section with the other WAGs. Being friends with TJ and Noah meant that I had met a few of them before, but I felt like I didn't belong. After tonight, he would be on the road for a week, so I didn't know when we would get to talk about what had happened. If it had actually happened, my brain was still not computing.

I cheered with the rest of the crowd when TJ checked Daniels hard into the boards. Revenge was sweet, and TJ was Noah's bud so he was always the hot-headed scrapper on the ice that was going to stand up for his teammate. I had to admit I loved their bromance. The team somehow pulled the win out of their ass, and everyone was in high spirits. The team was headed straight to the airport for a three game stretch starting in Detroit, but Brianna and Mia had invited me out with them to grab a drink. I still didn't feel like it was quite my place, so I declined and went home instead.

I laid on my couch playing video games and generally not wanting to go to bed when I got a text from Noah.

NOAH: *I feel bad I had to go right to the airport.*
ME: *I understand.*
NOAH: *Can we talk when I get back?*

I sighed. I had a feeling that was coming, and I wasn't sure what direction it would go.

NOAH: *In a good way...I think I'm making this worse.*
ME: *Okay...*
NOAH: *I'm sorry.*
ME: *For what?*
NOAH: *Are you mad about last night?*
ME: *oh, honey...no...def not mad.*
NOAH: *oh! Ooohhhh!!!*
ME: *I'll see you when you get back, okay? Good luck tomorrow.*
NOAH: *Will you watch?*
ME: *Always!*
NOAH: *Hey! Send me your book so I can read something on the plane.*
ME: *FIIIINNNE!*

I set my phone down, but internally I was screaming. I pulled my laptop over to the couch and emailed him the first draft. I honestly didn't think he was really going to read it. It was just a simple teen love story, why would he be into that?

My phone buzzed again on the coffee table, but when I looked at it, it was TJ, not Noah.

TJ: *Woman, give me details!*

I had to laugh at that. TJ was such a nosy fucker. He might be a smidge worse than my brothers.

ME: *NOPE!*

TJ: *You both suck.*

TJ: *ooh...or was that what happened?*

ME: *You're a perv, no.*

TJ: *TELL ME!!*

ME: *Mind ya business.*

I set my phone down and leaned back onto my couch with a sigh. My phone continued to buzz, but I ignored it. My head was swimming with thoughts of Noah. He wanted to talk when he got back, but I had no idea what that meant. Talk about what? Was he interested in me? Or was he trying to just get laid? I honestly would have been up for either.

I had an itch I really needed to scratch and I was willing to have the Canadian giant that lived next door to me scratch it, if he was interested. Based on the way he had looked at me and how he had kissed me, I was sure he would be up for it if I offered.

CHAPTER SIX

NOAH

Finally making a move on Dinah before a road trip was decidedly a super dumb idea, because now I just had all these pent up emotions about it. I wanted her to feel the same way, but most of all I wanted to kiss her until it hurt. It was affecting my playing, I was distracted and mopey and all my teammates kept ragging on me about it. The only thing that got me through were the text messages we had sent back and forth to each other.

So when I was sitting in an UBER with TJ finally on my way back home, I was surprised to get another text from her.

DINAH: *I need a man's opinion.*
DINAH: *That means you.*
ME: *LOL. Okay??*

She sent me a picture of herself. She looked nice in the photo, she was wearing a professional looking red pencil skirt, and an animal print blouse with a black cardigan over it.

DINAH: *I need this to say PROFESSIONAL. And not 'hey grab my ass.'*

ME: *Looking H-O-T!*

DINAH: *Fuuuuckkk. I have a meeting with a client, and I need to make sure he gets that it's NOT a date.*

My blood boiled at that thought. Dinah had told me that sometimes she meets with clients that seemed to not understand that she was a professional and they flirt aggressively and try to buy her drinks. I told her she should tell her boss and not work with these clients, but she just shrugged and said it didn't matter. It made me want to track down all the assholes who ever grabbed her ass and punch them in the face.

TJ leaned over my shoulder and saw my screen. He nudged me with his elbow. I swatted his hand away. "Tell her she's looking good," he teased.

ME: *TJ says you look good.*

DINAH: *FUCK!*

DINAH: *Thanks!*

I put my phone away and saw TJ was smirking at me. "What?" I asked.

"So when are you going to finally ask her out?"

I shrugged. "I told her I wanted to talk when we got back."

TJ groaned. "When girls hear you 'want to talk' they think that means you want to break up!"

I threw up my hands in defeat. "We're not even dating!"

He put his head in his hands. "Dude, you're hopeless."

I leaned back on the headrest. "Do you think the age difference is weird?"

"Why because D's thirty? Why should that matter?" he asked with a shrug of his shoulders.

It hadn't really bothered me at all, but I had a feeling

that it bothered her. She thought her life would have been different, but she ended up widowed and losing her baby before she turned thirty. Why would she want to hook up with a dumb hockey player like me for?

TJ nudged me. "It's not going to bother her either. She likes you."

I bit my nail. "You really think so?"

He rolled his eyes at me. "Yes! Or at least you two need to bone one out soon or you're going to explode!"

I stared at him with wide eyes.

He tipped back his head and laughed. "Seriously, you don't notice how she's always eye fucking you?"

"What?" I asked incredulously.

No way.

There was no way that was even true. I knew I caught myself staring at her and wondering what it would be like to slip her clothes off. I wondered what it would be like with her underneath me, or on top of me, or even what it would be like to take her from behind. I was a guy after all, but there was no way in hell that Dinah thought any of these things about me. Girls didn't undress guys with their eyes.

"She does!" he insisted. "You're both too oblivious to notice it."

I didn't say anything else for the rest of the drive back to our condo. I still didn't believe TJ, but I was tired after the road stretch and it would be nice to be back in my own bed. I planted my body onto my bed in exhaustion. We didn't play another game until Thursday, two days from now, so it was nice to have a break. These road trips could be a huge bitch, but I wouldn't have had it any other way. I loved that I got to play hockey for a living. It was truly a dream come true.

TJ knocked on my door. "Hey, Hallsy and Riley want to go out and get drinks, you in?"

I didn't want to move from my bed. "Nah, you go on ahead."

TJ eyed me carefully. "Uh huh."

"What's that face for?" I asked and threw a pillow at his head.

He smirked. "Use protection!" he yelled after me.

I rolled my eyes at him and settled back down onto my bed. I looked at my phone, but didn't see any more texts from Dinah. We still needed to talk, even though that wasn't exactly what I had in mind at the moment.

ME: *Hey...I'm finally home.*

DINAH: *Come over! I just got back from a work thing.*

I was really tired, but I was not tired enough that I didn't want to see her. Seeing her was all I could think of all week. I pulled myself off of my bed, grabbed my wallet and keys and walked next door. I leaned over the doorframe trying to look all cool when I knocked.

She opened the door with a smile on her face and pulled me down to her height into a hug. "Noah! How's your head?"

I let her pull me into her condo and smiled at her. "I'm fine."

She bit her lip. My eyes scanned her, and she was still in the outfit from earlier, I guess she decided not to change. The skirt was really short, and I wanted to see it pooled around her ankles. Even more so when she walked into the kitchen and rummaged around in the fridge for a beer. I cocked my head to the side as I checked out her ass. I had to calm myself down, sex could come later, right now I wanted to tell her how I felt.

I straightened up when she turned around, but I was

pretty sure she caught me staring. I took the beer she handed to me, but I didn't really want to drink it. She leaned up against the kitchen counter and looked up at me. I tucked my hair behind my ear nervously, I wasn't sure where I was even supposed to start.

"So," she began. "What did you want to talk about?"

I gulped. "Um...that wasn't just a fluke."

"What?"

"When I kissed you."

"Oh."

I cocked my head at her. "You said it was okay."

She nodded. "Noah, I kind of thought I dreamed it."

"What?" I asked confused.

She took a step towards me and pulled me by the collar of my shirt down to her height. Her breath was hot on my lips and my breath hitched in my throat. Damn, she knew how to work me. On their own, my hands settled onto her waist and my mouth hovered over her lips.

"Is this okay?" I whispered.

She pulled my lips to hers and I smiled against her mouth. My hands gripped her waist and I lifted her up onto her kitchen counter. I felt my cock pushing against the zipper of my jeans when she wrapped her legs around my waist and pulled me closer. She made a little noise in the back of her throat, of both surprise and contentment, so I pressed on kissing her, sliding my tongue across her lips. She opened to me and her tongue flicked back at mine. I dug my hand into the flesh of her hips pressing her further into the countertop.

There was no way this was actually happening. I must have been asleep in my bed dreaming. I should have pulled away, and just did what I came here to do, but I was definitely thinking with the wrong head tonight.

She moaned when I pulled my mouth away from her lips and kissed down her throat. I traveled down to her collarbone where she giggled at the ticklish feeling and then I slowly trailed my kisses up to her ear. She shed her black cardigan and I pushed back the sleeve of her top to move my lips down to her bare shoulder. She pulled me back up to her lips and continued to kiss me, licking into my mouth urgently. I clenched her thighs wrapped around me with my hands, and pressed myself into her center.

"Oh!" she exclaimed when she felt my hardness on her thigh. "Shit! I thought you wanted to talk?"

I sighed and tried to untangle myself from her, but she clenched her heels wrapped around the small of my back as if daring me to walk away. "D, we should talk," I said urgently, my breath coming out in pants.

She grinned up at me, and leaned forward to press a kiss gently on the hollow of my throat. "We could always do that later. I am fine with…whatever this is," she whispered huskily.

Oh, fuck…

"I—I didn't come over here to jump you, I do really want to talk to you about how I—"

She cut me off by snaking her hands around the back of my neck and slanting her mouth onto mine again. I moaned into her mouth when her nails grazed my scalp ever so gently. She pulled away just as suddenly as she pulled me down to her. Her green eyes were ablaze with a fiery passion and I knew there was no way we were getting through this night by talking about our feelings. Her movements were fierce and hungry and her eyes flashed like she wanted to gobble me up, and I was going to let her.

"Noah, take me to bed," she ordered with a sexy growl.

I'm not sure if she did that on purpose, but the sound of

the demand on her lips went straight to my dick. A woman who told you what they wanted was sexy as hell. I took a breath and looked her in the eyes, searching to make sure she really wanted to do this.

"Are you sure?" I asked, hesitantly.

"What do I have to say to you? Take me to bed and show me what you're made of!"

"You don't have to tell me twice."

I grinned at her, pulled her off the counter and carried her to her bedroom. Her hands clutched my shoulders and she kept her legs wrapped tightly around my middle. Once my legs crossed the threshold of her bedroom, she untangled herself from around my waist and planted her feet firmly on the floor. I sighed in relief when I heard the zipper of her skirt and I watched nervously as she pulled her shirt over her head.

My mouth watered at the sight of her in just her bra and panties, her small form ready for me to slip those off too. She crossed over to me and smiled at me seductively before she pushed me down onto her bed. How could a woman this tiny bring me to my knees like this?

"I think you have too many clothes on," she insisted in a low growl and climbed on top of me, straddling my hips and grinning down at me.

God, that growl, it was really turning me on. My hands reached up and traveled up her back. I kissed her, but I pulled away. "Are you sure?" I asked for the second time that night.

She rolled onto her back and pulled me on top of her. Urgently her hands went up my shirt to grip my back and she pulled my t-shirt over my head. "Stop asking for permission. Yes."

I paused. "This isn't exactly how I wanted tonight to go."

"Noah, shut up and fuck me."

She kissed me before I could protest, her hands furiously undoing my jeans and pushing the materials down my muscular thighs. I kicked them off hurriedly along with my boxers. I wanted this so bad, I was throbbing for her. I was a gentle guy in bed, mostly due to my size and not wanting to intentionally hurt a woman when I slept with them. Some women said I was a bit submissive, and I would admit I did like a woman who took charge in the bedroom. Dinah probably thought because I was a hockey player, I was like the rest of those alpha-male types hanging around the dressing room, but I was never that guy. I liked to please a woman, but I definitely liked a woman who took what she wanted.

"Dinah," I breathed. "Is this what you want?"

"Hell yes," she answered and shoved my hand into the waistband of her panties.

Fuck yes, Dinah did like to take charge. That was sexy as hell to me. She thrusted her hips up and I let my fingers do the talking. I had no idea that the first time we took each other to bed it would be with her itching to shed ourselves of all our clothes and me being the one with trepidation.

"I've wanted to do this for a long time," she admitted through a moan. I removed my fingers and she whined. I undid her bra and slid her panties off.

"Yeah? Me too," I panted.

I stopped asking questions then, and dipped my head between her thighs to please her with my mouth. I wasn't really good at this, at least that's what other girls had told me, but the way Dinah moaned my name made me realize maybe I just wasn't with the right people. Maybe I just hadn't found the right woman.

I felt her hands grip my hair and push me into her more, guiding my head to where she wanted my tongue to move. My tongue rolled around her, her moans acting as encouragement to keep going. I breathed in her scent and licked laboriously all up and down her slit, stopping to pay attention to the sweet nub of her clit.

She gripped my hair harder in her hands. "Oh...Noah...fuck!"

I lifted up my head to stop and saw her head was lying back on the pillow and her eyes were glassy. It was sexy as hell. "What? Did you want me to stop?" I asked with a wicked grin.

Her eyes snapped down to my level. "Hell no!"

"Tell me what you want."

"You. Right now, inside me."

I put two fingers inside her and she bucked against them as I dipped my head to kiss one breast then the other. I wanted her to come on my hand or on my mouth, but I hadn't decided on which yet. I just wanted to please her. It was sexy as fuck the way she was moaning my name. I never thought I would hear her moaning my name outside of my dreams.

"Fuck..." she trailed off in ecstasy when I returned back to her folds to lick and suck at her again. Her moans got heavier and I held her thighs down with my free hand feeling them start to shake as she came on my face. I gave her a few soft final licks before lifting my head up from between her thighs.

I wiped the back of my mouth and climbed out of the bed looking for my jeans. I didn't even know if I had a condom in my wallet, if I did, it might have been a little old. Fuck. I heard her fiddle around on her bedside table. "C'mere. I have one," she told me.

I climbed back on top of her, rolled the condom on and looked into her eyes before I pressed on. "Is this okay?" I asked.

"Yes," she moaned. "Please."

"No," I stared down at her serious now. "Dinah, I'm serious, are you absolutely sure you want to do this? With me?"

The look on her face kind of crushed me, because she looked so hurt at the question. "Why wouldn't I want to do this?" she asked.

I reached one hand down and cupped her jaw. "I just want to make sure you won't regret this."

She lifted her face up and kissed me tenderly. Her hands snaked around to thread through my flow, and then she gripped the back of my neck tightly. Her eyes were alight with passion. "Kennedy, you better get fucking inside me right this instance," she demanded.

Something jumped inside me at her using my last name and demanding I do this with her. That was all the answer I needed to press on. I didn't hesitate then and slowly inched myself inside of her, smiling at the happy gasp that exited her mouth. God, this was hotter than any fantasy I ever had. I might be on top tonight, but it was clear that Dinah was the boss lady, and I was one hundred percent here for it. She could order me around all night long and I would do it. God, I wanted her to just tell me what to do.

She raked her nails down my back and I reveled in it, but I saw the pained look on her face. I placed a gentle hand on her cheek. "You okay? Am I hurting you?" I asked.

She smiled and turned her face into my hand. "It's fine. It's just been a while since I've been with a man. Maybe..."

"What?"

She reached her hand to the side again for something in

the bedside drawer. I recognized the small bottle and pulled out of her. She uncapped the bottle and reached down to spread the lube on my sheathed dick. I groaned at her hand on me and she grinned up at me as she gave me a few pumps with her hand. The visual of her tiny hand pumping my erection was almost too much.

"I need to be inside you," I begged.

"Then do it!" she told me and tossed the bottle of lube to the side.

It felt smoother when I thrusted inside her again. She seemed to have relaxed, but I didn't want this to go too fast. I slowed to a gentle and painstakingly slow pace and kissed her a while. She leaned into the kiss, opening her mouth ever so slightly so I could slip her some tongue. She was gripping my shoulders as I kissed down her neck. She wrapped her legs tight around my waist and moved her hips in sync with mine in a slow, methodic rhythm. My name was a song she kept moaning on her lips, and it encouraged me to go faster. Her hand lingered past my back and she gripped my ass hard, pulling me deeper inside her. I concentrated so I didn't come before her.

"Go faster," she whispered and she pulled me in harder, her nails digging into my ass.

I ceased my movements, and cradled her face in my hands. "You sure?"

She visibly rolled her eyes at me. "Noah, it's just been a while, I'm all right. Go faster, please."

"I don't want to hurt you," I explained.

She smiled. "Oh my god! You are such a gentle lover, and I am totally into you letting me call the shots, but please hit me with the good stuff. You can go hard and fast with me, okay?"

"Yes, Ma'am!" I said with a cheeky grin and quickened my pace.

She laughed. "Is it bad that I like the sound of that?"

I grinned again. "Nope! You're the boss lady. I like it when you tell me what to do."

"Fuck yeah I am," she growled. "Now get back to work."

I knew how to take direction, very well.

CHAPTER SEVEN

DINAH

I didn't think that was how my night was going to go when I asked Noah to come over. I laid back on my bed with a sigh of contentment. He pulled me to him and laid my head on his bare chest. I cuddled into him, feeling at peace hearing his heart beat racing. He gently stroked my hair in silence.

"I need a beer, do you want a beer?" I asked him and untangled myself from his arms.

"I think you left mine on the counter," he said with a smirk and he watched my naked form get up from the bed.

I threw on a clean shirt before walking out of my bedroom and back into the kitchen. The now warm beer was on the kitchen island, but I didn't pay attention to it, rather just stood there thinking about what the fuck had just happened.

I had fucked Noah Kennedy.

My hot hockey player neighbor who was twenty-two! When Noah said he wanted to talk, I thought he was going to talk about how we couldn't do this thing. Then he had kissed me and it was like my brain turned off and my hormones were all like, 'Get out of here brain, we need to get that dick inside of us right now!' I couldn't say I was mad about it though, and Noah was so sweet about how he kept asking me if everything he did was okay. I always knew that Noah was the epitome of niceness, so I wasn't surprised by how gentle he was with me in bed. It was sweet. Getting tangled up in the sheets with him was better than I thought it would be, but I didn't know where it left us.

I must have been gone for too long, because warm hands wrapped around my waist and I felt him kiss me on my neck just below my ear. I sighed into him. "Hey," he whispered into my ear, his deep voice all thick and growly.

"Hey," I whispered back and strained my neck to give him more access. He peppered me with more soft gentle kisses that I felt all the way down to my core. I knew Noah was kind of a soft boy, but good god, he was such a gentle lover, and I loved it.

"It was okay, right?" he asked into my ear.

I turned around to face him. Noah was standing in my kitchen, his whole six-foot-two frame was clad only in his boxers. His hair was all mussed up and his pale face was red with a blush. I got the sense that he didn't expect this was how the night was going to go either. I guess we both just let our hormones control us tonight. I put my hands on his face, where the beginning of a beard was starting. It had felt scratchy on my thighs earlier, but that kind of always made it better for me. Beards were hot.

"Yes. You think I would have moaned like that if it hadn't been okay?" I asked him.

The corners of his mouth lifted up in a smile. "Maybe you were faking it."

"Oh, honey, no!"

He smiled and he kissed me again with all the passion that he must have had pent up for the last two years. My knees buckled, but he grabbed my waist and steadied me in his big arms. I knew he was a big man, but I kind of forgot how muscular his arms and chest were or how he could pick me up like it was nothing. My hand trailed down the planes of his chest, marveling at the rippling muscles. I shouldn't have been surprised at how ridiculous his body was. I knew he played hockey and worked out obsessively, but seeing him now here in my kitchen, kissing me in just his boxers was a different story.

I was eight years older than him, so this had to be weird. I mean, what would a hot twenty-two year old who just so happened to be a professional athlete want with a woman like me? I wasn't old by any means, but being a widow at thirty wasn't something I bragged about. It came with a lot of baggage, baggage that a kid his age didn't need to deal with. Although, Noah had been with me through it all. He was there comforting me in the wake of Jason's death. Then he was there for me when the worst thing I could ever imagine happened to me. That's what friends were for though — it wasn't as if Noah was trying to have a relationship with me. How could he?

I pulled away from the kiss suddenly, because you shouldn't be thinking about your dead husband when you were kissing someone else. My throat tightened at the guilt that I had betrayed Jason by sleeping with Noah.

Noah looked at me shyly, like he didn't know how to approach the situation either. "Listen, Dinah..."

I didn't let him finish that thought. "I need to get a shower. I have work tomorrow."

I didn't even wait for an answer, I just sprinted out of

my kitchen and back into the bedroom to the en suite bathroom. I shed my minimal clothes onto the tiled floor and cranked the water to hot before stepping inside the stall. I let the water cascade down my back while my thoughts turned to Jason. I didn't think my late husband would have wanted me to not have a life now that he was gone. I would like to think he would have wanted me to be happy, but I don't think he would have appreciated me finding love in the arms of our young neighbor. It made me feel so guilty, even though deep down inside I was thrilled at the fact that Noah and I finally took the plunge. It was nice to be with a man who was kind and gentle and asked if things were okay for me. God, a man who asked for consent was sexy as hell.

I stood in the shower for a minute longer than I would have normally, before I turned off the faucet and stepped out of the stall. The steam had fogged up the mirror, but I wiped it away with my hand and looked at my face through it. My pale skin was red and splotchy from the shower, but a part of me was wondering if it was also from what I had done with Noah earlier. My lips were swollen from his kisses, and I touched them thoughtfully thinking about what we had just done. To be honest, as much as I felt guilty, I kind of really wanted to sleep with Noah again. I think that scared me more than it should.

I wrapped a towel around my body and one around my long dark hair and stepped out into my bedroom. I froze in my steps when I saw that Noah was lying in my bed, in all his long-limbed muscular glory. He was looking at something on his phone and he hadn't heard me come out of the bathroom.

"Oh!" I exclaimed, "You're still here."

He furrowed his brow. "Was I supposed to leave?"

I shook my head and walked over to my dresser. Since

he had already seen me naked, I dropped all pretenses by just dropping the towel at my feet while I looked for a fresh pair of underwear. My back burned with his eyes on me, but I didn't give him the satisfaction of letting him know I knew what he was doing. I changed quickly, throwing on a tank top and shorts to sleep in. I wrung out my hair in the towel before depositing both towels into the hamper I had tucked away in my closet. I took my brush from off of my dresser and fought with the tangles in my hair.

"What are you thinking about?" he asked pulling me out of my thoughts.

"Nothing important," I answered honestly.

I still hadn't turned around to look at him while I smoothed out my straight hair with my hairbrush. I wasn't sure if I could look at him right now and not think about how much he had pleased me earlier. I don't know why I felt so guilty and shameful right now, sex wasn't anything to be ashamed of!

"You okay?" he asked with a hint of concern.

I slid my gaze over to him and my mouth watered at the sight of him. I knew he was a big guy, but looking at him leaning up on his elbow on my bed looking so sexy made me want to shed my clothes again. Geez, libido, where did you come from?

"I'm fine," I told him, but my mouth was a thin line.

"Okay, but that's the face you make when you don't want to talk about something."

I brushed out the rest of my hair, but was too tired to blow-dry it. Towel-drying it was all I had the patience for tonight. Luckily for me, I was one of those people with poker-straight hair so I could just brush it out in the morning and it would be fine. I was avoiding having this conversation with him, because he was right. It was the face

I made when I didn't want to talk about something. It was really hard to lie to your best friend.

"C'mere," he beckoned from my bed and like I was hypnotized, I went to him.

I slid into bed beside him and he put his arm around my shoulder, pulling me to him. It had been so long since a man had made me feel safe. So long since I had a man in my bed. Noah made me feel safe, and made me feel good, like really good. This was all really weird. I figured this was just a physical thing for him, and eventually things between us would just go back to normal. Or maybe we would just continue to sleep with each other and not catch feelings?

HA

HA

HA

Very funny, Dinah.

He smiled down at me and kissed the top of my head. "Just for the record, I didn't come over here for sex. Honestly, I didn't know that was on the table."

I smiled at him. "I didn't see you complaining."

He gave me a wicked grin. "No, definitely not complaining."

"It doesn't have to be weird between us," I told him. It really did not, because I totally wanted to do it again, but I wasn't sure if he felt that way.

My phone buzzed on my nightstand, preventing him from saying what he wanted to say next. I looked at it and laughed at a text from TJ.

TJ: *Did you get it in??*

TJ: *Tell me! Kens won't say anything.*

TJ: *TELLLLL MEEEEE!!*

ME: *None of your damn business.*

ME: *...yes*

TJ: *GET IT GIRL.*

ME: *I hate you so much.*

I laughed and put my phone down. Noah had an unsure look on his face. "Is that TJ?" he asked.

"Oh, was I not supposed to tell him?"

Noah laughed. "He would have found out anyway, he's a nosy little fucker."

I collapsed into laughter. "That's true."

Noah was biting his lip nervously now and pushing his hair behind his ear. I wondered if he knew that he did that when he was nervous. "Look, I have to tell you something."

"What's up?"

He sighed. "Speaking of TJ being nosy, I had to tell him about what happened to you, about the miscarriage. I'm sorry. I never wanted to tell your secrets."

"Oh."

"I'm sorry."

I reached my hand out to take his. "Noah, honey, it's okay. TJ's a bit of a goof, but I know he won't say anything about that. I actually called Coach LaVoie to tell him what happened so I assumed the team already knew."

He was shaking his head. "Yeah, I didn't know you did that. He told Girard, who mentioned something to me about it. But it was more supportive you know?"

I looked up at him in question. "What do you mean?"

"Oh, him and Brianna went through it too."

"Oh, yeah she told me that, but thank you for telling me."

He still looked nervous. "Are you mad?" he asked.

I shook my head. "Nah. So change of subject — I'm a bit worried about your head, you took some bad hits lately."

He shrugged me off. "I'm fine."

"Noah, I just worry! I'm a fan of this team, I lived

through LaVoie's playing days here. His concussions were dangerous."

He smiled down at me and bopped my nose. "You're so cute when you worry. I'm fine, the league's always doing concussion protocol."

I knew that, but this sport I loved and the sport this man played could still be dangerous. CTE was a real problem, and at least the NHL wasn't straight up denying it, but they needed to figure out a solution. I wasn't sure if *I* was the person to do that, but I did worry about Noah. I worried every time he took a bad hit on the ice, and every time he wouldn't tell me just what kind of 'upper body injury' he had.

I settled back onto his chest feeling the rise and fall of it with every breath he took.

"So, weird question, did I do all right in there?" he asked.

I looked up at him and saw that he was biting his lip nervously. God, what did he have to be nervous about? Also, did he know how hot he looked when he did that?

"Why are you asking again? I didn't know that you were so self-conscious about that."

He shifted around like he was uncomfortable asking the question. "I mean, when I—"

"You mean when you went down on me?"

He nodded his head. "Um...yeah."

I laughed into his chest. "Was I not vocal enough? I thought you got that I was enjoying it from all the moaning. I'm usually not responsive if it's not good, but when it's good bad things come out of my mouth."

He ran a hand through his hair and sighed. "I've had girls say I wasn't good at it."

I gave him a wicked grin. "But I mean if you think you need the practice..."

He shoved my shoulder lightly. "Yeah, yeah, I get it."

I exploded with laughter. "It's cute when you're so unsure of yourself."

He glared at me, and I just laughed again. He lifted my head up to him to kiss him again. When he pulled away, his thumb rubbed over my bottom lip. "You've got a dirty mouth."

"You loved it, shut up."

He smiled. "Not going to deny that one. I don't think I've ever been with a woman who told me exactly what they wanted. I always thought women were a mystery I had to solve, but maybe I just wasn't listening?"

I shrugged. "I've learned to not play games and to just ask for what I want."

"God, that's so sexy," I heard him mutter under his breath and I was pretty sure I wasn't supposed to hear that.

I pulled away from him and laid on my back. He slunk down onto his side beside me and slung his arm around my waist. I shifted my position in the bed so I could be the little spoon and he breathed into my neck, his breath tickling me.

"Do you want me to go?" he asked.

My arm rested against his and my fingers brushed lightly across his skin. "No, you can stay. Cuddling is nice."

He kissed my neck lightly. "Fuck yeah, it is!"

❄

I slept so well the night before that I slept through all three of my alarms and was late for work. I must have looked flustered as I dropped my purse onto my desk. Across from me, my coworker Matt was giving me a curious glance. I logged onto to my computer and started checking my emails. This job was necessary, and I was pretty good at it, but it was absolutely soul-sucking. All I wanted to do was write books, but I was stuck in a stable job because I'd only sold one book so far and it wasn't exactly paying the bills.

Matt threw a pen at me. "Oy!"

I dodged it. "What?" I snapped in annoyance.

He smirked. "You look like you're in a cloud." He mimed smoking a blunt. "And you're late, you're never late for work."

I shook my head. "Sorry, late night."

"You see yet?"

"See what?"

"The client's going to sign the contract, thanks to you."

I dropped my head on my desk. "Can you please take over that account? That guy skeeves me out."

Matt laughed. "I don't want it either, it's yours."

He cocked his head at me from across the open space of our workspace. The whole open concept design of the modern agency was for the birds. I kind of hated it, especially since it meant everyone could see the annoyed faces I made when I was on a call with an annoying client. I wasn't exactly good at being subtle. Matt was staring at my neck so hard, that I brought a hand up to it.

"What's on your neck?" he asked, but he was wearing a sly grin.

"What?"

I used the black screen on my phone as a mirror. That's when I saw the red mark on the side of my neck and it was pretty clear what it was and what I had been up to last night. Dammit, I would never hear the end of it from Matt. I also wondered if Matt would be the type of person to feel protective of Jason. Matt and Jason had been best friends and Matt was the reason that I had gotten this job.

My coworker was smirking at me now. "Oh shit, did you get laid last night?" he asked.

"Um..."

His brow furrowed. "You didn't sleep with the client, right?"

"Ew! No!"

"Good, good. I mean, I didn't think so, I just didn't know you were seeing anyone. Since Jason you've gone on what one date?"

I nodded. "It was kind of not planned."

"Okay, explain!"

I shook my head, but I couldn't keep the smile from my face.

"You look like the cat who ate the canary!"

"It's none of your business!" I insisted and knew I was starting to get all flustered. My face was probably beet red right now. Pale girl problems!

"Come on, I tell you about all the girls I date," he whined.

I just put my head in my hands and laughed. "Not that I want to know about them."

"Did you finally fuck your neighbor who has the hots for you?"

"What?"

"The hockey player...Kennedy right? Noah Kennedy?" he asked like he was unsure of the name. I saw him typing away at his computer, probably pulling The Bulldogs roster list up on his computer. He was nodding, so I knew he confirmed he got Noah's name right.

I held up my hands. "Wait, wait, wait, you think Noah Kennedy has the hots for me?" I asked. Yeah, we had slept together, but I thought maybe that was just all it was. Had Noah been pining for me this whole time?

Matt looked at me like I was the biggest idiot on the planet. "Yeah, you brought him to the Christmas party. He was like undressing you with his eyes the entire time."

Maybe it was just a physical thing then. I bit my lip and looked up to the ceiling hoping he wouldn't notice.

Matt's eyes widened. "Holy shit, you totally fucked." He started laughing. "Oh my god, good for you."

"NO COMMENT!"

"We're going to happy hour tonight and you're gonna tell me everything!"

"NO COMMENT!"

I tried to focus on work, but it was hard, because all I was thinking about was Noah and his big hands roaming all over my body last night. And how much I wanted to do it again.

CHAPTER EIGHT

NOAH

I honestly had no intention of going over to Dinah's to have my way with her, but I was so glad it had happened. Also glad she didn't get mad that I stayed over and held her while we slept. I was a little bummed I didn't get to tell her how I felt. That this wasn't just sex for me, and I had been harboring a crush for her for years. She seemed so cavalier about the whole thing, and that kind of upset me because I wanted her to know that this was something real to me. I did feel slightly guilty that I made her late to work this morning.

I laid in her bed after she left, and drank in her scent. I smelled her all over me, and I didn't want to wash it off, but I should probably shower. We had practice later and then a game tomorrow, so it wasn't like I really had time to think about it. I just really didn't feel like going next door and having to deal with TJ razzing me.

Speaking of which, my phone buzzed with messages

from him that caused me to finally decide to get up out of her bed and put some clothes on.

TJ: *Are you done fucking our neighbor?*
TJ: *Kens! We have practice today!*

I put my phone into the pocket of my jeans, locked up Dinah's place and walked into my shared condo with my teammate. TJ and Hallsy were in the living room playing on our gaming console. Hallsy looked at me curiously. "Weren't you wearing that yesterday?" he asked. His lips were curled up into a sly smile and his dark eyes twinkled in mirth, so I knew he was just teasing me.

"No comment," I deadpanned.

TJ smirked. "Ask him where he's been all night."

Hallsy smiled. "Oh shit, did you finally do it with your neighbor? NICE, bro."

I gave them both the finger and walked into the shower attached to my room. I was glad when TJ and I signed this mortgage together that both of the bedrooms had their own bathrooms. I wasn't sure exactly how to approach things with Dinah. I didn't want it to just be sex, but I think I could handle that if that's what she wanted from me. I wanted something more, something real with her. I had to remember that she might not be feeling the same way. She wasn't the one who harbored feelings for me for the past couple of years. For her, this was completely new and I had to keep on reminding myself of that.

After I got out of the shower and dressed, I flopped on my bed and looked at my phone. We had practice in a little bit, but I couldn't help myself from texting Dinah. Even though I knew she was at work and she might not see my messages for a while.

ME: *I hope things aren't weird between us now.*
ME: *I hope that doesn't make it weirder now.*

ME: *I have a game tomorrow, but do you want to do something tonight?*

DINAH: *I'm being forced into happy hour with coworkers.*

DINAH: *Please send help. Also you gave me a HICKEY. Who does that outside of fifteen year olds?*

I smiled at that and texted back.

ME: *I can come rescue you, tell me when and where.*

DINAH: *FIIINNE. I'm in meetings for the rest of the day.*

I put my phone away and TJ walked into my room. "You ready to head out?" he asked.

I nodded and walked with him and Hallsy out to my car. TJ had driven last time, so I agreed to drive us to the practice facility in the suburbs. Even though things were weird between Dinah and I, or at least I thought they were, I couldn't wipe the smile off my face. So much so that even the Captain had to say something while I was lacing up my skates.

"I don't think I've ever seen your face look like that," Girard commented with a laugh.

"What?" I asked.

TJ threw a towel at my head. "He's been like that all morning."

Riley cocked his head at me. "So does that mean I can't ask out your neighbor?"

"NO!" I yelled.

Riley smirked. "About damn time. You deserve happiness man, congrats."

At twenty-seven, Riley was like an old guy in the dressing room. He was a vet in the league and he tended to always take us younger guys under his wing. I joked that he was a fuckboy, but he really was a good guy at his core. He just tended to be a guy into casual hookups, like TJ. Nothing wrong with that, but I was never that guy. Also, he was like obsessed with watching game tape. Like no other player I have ever seen.

Benny who sat on my other side in the dressing room, clapped me on the back and smirked. Benny was the biggest guy on the team, so I think a lot of people thought he was a stoic giant, but I had a feeling he was a lot more sensitive than everyone gave him credit for. I mean, he had come to me when him and his girlfriend of about a year were on the rocks and asked for advice. He had seemed genuinely conflicted about the whole thing, which was interesting to me since everyone painted him as this big playboy. He so wasn't.

I nodded but didn't say anything and before I knew it, I was out on the ice running drills and shooting pucks at our goalie until I felt like I was blue in the face. I felt good about our game tomorrow. My body felt loose and I was finally in a good head space.

Hallsy's girlfriend worked near the practice facility, so she gave him a ride home. I liked Mia, she was sweet and always seemed like someone who would welcome someone into the fold. The two had been together forever, so it was like they were practically married. I drove TJ home with me, but still hadn't heard from Dinah. I was pacing in the kitchen when we got home so much that TJ made me take a shot with him.

"What's your problem?" he asked.

I sighed and ran a hand through my long hair. "Nothing. I'm just waiting to hear from Dinah. I think I'm going to meet her for a drink tonight."

He raised an eyebrow at me. "This isn't just a casual fuck for you is it?"

"What?" I asked confused. "Of course not. You know I don't do casual."

TJ hung his head with a sigh. "She was married before, she might not be ready to have something serious yet."

I was kind of afraid of that. I bit my lip.

TJ clapped me on the shoulder. "Just don't fall in love with her too soon."

I wasn't sure how to tell him that was impossible, because I had fallen in love with her a long time ago.

"You want to get something to eat?" he asked.

"Sure."

We were on our way back from dinner when Dinah finally texted me.

DINAH: *Mac's Tavern. Please give me an excuse to leave.*

ME: *What's in it for me?*

DINAH: *HAR HAR HAR. Don't be a dick.*

ME: *OMW.*

I changed when we got back to the condo, but was unsure if I looked okay, and I messed with my hair so much that TJ finally threw me out of the condo and told me to go get Dinah. He had plans with this girl he had been casually seeing, so I had a feeling he was just trying to get rid of me. Not sure TJ was the kind of guy that would ever settle down. I was hoping to end up at Dinah's place tonight anyway where there were no room for interruptions or roommates complaining about noise. I smoothed down my hair in the UBER I caught, and realized how nervous I was. I shouldn't be nervous, it was just Dinah. She was my best friend and we had already spent time together between the sheets. That made me nervous even more because I wondered if she regretted it now.

When I walked into the bar, I saw her standing there

with a beer in hand laughing at something some guy was saying to her. I was pretty sure I had met the guy before, her coworker Matt, but they were just friends. Although, I guess we were just friends at one point too. Her dark hair was still pulled back in that tight bun on top of her head and I wanted to unravel it and run my fingers through her hair. She was wearing a black pencil skirt with one of her work blouses, and she looked so damn good. She glanced down at her phone, and when she looked up and spotted me I swore her eyes lit up. She waved a hand to beckon me over to her.

I swiftly moved across the bar towards her. She smiled up at me and I bent down to her height to hug her. I planted a small kiss on her cheek, and she made a surprised face. Was I not supposed to do that? She smiled at me and I put my arm around her waist.

She pointed at me and said to her coworker. "Matt, you remember my friend Noah, right?"

Matt nodded and had a grin on his face. He put his hand out and I shook it. "Hey man, nice to meet you again."

"Likewise," I said.

"You want a beer?" Dinah asked.

"Sure."

She waved over the bartender and I ordered a beer. She took a sip of her pint that she drank in the can. It was cute how much she gave exactly zero fucks about anything. I had met her insane brothers, so it seemed to be a family trait, but I liked it so much better on her. I didn't pull my arm from around her waist though, and she leaned into me. It was nice to feel wanted, and it was nice that none of her coworkers were asking me about hockey. None of them really seemed like the hockey type anyway, but I think Matt knew who I was since we had met before.

She finished her beer and gave me this look that I

couldn't decipher. There was a twinkle in her eyes, so I gulped down the rest of my beer and called an UBER.

"Hey, man, it was good to meet you again." I said to Matt.

He smirked at Dinah and she glared. "Don't," she growled.

"Get some!" he laughed as we walked away.

"Did you tell him?" I asked.

She shook her head. "I tried not to. He guessed. Apparently it was obvious to everyone but me that you had the hots for me."

"Really?" I asked. "You never knew?"

Dinah shook her head and her eyes were wide. "No, you're so subtle. Until last night I thought maybe that kiss before your road trip was a drunk kiss."

I slipped my hand into hers and she seemed to freeze at that, but then she leaned into my arm. Our UBER came soon so I didn't have a response to that before we got in. The ride to our complex was silent, but it didn't feel uncomfortable. I wasn't sure if she wanted me to come to her place but when we got to our floor she beckoned me to follow her.

"You coming?" she asked.

I nodded and followed her inside.

I followed her into the kitchen where she got a glass of water. I heard a thump from the wall next door. We shared a look and then I heard a loud moan. Oh, TJ definitely wanted me to get out of the condo tonight.

She laughed. "Well, I guess I know why TJ didn't come along."

I laughed with her, and crossed over to her. I just wanted to hold her in my arms and have a repeat of last night, but I wasn't sure if that was on the table.

"You want a drink?" she asked.

"I'm good."

She nodded her head. "Look, I don't want this to be awkward between us."

"I don't want it to be like that either."

She looked down at the floor. "Um...was it a one-time thing?"

"If that's what you want," I explained, even though I was really hoping it was not.

I wanted to tell her how I felt, that I was crazy about her and had been harboring a crush for her for two years. That spending one night with her hadn't changed that. That it wasn't just a physical thing, and that I was in love with her. But I kept thinking about what TJ said about maybe she was not ready for a relationship with me. I felt like laying out my feelings could ruin our friendship.

"Noah, what do you want?" she asked looking up at me hopefully.

I looked down at her. I always forgot how small she was. She had such a big personality, her don't give a fuck attitude made her seem like the tallest person in the room. I put my hands on her hips and lifted her up onto her kitchen island so she was at eye-level with me. She looked shocked at first, but then she laced her hands at the back of my head. I pulled her mouth to mine and kissed her with all the passion I could muster.

CHAPTER NINE

DINAH

*O*h.
 Oh, he was good.

I liked this aggressive Noah. I liked the way he didn't even think and threw me up on the island kissing me fiercely. I didn't care if this was casual or serious or whatever, I just knew he made me feel good and I hadn't had that in a very long time. And...it was Noah! Sweet, kind Noah, who I loved hanging out with and was probably the reason that I was alive right now. Noah, my best friend who knew all of my secrets and had held me when I cried after going through an awful miscarriage and finding out I couldn't have kids. The man with the kind eyes and the big heart who was always there for anyone in a pinch. Even if he didn't really know them that well.

We heard a moan through the shared walls of our respective kitchens, and we both pulled away so we could cackle with laughter. Noah's eyes were shiny with amusement. "I think it's safe to say TJ thought I wasn't sleeping in my bed tonight again."

"Oh."

Noah twirled his hand around my long hair. "Dinah, I'm not trying to pressure you to do what we did last night again. Okay?"

I nodded. "Okay."

"We should probably have that talk, eh?"

I frowned. I really didn't want to have this talk he wanted to have. Because deep down I knew what it would be. Noah was young and hot and he had his pick of all the beautiful women in this city. Why would he ever want someone like me? A pocket-sized sleep-deprived widow with a lot of baggage? No thank you.

He reached down to grab my hand and stroked his thumb across the back of it. "It's not a bad thing, you know?"

"What isn't?" I asked, generally confused about what the hell was happening. I just wanted him to keep on kissing me rather than talk about how this could never be real for him.

He sighed and put a shaky hand in his hair nervously. "Look, I really like you, always have, and I...well...it wasn't just sex for me. So you let me know when you're ready."

I stared at him dumbfounded. "What?"

His smile crinkled around his eyes. "Dinah, I like you. A lot."

"I like you too."

He sighed again. "No, I mean, I want to leave what this is between us up to you."

I stared at him some more. Oh...was he saying he had feelings for me but he wanted me to decide if we turned this into something more? I felt his big hands go to my cheeks and he kissed me softly. He pulled away so he could lift me off the kitchen island.

"I should probably go. You have work in the morning."

It seemed like he wasn't waiting for me to give him the answer tonight, and I wasn't sure if I had an answer yet. I knew I liked Noah, I loved hanging out with him and I enjoyed kissing him, but something serious? Was I ready for that? Would Jason have been okay with me dating again?

"You can stay," I heard myself saying.

His dark eyebrow shot up in question. "Don't you have to work on edits?"

I glared at him and put my hands on my hips. "How do you know that?"

He chuckled. "You told me. I respect your writing time. I don't want to ever come between that."

My heart nearly flipped over in my chest at that. Who was this guy? Noah was unlike any man I had ever known before. The fact that he was so respectful of my time and my need to work on my craft meant so much to me. There was something inside myself that was digging into me, but I tried to push it down. Last night had not just been a physical thing for me either. Noah might be my best friend, but if we hung out and it continued to involve kissing, I was pretty sure I was going to fall in love with him.

I squinted at the clock on my stove, it was already ten-thirty but I could get some writing in before bed. It wasn't like I ever went to sleep at a decent hour anyway. I looked up at Noah. "Can you give me like a half-hour?"

He nodded. "Whatever you want."

I reached up on my tip-toes to kiss his cheek, but since he was an entire foot taller than me he had to bend down so I could reach him. I walked away and shut myself into my office. I opened my laptop and started getting to work.

My editor had emailed me big picture edits earlier today, but I hadn't even looked at it yet. I opened my email and started making notes for where I needed to fix things. No one had really prepared me for what it was going to be like once I got my first book published. The first book was doing okay, not a bestseller or anything, enough that my publisher bought another book. I had to learn to pivot from edits on this current novel, to drafting a third novel. I wanted to write something completely different. Oh yeah, all of this on top of working a full-time demanding job in marketing that was slowly sucking my soul out. Seriously, I was about ready to just up and quit, but I kind of needed the job to pay my bills. I loved being a writer, but right now it wasn't exactly a living wage.

I pulled my hair up into a bun so I could focus and shoved my headset on my head. The video game soundtrack I was listening to was going to get me through this. My fingers flew across the keyboard and I got into the zone working on a new chapter. I felt confident and good about it, but it might be a different story in the morning when I re-read what I had written.

"Hey, you there?" I heard Noah's voice behind me and I nearly jumped out of my seat.

I yanked my headset off my head, and saw he was standing in the doorway of my office. His long and lean body was leaning up against the doorway and it made him look so sexy. God, what was wrong with me? I put a hand on my heart. He smiled at me sheepishly.

"You scared me!" I chastised him.

He crossed the room and put his hands on my shoulders. "You did tell me to give you a half-hour but I gave you forty minutes."

I reached up a hand to my shoulder to rest on one of his.

His hand felt warm and sent a shockwave of pleasure down my spine. I didn't know if it was just hormones or if it was just my feelings for this man seeping out. "Thanks, I think I needed the extra ten minutes," I thanked him.

"I know you have a real job, so you should get to bed," he insisted.

I couldn't focus on the actual words coming out of his mouth right now though, because his big hands were rubbing the tension out of my shoulders. He was a little too good at relaxing me, and he was really good at shoulder rubs. I saved my place and closed the lid to my laptop.

Noah continued to rub my shoulders. "Mmmhmm... you're good at that, thanks," I told him.

"Come on, come to bed, it's late," he urged and pulled his hands away from me.

I took his hand and he led me to my bedroom. Even though he saw me naked last night, I felt awkward changing into my pajamas in front of him. It was like exposing myself to him, but it wasn't like this man didn't know everything about me. He must have felt my self-conscious thoughts, because he distracted me by slipping his shirt over his head and taking off his jeans. I tried not to stare at the hard planes of tight muscle on his body, but damn Noah hid how built he was until you got him naked. I really didn't want to think about all the other girls who may have gotten to look at this view right now. A stab of jealousy hit me in the chest when I looked at him, because I wanted to be the only woman who got to see him like that.

Whoa. Calm down, Dinah.

He joined me in my bathroom, where I handed him the extra toothbrush I had underneath the sink. We joked while we brushed our teeth and I washed my face. It was all so weirdly domestic. I mean, he was going to stay over again tonight and he wasn't even pressuring me to get naked again.

Why wasn't he pressuring me to get naked with him again?

I wanted to put my mouth all over him right now and ride his cock until he couldn't handle it anymore. I sighed to myself, because he was the kindest and most decent man I had ever met. EVER. I swear, I built this gentle giant in a factory.

I slid into the bed and he pulled me close to him, my head lying on his chest and his big arm around me. I felt my eyes starting to close while his finger stroked up and down my arm.

"D?" he whispered into the quiet of my bedroom.

"Yeah?"

"What's your day like tomorrow?" he asked.

My brow furrowed in confusion as I thought about what my schedule was like. I honestly couldn't even remember. I pulled away from him to grab my phone off the nightstand and I scrolled through my work calendar. "Um...pretty okay. I have a meeting at three, but otherwise it's open. Why?"

I wasn't looking at him when I double checked that my phone was plugged in and my alarm was set for the morning. I set it back on the nightstand, and when I crawled back over to place my head against Noah's heart he looked like he was thinking a little too hard. His hand absent-mindedly stroked my hair. It took all my composure not to moan at that, because seriously getting my hair stroked while a man I had feelings for held me in his arms was such an intimate gesture.

"You have lunch plans?" he finally asked.

I racked my brain for an answer. "I don't think so..."

"Can I take you to lunch?" he asked, and I noticed a nervous hitch in his voice. God, he was adorable.

"Sure...wait, don't you have practice?"

He shook his head slowly. "Nope! Let me take you to lunch tomorrow."

I was nodding, but mostly because his stroking of my hair was hypnotizing me into agreeing with anything he said. He could have told me to get on my knees and take off my clothes and I would have done it. Not that Noah would have done that right now. Although, I wouldn't have minded it.

"Okay, sure," I agreed.

He kissed the top of my head gently. "Come on, let's get some sleep."

I let sleep take me, curled up into the side of the first man to sleep in my bed since my husband died. The man that I used to call my best friend, but I wasn't sure what he was to me now that we crossed that line.

CHAPTER TEN

NOAH

She was asleep within minutes, and it made me want to just shake her awake and say, 'HA! I knew you were lying about not being a good sleeper.' But she looked so cute asleep in my arms, with her head lying on my chest and her arms clutching onto me. It made me feel all warm and fuzzy inside. I wasn't sure what was going on with us right now, but I thought it was good enough that I told her how I felt and left the puck on her stick. Now she had to decide if she wanted to take the shot.

I mean, what could a woman like her want with a dumb jock like me? There was no way that Dinah had feelings for me, and I couldn't help but wonder if the other night was just sex. I was just her young neighbor who she happened to be best friends with. I would be lying if I said I didn't want to sleep with her tonight. I was a man after all, but I didn't want her to think I was just some horny bastard out for sex and nothing more. With Dinah, I wanted all the mores and I wanted her to know that. I wasn't sure if my lame explanation tonight had even gotten through to her.

I heard my phone buzz on the bedside table and I glanced at it to see a text from TJ. I shifted slightly in the bed, afraid to wake the small woman curled into my side.

TJ: *It's safe to come back now, Taylor left.*

ME: *K.*

TJ: *K??*

TJ: *Do you even live here anymore?*

ME: *It's been two nights! Why are you obsessed with me, bro?*

TJ: *Kens...don't make this weird with D or she'll never hang out with us again.*

ME: *I'm not.*

TJ: *Sure...*

I set my phone down and stared up at the ceiling waiting for sleep to take hold. The sound of Dinah's breathing eventually lulled me to sleep too.

I slipped out in the morning while she was getting ready for work with a quick wave. "I'll see you later, okay?" I said to her.

She nodded while she blow-dried her hair. "Is noon okay for you?" she yelled over the noise.

I nodded and slipped out of her condo to go next door to my own place. I was surprised to see TJ was already up, and he was in gym clothes. Even though we had a day off, it didn't mean we gave our bodies a break. Especially when we really needed to figure out if we could make it to the playoffs this season.

He smirked at me. "Do you need to come with me to the gym today, or did you get a good enough workout last night?"

I sighed. "Um...no."

"What do you mean no?"

"We just talked and fell asleep," I explained.

TJ was a casual hookup guy. Taylor was actually the first girl I had seen him hookup with for longer than a couple of weeks. I liked her, she was a sweet girl, but I think she was trying to see if she could change him. I loved the guy like a brother, but when it came to women we were just very different. I was a serial monogamist, happier to be in a relationship and he was happier to just never call women back. I don't think he understood that talking with Dinah and trying to lay out my feelings was more important to me than trying to get her naked again. I kind of felt bad for Taylor, she was a nice girl and she deserved happiness, but I didn't think she would find it with TJ. I guess that made me a bad friend, but I just didn't think he was the kind of guy into that.

"Wait, so you didn't sleep together?" he asked with a raised eyebrow.

I felt the blush color my pale face. "We did...just not last night."

His face was still scrunched up in confusion and then he just shook his head. "Man, I will never understand you."

"You going to hit the gym?" I asked, changing the subject so I didn't have to explain to TJ what it was like to actually have feelings for a woman other than wanting to sleep with her.

"Yeah, no practice today, but like we are kind of fucked this season," TJ explained with a grimace.

"Wait for me to change? I have some time for a workout this morning."

I didn't wait for his answer, but went into my room to change out of my clothes from the night before and into gym clothes. I changed into gym shorts and a red Bulldogs t-shirt. TJ was waiting for me at the kitchen counter, grabbing our water bottles and checking his watch. He looked up at the sound of my footsteps.

"Come on, let's go lift some weights and you can tell me all about what's going on with you and Dinah."

I sighed, but followed him out of our condo. He drove in his car to the gym and peppered me with questions about how the sex was with Dinah. I was not a kiss and tell guy, and there was no way I was going to describe it to him. That was between the two of us, and no one else needed to know about it. I was sure Dinah wouldn't appreciate me talking in vivid detail with the boys about the night we spent together. It wasn't their business.

At the gym, I spotted TJ while he used the bench press and gave him a taste of his own medicine. "So what's up with you and Taylor?" I asked.

He glanced up at me in annoyance, the sweat beading on his forehead while he grunted and lifted the bar above his head. "We're just hanging out," he offered.

"Uh huh."

"It's just casual."

"Does she understand that?"

He set the bar back down on the rack and stood up. He wiped down the bench and we swapped positions so now I was raising the bar above my head. "She knows what I'm about," he argued.

"Okay..."

He glared down at me. "What does that mean?"

"Listen, man, Taylor's a nice girl."

He crossed his arms over his chest. "What are you saying?"

I sighed and grunted while I did a couple more sets.

"She might say she's okay with the casual stuff, but in my experience that always leads to feelings."

"Yeah, I'm kind of worried about that," he admitted with a frown.

"T, you know it's okay to have feelings and to want a partner, right?"

He shook my head. "Nah, that's not me, man."

I rolled my eyes at him. He was hopeless. I got the feeling that something had to have happened for TJ to be so anti-relationship. The last time his twin had visited, she had mentioned some girl named Natalie they knew from back home in St. Catharines. I swear I saw him flinch at the sound of her name. When I asked him who Natalie was later he just shrugged and said, 'Some girl from high school.' I had to remind myself to ask Rox what the story was.

I finished my set and wiped down the bench. TJ went to go run on the treadmill and I opted for the bike. I put my headphones on and saw a text from Dinah.

DINAH: *Hey...can we make it one instead? I just got a meeting added to my schedule today last minute at noon.*

ME: *Sure! Anywhere close to your office you want to go?*

I pumped my legs into circles on the bike and waited for the three dots to finish while she typed her reply.

DINAH: *Let me think about it. The sandwich shop a block up is pretty good.*

ME: *Sounds good to me. See you later.*

DINAH: *Can't wait!*

I smiled at that and I didn't care if it made me seem like that weird guy in the gym. If I got to see Dinah and our relationship was moving to where I wanted it to be, I would be the weird guy in the gym. I finished my workout and met up with TJ so we could head back to our place together. He had finished before me and took a shower at the gym, but I wanted to shower in my own bathroom. I took a quick shower and examined my face in the mirror holding up my razor in my hand. I scratched a hand across my jaw, where scruff was starting to appear already. Having been friends with Dinah for so long, I knew the type of guys she liked. Especially when we were the type of friends that got drunk together and teased each other about our 'types.' Dinah liked a bearded man, and I knew she liked the hockey flow look. Hence why I kept my hair on the longish side, even though my mom hated it. The amount of 'get a haircut' texts that came through from my mom after games could fill a book.

I put the razor back into the medicine cabinet and combed out my hair. I shook my head and let it air dry and walked out of the bathroom. With my towel wrapped around my waist, I peered into my closet. What do you wear to a lunch date? I mean, it was just lunch. The part of me that was still trying to win over this woman's heart wanted to impress her. So I called Rox.

"You do know that other people have day jobs they have to be at?" she asked in way of greeting.

I stifled a laugh. "You didn't have to answer, you know."

"What's going on?" she asked.

"Um...so weird question, what do you wear to a lunch date? Or if you're not sure if it's actually a date but you asked if you could meet a woman on her lunch break?"

She barked out the loud laugh that she would kill me if I told her sounded exactly like her brother's. "Oh my god, Noah! Are you and Dinah finally a thing?"

Rox had visited a few times since I moved in with her twin, so of course she knew Dinah. She was actually the first person to call me on my bullshit about how I was in love with the older woman.

"Um...not exactly. I don't know?"

"What do you mean, you don't know?"

I dragged my hand through my hair and walked across my bedroom to my dresser to at least put on a pair of boxers. I felt a little odd talking to Rox when I was naked. I sighed. "Um, it's complicated, but I basically told her how I felt and left it up to her."

"Oh my god! You so went to Bone Town!" she squealed.

"Ugh, will you and your brother stop saying that?" I groaned.

She laughed some more. "Oh my god! Noah!"

"ROXANNE!" I yelled back at her sarcastically.

"Boo! Give me details!" she demanded.

I opened my closet door and surveyed a plain light blue button-down that might be okay. "Nope! You know I don't kiss and tell."

I could practically see her pout through the phone. "It's just Dinah, okay? You don't have to impress her. She already tolerates your existence," she assured me.

"Wow, thank you for the vote of confidence."

"No, seriously! I don't know what's in her head, but I think things will work out between you two. I mean, shit, you both have been too busy eye-fucking each other to notice."

"What?"

She cackled on the other line again. "Oh, Noah, I love you, but sometimes you can be a bit thick. Just wear like a nice pair of jeans and maybe one of your button-downs."

I pulled the shirt I was eyeing out of my closet and laid it on my bed. "Thanks, Rox. You're the best."

"Ha! Sure."

There was something odd in the tone of her voice. "You okay?"

"I'm good. You'll have to remind me when you guys are next playing Toronto and I'll try to come meet you. Tristan always forgets."

By Tristan, she meant TJ. She was the only one who called him by his first name.

I smiled. "Okay, but you are not allowed to fight with Benny again, okay?"

She scoffed. "Ugh, Michael fucking Bennett can get bent. On that cheery note, I have to get back to work. Good luck!"

I hung up with her and got dressed. I thought I looked okay, and I really hoped that Dinah was as nervous as I was. Even though it was just lunch with a friend. But it was with a friend I had a thing for and whose kisses I couldn't stop thinking about.

CHAPTER ELEVEN

DINAH

I clicked my pen furiously as my boss Stacey droned on and on about new media buying strategies. We had this last minute Media Team meeting added to the schedule this morning and I was freaking livid about it. Who schedules a meeting over lunch time? Also this meeting so could have been an email, instead it was just another colossal waste of time. It's like the company just thrived on having meetings for the sake of having meetings. Thank the hockey gods that Noah had a flexible schedule today.

Matt sat next to me and kicked my foot to get me to stop, to which I just flicked his Dire Wolf tattoo on his forearm in retaliation. Since Jason had died, Matt and I had grown close, but not close like Noah and I. Between Matt and I, it was strictly platonic, plus the whole working together thing had always turned me off to men. I was there to work, not find a husband!

We shared an annoyed look while Stacey droned on

some more. Seriously, the mundaneness of all the bullshit meetings I had on a daily basis was starting to get to me. This whole job itself was starting to get to me. Each day I woke up with the alarming fear that this was what I was going to be doing for the rest of my life. I freaking hated it. I wanted nothing more than to quit and write full-time, but I just didn't have that luxury. Even writers that did that, usually had a support system to fall back on, or they were supported by a partner. I didn't have either of those.

I felt my phone buzz in my pocket, and I stealthily looked at it from below the table.

NOAH: *Hey...I'm kind of early. Waiting in the lobby now.*

CRAP!

ME: *Sorry, hopefully almost done. Stuck in this meeting.*

NOAH: *No worries. I'll be here.*

I felt Matt elbow me and I looked down at the table to see he had slid his notebook over to me. I read the note.

You got somewhere to be?

I picked up my pen and scrawled back, *Lunch plans.*

He wrote back, *with the hockey boy???*

I didn't pick up my pen to answer that one. I was pretty sure the blush blossoming across my face told him the answer he was looking for. I pushed the notebook away and was relieved when we ended a whole three minutes early. It was kind of a record. It was almost spring but winter was lingering on, so I grabbed my jacket off the back of my chair. I checked my work email on my phone on the elevator ride down, where I saw that building management had emailed me about having a guest. Old news, buddy.

I strutted out of the elevator as soon as the doors swung open with a ding. I saw Noah was sitting in the reception area, studying one of the hipster modern art paintings that was hanging on the wall. "It's ugly, right?" I asked.

He looked at me with a smile. "Hey, girl," he greeted and ugh, I think my insides melted a little bit at those two casual words. This kid was too much.

He stood up, his whole six-foot-two frame towered over me as he straightened up. He looked nice in his black long jacket, neatly pressed baby blue button-down and the nice jeans that made his tight butt look so yummy. I'd never tell him that, because then he'd probably always wear it and that would be dangerous for me. He bent down to wrap me in a hug, lifting me a few feet off the ground. I laughed until he set me down.

"Let's go, I'm really in need of a cheesesteak right now," I urged.

He chuckled, and surprised me by sliding his big hand into mine as we walked out the door to the streets of Philadelphia. I didn't have time to process that little move of his, because I was hungry and needed food. We must have looked pretty comical next to each other though since he was like an entire foot taller than me. I dragged him through the streets, down the block to the one hole-in-the-wall pizza/sandwich shop I liked to go to on my lunch hour.

The one that my oldest brother Frankie owned.

I froze in front of the doorstep.

Noah rubbed my hand. "What's wrong?"

"Maybe we should go somewhere else?" I suggested.

Noah eyed the doorway of the place with indifference. "What's wrong with this place?" he asked.

"Nothing, it's fine. You remember my brother Frankie?"

Noah's sapphire eyes lit up in recognition. "The one who talked about all his gains?"

I shook my head with a laugh. My brother Tony was

kind of a meathead, which said something when I was standing on the street talking to a professional athlete. "No, that's Tony. Frankie's the oldest, he's kind of got that brooding, stoic thing going."

"Sleeve tattoos?" Noah asked, and I saw the wheels turning in his brain. I was one of four and came from a big loud-mouth Italian family, even Jason had a hard time remembering everyone.

"Nope, that's Eddie."

"Okay, so why are you bringing up your brothers?"

I pointed at the sign that read Mezzanetti's above the door. "Frankie owns this place, only reason why I come here."

Noah smiled then, understanding what I was getting at. "We can go someplace else if you want," he offered.

I sighed. "No. They do make a really good cheesesteak."

He laughed. "Then let's eat here. Maybe we won't run into your brother?"

"If the hockey gods are on our side today."

He laughed at that.

He held the door for me like the gentleman he was and we went inside. I sighed in relief when I didn't see my oldest brother anywhere near the front counter. He was the owner, but that didn't mean he was always in the shop. Thank the hockey gods for that. Behind the counter, a college-aged kid with floppy skater hair waited for us to order. I ordered a cheesesteak, but Noah went with the healthier option by ordering the grilled chicken wrap. Even though it was the tail-end of the season, he still stuck to a pretty strict diet.

He held out his credit card to the cashier, but I tried to stop him. "Hey, you don't have to pay for me!" I whined.

The college kid laughed at me. "Lady, just let your boyfriend pay."

Noah smiled and put an arm around my shoulder. "She's a feisty one."

The kid smirked at him while he took Noah's card and rung up our order. "Those Italian ones always are."

"Thank you," I said under my breath.

Noah rubbed my shoulder soothingly and kissed my temple. "Of course. I did ask you to lunch, so it's only fair I pay."

I didn't argue with him, but I noticed neither of us jumped to correct the kid behind the counter that Noah wasn't my boyfriend. He told me that he liked me and then left it all up to me and I still hadn't given him a clear answer. Maybe this was why he wanted to meet for lunch?

We squeezed into a booth across from each other while we waited for our food to be ready. I cracked open my bottle of water and took a sip of it nervously.

Why was I so nervous?

Noah eyed me. "You okay?"

"Shit day," I explained.

"Hence, the cheesesteak."

I nodded. "You know it. How was the gym?"

He gave me an amused look. "How did you know I hit the gym today?"

"Best friends, remember? I kind of know your schedule."

He looked amused. "I'm not sure if that's sweet or kind of creepy."

I grinned. "Little of both."

"What's going on with work?" he asked and he seemed genuinely interested in what I had to say. Maybe boring mundane jobs were interesting when your job was to always be in the spotlight?

I shrugged. "Work is work."

I didn't elaborate because our order was up and Noah jumped up to go grab it. It seemed like he was taking a long time, so I glanced over to see him talking with the guy at the counter and my oldest brother. Damnit, hockey gods, couldn't you give me a win today? Frankie raised a dark eyebrow at me and I just glared as if to say, 'Don't you dare tell, Mom.' Noah was signing something for the college kid and shaking his hand. He said something to Frankie and my brother smiled at him. At least that was good? Then he walked back over to me to set down the tray with my cheesesteak. I was so hungry that I dived right in.

Noah was laughing at me. "Damn, I forget sometimes that you vigorously enjoy food."

"You know that I'm one of four right? It's eat or you don't eat in the Mezzanetti family!" I exclaimed.

"I forgot that Lace is your married name," he mused. "Why did you keep it?"

I bit my lip and took another big bite of my sandwich so I didn't have to answer.

"Shit," he cursed. "Was that a rude question?"

I shook my head and swallowed. "Nah. Just lazy. It's a bitch to change everything back. I don't know, if I ever get married again maybe I'll change it, but Dinah Lace is such a better writer name than Dinah Mezzanetti."

His lips curled up into a smile. "The latter's quite a mouthful."

"Truly."

Noah took a bite of one half of his wrap with a smile and I continued to eat my insanely greasy cheesesteak. This was probably a bad thing to eat on a first date, but also was this a first date? Noah and I hadn't exactly defined what was happening between us. Getting in the sheets had been great, and he made it clear that he wanted more, but did I? I was racked with guilt over Jason just thinking about it.

I jumped when Noah's hand brushed across mine on top of the table. "Hey, you okay?"

I shook my head. "Sorry, spacing."

"You story plotting over there?"

"Yup!" I lied.

His clear blue eyes bored into me, and I could tell that he knew I was lying. We had been friends for too long and knew each other too well to not recognize it in each other. But Noah being the kind-hearted soul he was, didn't call me out on it.

"Hey, so what are you doing tomorrow?" he asked, changing the subject.

I searched my brain for my plans. It was a weekday, so I had to work, but after that my only plans were to drown myself in editing my book. I frowned. "Working on my book. Why?"

He shook his head. "Oh, never mind."

"Noah, what?"

He ran his hands through his hair, and I was reminded how it felt to run my own hands through his silky tresses while his big hands had roamed all over my body. Did somebody turn up the heat in here? Because I felt a little flushed just thinking about what I had done with Noah Kennedy. And how much I really wanted to do it again.

"I just wanted to know if you wanted to come to our game tomorrow night. We're on a road trip again right afterwards," he explained, but he was looking down at his plate, like he was shy about asking me. My heart melted at the sight of this hulking man being so shy around me.

"Sorry, I want to come, but I also really need to stick to my writing schedule," I explained.

He waved me off. "No, I totally understand that. I was being honest when I told you that I never wanted to keep you from that. I know how important that is for you."

If I could be more of a deliriously happy person to hear him say that, I would be a puddle of joy underneath his feet. "I'll watch from home, though."

He smiled big at me. "I know you will. Glad I got to see you today at least." He glanced at his watch. "How much time do you normally have for lunch?"

I checked my phone and frowned. "Crap, not much. I better get going. I need a box for this."

"I'll get it!" he offered and before I could protest he was jumping up to the counter to ask for one for me. I glanced over to see my brother grinning over at me, and that's when my phone buzzed and all the family group texts started coming in. Oh, fuck you, Frankie.

FRANKIE: *Dee-Dee's on a lunch date in my restaurant!*

MOM: *D's dating again? Who's the guy? Why don't you ever answer your phone??*

EDDIE: *It could be a woman, you never know!*

TONY: *Who is it, do we have to rough him up?*

FRANKIE: *Noah Freaking Kennedy!*

DAD: *The hockey player??*

MOM: *Oh Noah! He's such a nice young man.*

FRANKIE: *Bit young for her.*

EDDIE: *Get it, sis!*

DAD: *He better bring us the cup.*

ME: *I hate all of you.*

I gritted my teeth, so by the time Noah came back to the table he was concerned by how angry I looked. "Hey, what's wrong?" he asked.

I shook my head and shoved my phone back into my purse. I boxed up my sandwich and stood up. Noah took it from me and helped me back into my jacket. I gave my brother the finger behind Noah's back as we walked out. Noah slid his hand into mine once we were back on the street and walking back to my office building. I totally didn't hate it, I actually really loved the feeling of his hand in mine. My chest felt so warm, and I knew it wasn't just from the hot cheesesteak I had for lunch.

"Are your brothers going to hate me now?" he joked.

I scoffed. "They better fuck right off."

Noah's big shoulders shook with laughter. "Sorry if I caused any unnecessary family drama."

I laughed. "You've met my family, there's always some sort of drama, but Frankie did text everyone that I was on a date, which was awesome!"

He slowed his pace as we stood outside of my office building. "Was it a date?" he asked.

I looked up at him. "Didn't you want it to be?"

His hand brushed across my cheek softly, like light kisses on my skin. "Very much so, but you're the boss lady."

I felt my heart in my throat. I very much liked the sound of that. "Yes," I whispered and sighed in relief when he dipped his head down to mine and kissed me goodbye.

CHAPTER TWELVE

NOAH

Today was game day, so that meant we needed to prepare. I needed to get to the arena, do my rituals, and have my pre-game meal, before getting back out there on the ice. Dinah once made fun of me because my pre-game meal was a ham and cheese sandwich. One time the media asked me why I was playing better, which I thought was such a dumb fucking question, so I sarcastically said I ate two ham and cheese sandwiches, instead of the one. Fans ate that shit up though, so I couldn't be bothered by it.

I was bummed Dinah couldn't come to the game tonight, but I got to see her yesterday and kiss her goodbye after our lunch date. Her brother Frankie had only razzed me a little bit, and just said to not hurt her, which I never dreamed of doing.

"What did your sandwich ever do to you?" Riley asked me.

"Huh?" I asked, pulling myself out of my thoughts. I

was staring intently at the sandwich in my hands. "Nothing, just thinking."

He shared a look with TJ. "You all right, man?"

I nodded and rubbed my hand over my growing stubble. I usually liked to be clean shaven, but I knew Dinah thought beards were hot, so I was trying to see if I could do it. It was a little too scratchy for me right now.

"I'm fine," I insisted.

"Get your head in the game!" TJ exclaimed.

I gave him the finger. "I'm good."

"You sure, man?" TJ asked with a raised eyebrow. "You ask D to come tonight?"

"She can't. It's fine."

"Ooohhhh," they both said in unison and shared a knowing look.

"Shut up, it's fine," I argued.

"Man, I've never seen a chick twist you up like this," Riley commented with a shake of his blonde head.

I really didn't want to be talking to them about Dinah. She definitely did not have me twisted up in anything. She had texted me earlier and said she felt bad, but it wasn't a big deal. It wasn't! I really respected that she worked just as hard as I did, and in two jobs. I only ever wanted to support her passion, not steal her time away from it.

I had to stop thinking about it because the guys were right, I needed to get my head on straight. We were a couple points out of the wildcard spot for the playoffs, and we needed to focus on the game. The subject changed to our special teams and what we needed to do if we honestly thought we had a shot at the playoffs. This was my third season with this team, and I had been enjoying playing in this city, but now I really wanted to buckle down and bring some pride to Philadelphia. They were desperate for the

Cup, and I wanted to be on the team that brought it to them. I just wasn't sure if this year was our year to do it.

"You gonna do your pre-game nap?" TJ asked after we cleaned up after the pre-game meal at the arena.

I nodded. "Always. We carpooling together?"

"Tradition man!"

I shook my head with a laugh and we headed home together. TJ and I went our separate ways when we got home, and I stripped down to my boxers before sliding into my bed. I checked my phone to set my alarm and saw a text from Dinah.

DINAH: *Good luck with your game today, I know you're probably taking your pre-game nap, so I don't know when you'll see this.*

ME: *Just sliding into bed actually, you caught me.*

DINAH: *Sorry!*

ME: *Don't be. Good luck with writing tonight. Bummed you can't make it tonight, but I understand.*

DINAH: *Maybe I can come to the next one?*

ME: *You know you can.*

I fell asleep with a smile on my face and ready to take on Carolina.

❄

By the time I was walking down the tunnel with the rest of my team, I had my game face on and I was ready to take on whatever the Carolina Thrashers had to throw at us. I was on the starting line-up tonight, so it was nice to skate out onto center ice with my teammates. I fist-bumped the little flag-bearer who was standing next to me for the National Anthem, and then I was ready for this game.

Girard took the face-off and he won, taking the puck up

past the blue line and passing it back to me. I passed it back and he took the shot, but it went off the post. I scrambled for the rebound and passed to TJ, who whacked it in. TJ and I threw our hands up in celebration and we hugged it out.

Tonight I was feeling good, and it must have been spreading, because we ended up winning the game, 2-1. Metzy was hot in goal tonight, and everyone was hungry to win. I wished we could keep it going, but I had been studying stats with Riley lately and it wasn't looking good.

The team walked into the dressing room with smiles on their faces. I had to do a post-game interview about the assist, probably because TJ had hopped in the shower and they were tired of waiting around for him. Things felt really good, like we could make up for a shitty first half of the season and could turn this ship around. I was working hard at this, and I wanted to bring that glory back to this city. Our young goalie Seamus Metz, who was like twenty going on forty, kept telling us we had to take this one game at a time. I think he was right.

We were on the road for a game tomorrow night in Newark, but at least that meant I could sleep in my own bed tonight. I drove TJ and I back to our place and pretty much crashed as soon as I got into bed. I checked my phone for the first time since getting to the arena and saw Dinah had texted a few times since our conversation earlier today.

DINAH: *Sorry, I couldn't be there tonight.*

DINAH: *These edits are killing me, I think I need to rewrite this whole thing.*

DINAH: *YAY! I saw your assist. GET IT!*

I smiled to myself, and looked up when TJ stepped into my doorway. "You have the dumbest grin on your face right now."

I shook my head. "That's just my face!"

He pointed at my phone. "That who I think it is?"

I nodded.

He shook his head. "I know I warned you about falling in love with her, but you already are, aren't you?"

I ignored him and started typing out a response to Dinah. "I don't know what you're talking about."

"Bro, you're hopeless!" He shook his head and walked away. I got up and shut my bedroom door. It was late, so I felt bad about texting her back, but I figured she wouldn't see until the morning.

ME: *NOOOOO don't rewrite it! I'm almost done reading it, and I'm really enjoying it.*

I saw three little dots appear so I knew she was typing.

DINAH: *...really?*

ME: *Yes, really. Girl, you have to be confident in your writing!*

Dinah was a mystery to me, she always came off as so sure of herself, but when you got to know her you saw that she didn't really know what she was doing. Like the rest of us. It wasn't until you really got to know her that you could see the cracks in her facade. Writing was her ultimate passion, so I think she was just extra hard on herself about it. I definitely understood that, as I was the same with hockey. I talked her off a ledge when she was editing her first book, and she had helped me in the past when I would think about that empty net goal I missed seven years ago in juniors. It's always the missed goals that you remember.

It was crazy to me that she didn't think she was good at writing. I wasn't really her audience, but her books appealed to me because of the hockey in them. I think she thought men didn't want to like love stories.

My phone buzzed in my hand again. I smiled at seeing her typing back.

DINAH: *Your support means so much to me, I don't think you really understand how much your opinion means to me.*

ME: *AW!*

DINAH: *SHUT UP*

ME: *HEY! Why are you up so late, don't you have work tomorrow?*

DINAH: *Ugh, yes. 'Night. Good luck with your games this weekend.*

ME: *Night!*

I laid back on my bed with a sigh. I had never felt lonely before being alone in my bed, but having spent the last two nights with Dinah at my side, it felt cold. I set my alarm, we had to be down the turnpike early tomorrow for morning skate, so I had better get to sleep as soon as possible. Of course, I had a hard time sleeping and ended up finishing Dinah's book before I could go to sleep. When I did fall asleep I just was tortured by dreams of taking Dinah in my arms and having my way with her multiple times. I had fallen deep into love with her, and I wasn't sure I would ever come out of it.

CHAPTER THIRTEEN

DINAH

I spent the weekend working on edits, which no one ever really told me how much they fucking sucked before. Why did I want to be a writer? Noah had texted me his feedback about my book, and a lot of his issues with it were the same as my editor. So at least I had consistency. I got so busy, that I basically never left my apartment, and barely even ate dinner. Unless you counted bowls of pretzels as dinner, which I didn't think really counted. I had kind of become a shell of a person after Jason died. He always made sure I ate, but now it was like I was just pretending to be an adult.

Since Frankie spilled to my nosy family, I had been skirting their calls and leaving them unread. So much so that when I got home from work on Tuesday night, I wasn't that surprised to find Eddie loitering in our lobby, much to the chagrin of the management. I was annoyed to see him here, but that was mostly because Noah and TJ were due back tonight and I wasn't sure if Noah and I were going to see each other tonight. He had seemed really tired when we video chatted last night and when I hung up I realized with a pang that I really missed him when he was on the road.

Eddie smirked at me, and pulled me into a big hug. All of the Mezzanetti boys were on the tall side, so I think there must have been a mix-up in the factory when I was born. Eddie was barely a year older than me, so we were pretty close compared to Tony and Frankie. But it didn't mean I was happy to see him. He was holding a pan of something and I cringed.

"Why are you here?" I groaned.

Eddie laughed and shoved the pan at me, his rose tattoo on his right wrist peeked out from his jacket sleeve. I sighed and took it, while I hit the up button on the elevator. The condo I lived in was super nice, but if it wasn't for the fact that Jason had bought it outright with his inheritance money from his grandmother, I didn't think I would still be living here. Especially now that I was the sole earner.

"From Frankie," Eddie explained and nodded his head at the casserole dish. "He said you were on deadline and knew you would forget to eat."

I might think Frankie was an overprotective asshat, but my oldest brother was such a caregiver. "Wow, could he 'mom' me even more?" I asked sarcastically.

Eddie laughed. "Probably? I think he actually does it because Mom tells him to."

We both scoffed. Frankie was Mom's favorite and she didn't even try to deny it anymore. Everyone thought since I was the baby and only girl in the family that Mom just wanted her girl, but my dad was blunt enough to admit I was an oops baby. Thanks, Dad!

We stepped out of the elevator on my floor and I unlocked the door to my condo. Eddie kicked off his shoes and shed his jacket tossing it across my armchair. I took the casserole into my kitchen and peeled back the tinfoil to reveal the homemade lasagna.

"You want a plate?" I called into the living room to my brother.

"Nah, I've got plans!" he yelled back.

I heated up a plate for myself and came back into the living room with it. I tucked my feet underneath myself on my couch and dug into the lasagna. I moaned at the delicious food hitting my taste buds. My oldest brother was an amazing cook. It was why I always went to his sandwich shop when I needed to get out of the office.

Eddie didn't say anything, just checked his phone and waited for me to start the conversation.

I swallowed a bite and looked over at him. He looked up in question, feeling my eyes on him. "So what's up?" I asked.

He shrugged. "I just came to see if you were all right."

"Fine, big brother," I scoffed.

He smiled, and flipped his long bangs out of his face. "Okay really they wanted me to find out about you and the hockey boy."

I rolled my eyes. "Knew it! You spy!"

He laughed. "You know I don't care. I just want you to be happy."

"I am happy."

"D, are you?"

I took another bite of my dinner. "Yes."

"Noah's treating you right?"

I sighed. "I'm not sure what we are yet."

Recognition dawned in my brother's eyes. "Oh. Did he tell you how he feels yet?"

"What? How did you know? Yeah, he basically left it all up to me."

Eddie furrowed his brow. "Look, D, don't be stupid. That man really loves you. I spent years fighting my sexuality, fighting who I was, don't fight what's happening between you and Noah just because you're scared."

I just stared at my brother for a long time. "I'm not scared," I argued.

Eddie gave me a hard look. "Yeah, you are. You think that moving on is betraying your dead husband. Jason liked Noah a lot, Noah's a good man and that's what makes it worse for you."

I chewed softly. Fuck, how did Eddie know me so well? "Wait a second, you said he loves me?"

Eddie looked at me like he was talking to a child. "Duh! What man would come to the funeral of another woman's husband, deal with our batshit insane family, and let her cry as much as she wanted on his shoulder?"

"Noah's Canadian!" I argued. "He's just really nice."

Eddie put his head in his hands. "Oh my god, I thought Tony was the dumb sibling. Noah did all that shit because that man's smitten with you and probably has been for a really long time. Probably even before Jason passed."

I chewed my fingernail. That was a lot to process.

"He never tried anything when Jason was alive."

"Of course he didn't! He's a good guy, not a homewrecker." Eddie put a tatted hand on my knee in comfort. "Hey you like this guy, right?"

I nodded.

"Then what's the problem?"

"He's a bit young for me, Frankie even said," I admitted in a low voice.

"Oh, fuck, D! He was just teasing. I like Noah, he's a

good guy, you shouldn't be worried about your dead husband if you really like him."

"But—"

He cut me off, "Jason's gone, worrying about if he would be okay with you moving on with a hunky hockey player will do neither of you any favors. I don't want to see you lose something good."

I put my empty plate on the coffee table and sighed. I felt a buzzing in my purse and pulled out my phone to see a text from Noah.

NOAH: *Do I get to see you tonight?*

I typed back to him quickly.

ME: *Maybe...my brother Eddie came to check up on me.*

I eyed my brother over my phone, but it seemed like our conversation was finally over. I set my phone down on the coffee table next to my empty plate. "How did the shop opening go?" I asked.

Eddie beamed at my question. Eddie wasn't just tatted up for show. He was a tattoo artist and he and his partner Alex had just opened up a new place on South Street. I still didn't know how they got such an amazing location. I touched the tiny quill tattoo on my wrist in remembering the one and only tattoo I let my brother give me.

"It went really well. Business is good. Thank god for Alex's sister Veronica finding our receptionist or we might be fucked. You ever going to let me give me another one?" he asked.

I shook my head. "Nah, I'm good with my little quill. It suits me. How's Alex?"

Eddie beamed even more. "Good, things are really good."

"Eds, I'm really happy for you."

He nodded. "You think I need to tell the family?"

I shrugged. "That's your business. I'm so pissed at Frankie for telling you all I was out with Noah. It was our first date!"

Eddie hung his head. "Oh, sis, I'm sorry!"

I saw my phone light up some more. Eddie nodded at it. "That your man?"

I nodded and smiled, really liking the sound of that. Noah Kennedy being called 'my man' made my heart and maybe also my girl parts sing. "Yeah, I think the team just got back."

Eddie stood up and was shrugging his jacket back on. "I got to meet Alex for dinner. I think you should tell your hockey player that you like him too." Eddie bent down to kiss my forehead. "Seriously, baby sis, don't lose him."

Eddie let himself out of my condo and I sat on the couch thinking about what he said. He was right, but that didn't mean I wasn't still scared. Noah had laid all his cards on the table, so maybe I should give him a real chance at this thing. I put my plate away and changed out of my work clothes and into comfy leggings and a big t-shirt.

I walked back into my living room and texted Noah asking him if he wanted to come over. Within seconds there was a knock on my door. I smiled and opened it to him standing there looking casual in a Bulldogs t-shirt and athletic shorts. He looked so boyishly cute, and I loved it.

"Hi!" I greeted and he hugged me before pushing me inside and shutting my front door.

"Hey, yourself," he breathed and bent down to kiss me. I pouted when the kiss ended too soon.

I disentangled myself from him. "Did you eat?" I asked.

"Actually no," he admitted.

"Oh good! Eddie brought lasagna from Frankie, I'll make you up a plate," I told him and sprinted off into the kitchen. I grabbed two beers and sectioned off a big helping of the lasagna on a plate for Noah. I walked back into the living room and handed Noah his food.

He thanked me and I watched amused as he scarfed down the big helping I had given him. He was a hockey player, maybe he needed to eat more? I took a sip of my beer. "There's more if you want," I offered.

He smiled as he damn near licked the plate. "This is good. Damn, your brother's a good cook."

I laughed. "Which is why I go to his shop on my lunch break, even if he's a nosy fucker."

He set his plate down and took my hand in his. He brought it to his lips and kissed it. "I missed you. Tell me about your week."

I was pretty sure I melted into the couch right then and there. "Tell me about your games."

"You first."

"No!" I exclaimed with a laugh. "Tell me if you're okay after taking that hit last night."

He ran a hand through his long hair and shrugged. "I'm fine, like I told you last night. Hey, so I did want to ask, do you want to come to the game tomorrow?"

"You want me to come?"

His thumb was rubbing across the pad of my hand. "Definitely."

I nodded. "Then I definitely want to be there."

"Now tell me about your day and how the editing's going," he insisted and I did, but I couldn't sum up the courage yet to tell him how I felt about him.

❄

"Whoa! Look who's here!" Mia announced as I slunk into the seat next to her with a beer in my hand. She rushed over to give me a hug. I always liked Mia, she was sweet, and at least she didn't make me feel like a complete outsider.

"Hi, Mia," I greeted with a smile. I had somehow managed to get down here in time to see the puck drop. I took SEPTA because I was just not dealing with the nightmare traffic.

I hugged her back and tried not to spill the beer all down her back. Brianna Girard was sitting down in one of the seats and she gave me a small wave. I waved back.

"Oh my god! So, I didn't know you were a writer!" Mia squealed.

I took a sip of my beer, I was pretty sure I had mentioned it before. "Oh?"

"Yeah, my sister really loved your first book."

"Oh, really?" I asked perking up.

Mia nodded. "I love YA! The love story you wrote was so cute."

"Mia, that means a lot to me, thanks. Hey, if she wants a signed copy, I can get you one."

Her eyes nearly bugged out of her head. "Really? That would be awesome."

"Yes, really," I said with a smile.

I was still a newbie writer, so if I had a fan in Mia's sister, I wanted to keep that fan. Last night, Noah and I had recapped our time away and cuddled in my bed until he fell asleep. I had been slightly disappointed because I wanted to tear his clothes off as soon as he walked in, but I knew traveling could be exhausting. Also it gave me the chance to sneak away to work on my edits. Noah pried me away from my desk around midnight just so I could get some sleep. I was waist-deep in rewriting a huge chunk of the novel, and I wasn't sure how I was going to get through it. I had been bouncing it off with my writer support group, and they had been super helpful, but I guess I needed to take a night off.

I looked down on the ice and watched the guys. Our team wasn't aggressive enough, they were slow on the forecheck, not getting enough shots on goal, and there were way too many turnovers in the neutral zone. I chewed on my bottom lip. I watched in horror as a second goal slipped past Metz, and the feeling on the bench was not good. Noah had his head in his hands sitting on the bench. This was not good.

Mia and I shared a worried look. I gulped down my beer while the horn sounded ending the first period 2-0.

"So..." Mia started, while I watched the mites on ice. Baby hockey players, how cute!

"So what?" I asked, but I had a feeling I knew where this was going.

She smirked at me, and next to her Lacey, Metzy's girlfriend, had perked up. "Oh?" Lacey asked. Her golden-brown eyes twinkled. She pushed her black braids behind her shoulder and ran a hand down her brown cheek. "Wait, are you like THE Dinah?"

I raised an eyebrow. "Wait, what?"

Lacey glanced over at Mia and then at Brianna, who was cutting her hand across her neck. I glared. "What in the actual fuck?" I exclaimed.

"Uh, wait, do you not know?" Lacey asked.

"Know what?"

"Oh, girlfriend, Noah's in love with you," Mia admitted.

"Excuse me?" I asked.

Mia turned to Brianna who just shrugged. "Apparently he talks about you a lot. You should really just talk to him."

I didn't know what to think about that. Wasn't it exactly

what Eddie had said to me last night? It was true that my favorite part of my day was hearing from him, and I couldn't help the smile spreading across my face whenever a text message from him lit up on my phone. I knew I had feelings for him, but Eddie was right, I was just afraid. I pushed the thought to the side as the second period got underway. I tried to focus on the game, but all I could think about was the way Noah looked at me, and how it felt when he kissed me.

But I didn't miss when he scored the game winning goal with TJ getting the apple.

"Come on," Brianna urged. "Let's go get a drink. The boys will be a while with press and everything."

I checked the time on my phone. It was just after ten, and I had work in the morning, but I was debating if I could just work from home tomorrow. I wanted, no, I needed to see Noah again tonight. I wanted to really pay close attention to the way he looked at me when he saw me.

Mia grabbed my arm. "Come on, girl!"

I stood up and followed her to her car, where she drove us to the bar they usually went to for drinks after the game. It was a local place, and I think it was owned by an ex-Bulldog because there was a ton of hockey stuff along the walls. A lot of it for Philadelphia.

"I have to ask, do you not have feelings for Noah?" Mia asked.

I took a sip of my beer. "Honestly? I don't know."

She cocked an eyebrow at me. "How come?"

"I never did the whole dating thing before," I explained.

"What do you mean?"

"I met my husband in college, we dated for years before we got married and then he died. I've only been on one date since then. I'm not sure how this goes."

She surprised me by hugging me. "Oh, I had no idea. But I get it, Adam and I have been dating since high school. I would be just as clueless if we broke up."

I almost didn't know who she was talking about, because I only ever knew her boyfriend as Hallsy. I guess it was the same for me since Noah was Kennedy or Kens to the guys, but he always wanted me to call him by his first name.

I couldn't really say anything because then I heard. "Hey, you came!"

I looked up and saw Noah, TJ, Hallsy, and Riley all coming over to us. Noah leaned down to hug me and he kissed me on the cheek. It made me feel all warm inside, and that's when I knew I was in deep trouble. I didn't even notice if he was looking at me the same way, I just knew that I wanted something more with Noah, and I didn't know if that would ruin our friendship. But he had told me he liked me, so what was the worst that could happen?

CHAPTER FOURTEEN

NOAH

God, she was so cute when she blushed. I hadn't even thought about it when I kissed her on the cheek, because we hadn't really talked about if I was allowed to kiss her in public. I wanted to, I wanted to show the world how much I loved her, even if she didn't love me. She didn't flinch away or laugh it off, she just blushed and hugged me back even tighter. I shamelessly nuzzled her neck and breathed in the vanilla scent of her perfume. I had missed that when I was on the road, so when I woke up in her bed this morning I realized I was in way deeper than I realized. And we hadn't even had sex last night, even though I knew she wanted to.

From behind her back I saw TJ making the motion of a 'V' with his two fingers over his mouth and he waggled his tongue in-between them. Riley laughed and I gave TJ the finger.

"Hey, I saw that," she called him out for it. I loved that she didn't take any of our shit.

I pulled away from her. TJ laughed and gave her a hug too. "Hey, D. You see this guy's sick-ass goal?"

I ran a hand down my face and blushed now.

She nodded at TJ. "It was awesome. And here I thought I was such a jinx."

Hallsy was in deep conversation with Mia now, and Riley had sidled up to the bar to talk to some leggy blonde. I turned back to my two best friends in the entire world, who were now looking at me expectantly. "What?" I asked.

They both just laughed.

"Nothing," Dinah said with the shake of her head.

"Hey, how's the editing going?" I asked her.

She groaned and dropped her head into her chest. "Don't remind me. I have a lot of rewriting to do."

"On your book?" TJ asked. "Will you let us read it?"

I bit my lip, and she just stared at me. TJ looked back and forth between us. He put a hand over his heart and looked offended. "You wound me, D. You gave it to this dummy, before me?"

She waved her hand at him. "You wouldn't like it."

"Why not?"

"Not enough sex in it," I joked.

Dinah laughed that hearty laugh of hers and tipped her head back. Her long dark hair whipped back and forth in the ponytail she had put it up in tonight. My eyes roamed over her outfit, she looked way too good in that tight striped dress, black tights, and heeled boots. She must have come straight from work, but I didn't mind because she looked *good*. I had showered after our game and was back in my suit. I straightened my tie nervously. She glanced up at me with a questioning look, and I realized I had been staring.

TJ jabbed me in the elbow. "Dude," was all he said.

I shook my head, my long hair getting messed up. TJ

shook his head at me and went over to talk to Riley. Dinah wrapped her arms around herself.

Nervously I pushed my hair out of my eyes, and she smiled up at me sweetly. This woman had no idea what she did to me. "I'm really glad you came," I told her.

"Me too. It was a really good goal."

I eyed her suspiciously. "But?"

She sighed. "You guys kind of pulled that win out of your asses."

I barked out a laugh and she just shrugged. "What? Am I not supposed to tell you the truth anymore?"

I just shook my head. "No, you can. I like when you call me on my shit."

She smiled and sipped down the rest of her beer. She checked the time on her phone and stifled a yawn behind her hand.

"You look really tired."

She nodded. "I am. I should have taken tomorrow off, but now I have a meeting first thing. COOL!"

"Why don't I take you home?" I offered. I waved TJ over, but he shook his head. Now he was talking to the leggy blonde at the bar. More power to him. I wondered what happened with Riley, she seemed like his type. He was a little too engrossed in his phone, so maybe he was just oblivious.

She paid out her tab, and I slipped my hand in hers while we walked out the door. When she had looked at me when I got to the bar, her eyes had this shining look in them. Like they had lit up when she saw me, but maybe it was just the alcohol. Maybe she didn't feel about me the way I felt about her. Because as much as I wanted to take her to bed again, I also wanted to just hold her in my arms and tell her I loved her.

She ended up falling asleep in my car on the way back home. I had to shake her awake in the parking garage. "Hey," I said softly.

Her eyes fluttered open sleepily. "Hmm?"

"Come on, you fell asleep in the car. Let's get you upstairs and to bed."

Her lips curled into a smile. "Is that the line you use on all the girls?"

I laughed and ran a hand through my shaggy long hair. "Why, did that work on you?"

She laughed, but let me put my arm around her shoulder as we walked to the elevator that took us to our floor. We stopped at her door where she fished around for her keys in her purse.

I put my hands in my pockets nervously, and then removed them, pushing my hair out of my eyes again. After I took her to lunch, we hadn't had a chance to go on another date, and I wanted one so badly. I had to push down my nerves and just ask her out again. But then she smiled at me and was pulling on my tie to pull me down to her level, and the next thing I knew we were making out against her front door. My hands were gripping her waist, and her small hands were threading through my hair. I kind of liked how aggressive she got and pulled my hair to get me closer to her.

"Ew, get a room you two," I heard TJ say from behind me.

We pulled away suddenly. I straightened my tie, and Dinah smoothed down her hair, but the blush wasn't leaving her face. TJ just laughed and shook his head before heading into our shared condo.

"Do you want to come inside?" she asked.

The tightening in my pants was screaming yes, but my heart was screaming no. I had stayed over her place last night, but we just talked and held each other until I passed out from jet lag. She must have snuck away when I fell asleep because when I woke up an hour later I pried her away from her desk and made her go to sleep.

"Um, it's late," I explained.

Her face fell, and the look of disappointment nearly broke my heart in two.

"I mean, you have work in the morning. I don't want to keep you up late."

She nodded and smiled, but it didn't quite reach her eyes, so I knew she was faking it. I saw the turmoil in her eyes.

"What's tomorrow like for you?" I asked.

She checked her phone. "You mean after I get done work?"

"Yeah, I want to take you out to dinner."

"Like a second date?"

"Yes, that's exactly what I mean."

Her cute mouth made a little 'O'. Oh no, she was going to say no, she just wanted this to be physical. She was going to tell me she didn't feel the same way I did, even when I had laid all my cards on the table for her to see.

But then she smiled big and nodded. "Okay."

"Okay?" I asked surprised.

She rolled her eyes at me. She leaned up and I bent my head down again so she could kiss my cheek. "Yes, Noah. I am saying yes to another date with you."

I moved my mouth, so it was on her's again. She sighed into the kiss, and I just wanted to pull her legs around my waist and ravish her right here, but I could wait until tomorrow night. She said yes! She actually would let me take her out again, that had to mean something. That had to mean that she liked me more than she liked my dick. At least I hoped so.

She pulled away from me, her hands pushed lightly on my chest. "You better get out of here now, or else I'm going to drag you into my bed, and as much as I want to do that, I'm really tired."

I smiled down at her. "Goodnight, Dinah."

"Goodnight, Noah," she called back as she opened her front door. I waited for the click of the lock before opening my own door.

I walked inside and TJ was sitting on the couch with a beer in hand and a game controller in the other. He looked up at me with a confused look. "The sex must be bad if you're that quick."

I gave him the finger, and flopped down on the couch beside him. I loosened my tie enough so I could take it off and threw it on the couch next to me. I kicked off my shoes and watched him play on our gaming console.

"So, this thing with D, is it serious?" he asked.

I shrugged. "I want it to be. I asked her to dinner."

"She said yes?"

I nodded.

"Where are you going to take her?"

I leaned my head back on the couch and stretched out my impossibly long legs. "I hadn't even thought it through yet. I was more worried she would say no. I should call Rox, she'd know what to do."

He raised an eyebrow at me. "Aren't you two already fucking? Why would she said no?"

"Yeah, but I don't want it to just be physical. I want her to know that."

He shook his head at me and rubbed his two fingers between his eyes. "Kens, you're so done for."

I punched him in the shoulder. "Is it so wrong to want love?"

He shrugged. "I don't think I'm wired that way."

I clapped him on the shoulder. "Maybe one day. How are things with Taylor?"

He groaned. "Don't change the subject!"

"I'm not, just how are things?"

"Done with her."

"Why?"

He shrugged. "She wants what you want, and I don't want that. Unlike you, I don't want to be tied down."

I ran a hand down my jaw at the beard that was starting to come through. I was debating if I should shave it off tomorrow, but Dinah did like beards. "You think I should shave?"

He eyed me. "I was kind of wondering why you hadn't in a few days. Is it because D likes beards?"

"Yes," I grumbled under my breath.

He cackled. "Then keep it. I have to ask, what's she like in bed?"

"NOPE! Some secrets belong behind closed doors," I urged and stood up from the couch.

I heard him still asking inappropriate questions as I walked into my bedroom and started getting ready for bed. I couldn't believe it, Dinah was actually going to go out with me again.

CHAPTER FIFTEEN

DINAH

My knee bounced up and down underneath my desk. Matt looked around his monitor to glare at me.

"Did you have too much coffee today or what?" he seethed.

I shook my head. Not enough. I was nervous. Noah was taking me on a date tonight. A DATE! Okay, technically it was a second date, since we went to lunch before his last road trip. However, a dinner date was completely different from a lunch break date. A dinner date meant we were probably going to have sex again, and I was super nervous about that. Sex with Noah the first time had been great, he was gentle and tender in bed and I was itching to do it again. But since we were going out for a second time, I knew it was time to woman up and tell him that I liked him too and I wanted this to be a real thing. I had no idea what I was supposed to wear!

Matt threw a pen at me. "What's with you today? I thought you would have been in a good mood today?"

I shook my head and threw the pen back. "What, why?"

He stared at me blankly like I was an idiot. "The hockey team won. I figured that meant you got it in last night."

"Nope!"

Matt's eyes narrowed to slits. "What do you mean 'no'?"

"I mean, I didn't get laid last night, if you really needed to know."

"What, why not?"

"Becauseheaskedmetodinnertonight," I rushed out in one breath.

"What?" he asked, completely confused. I spread my fingers across my face to peek out from them, and Matt had the biggest grin on his face. "Get it, girl!" he exclaimed. His reaction was kind of a relief, because I had been worried he would feel some protectiveness about his late best friend.

"Oh, I intend to."

I felt like the hours were going by so slowly, but maybe it was just because I was too excited about going out with Noah. He wouldn't tell me where we were going, so I had zero clue what to wear. It was super frustrating, but he wouldn't tell me even when I begged. I even tried to get TJ to coax it out of him, but TJ hadn't answered any of my texts.

Dick.

At lunch, I went down into the courtyard and I called my sister-in-law Chloe. Chloe was my best friend in the whole world, but she lived across the country, so we didn't get to see each other much. Chloe was also Jason's younger sister.

"Hey, girl!" she exclaimed.

"I'm on my lunch break, is this an okay time to talk?" I

asked. Chloe worked from home, so I knew my lunch time was usually an okay time for her to talk.

"It's fine. What's going on?"

I chewed my bottom lip. "Why does something have to be going on?"

"I already finished reading your book, so that's not it. Come on, girl, spill!"

"Um..." I trailed off not sure how I was supposed to start this conversation. "Do you think it's too soon for me to start dating again?"

"Wait, what?"

"Oh..." I trailed off. This was probably a bad subject to broach with her.

"No, girl, yes! You should be happy. Just because my brother's dead doesn't mean your love life has to be too. Is there a guy?"

"I have a date tonight," I admitted.

I had to pull the phone away from my ear from all her squealing. "Oh my god! I'm so happy for you. Anyone I know, not that guy who—"

I cut her off, "Oh god no."

"Dinah, have you already fucked this guy?" she accused.

Shit, she did know me too well.

"How did you know that?" I demanded.

She laughed. "Because you got this dreamy sound in your voice. You have to tell me who it is!"

"No! You will judge me."

"Girl, no judgement here."

I paused a beat. "He's younger."

"No!" she exclaimed in disbelief. "Did you fuck Noah Kennedy?"

"Um..." I trailed off not sure how to answer that.

Chloe just laughed on the other line. "Your brothers told me that you two had a cute little lunch date at Frankie's shop."

I groaned. Ugh, I was so going to kill Frankie. Good lasagna be damned, he was a rat bastard.

She laughed some more. "Girl! Good for you. How was it?"

"That's not why I called you!" I scolded.

"Oh right. No, it's not too soon. Do you like Noah?"

"I think so. He told me he likes me, but left things up to me."

"Then go for it. You should be happy."

I paused for a moment, letting it all sink in.

She sighed on the other line. "You shouldn't feel guilty because Jason's gone. I don't know how he would feel about you dating a hockey hottie, but he wouldn't want you to be unhappy."

"I have no idea what to wear tonight!"

"Let me think about it, and I'll let you know. I got to jet."

I hit end on my phone and slid my phone back into the pocket of my dress pants. She was not helpful at all. I walked back up to my building and got back to work. I had digital reporting to get done, so I put my headphones on and buried myself in the very boring numbers. Which was hard to do when I was just daydreaming about what Noah was going to do to me tonight. Maybe we didn't even need the dinner. Could I just ask him to skip it so I could drag him into my bed instead and do dirty things to him? I clenched my thighs just thinking about his head between my legs again. God, how could anyone ever tell him he was bad at going down on them? That boy had a magic tongue. Plus he knew how to use his stick.

Chloe made good on her promise to help me, telling me to go with the classic black dress and heeled boots. I had to wear a cardigan over it, because the only black dress I owned was sleeveless, but I thought it was okay. I was just finishing up applying red lipstick when there was a knock on my door. Noah was nothing if not punctual.

I opened the door, and he was standing there leaning up against it, wearing a nice gray suit. His long hair was pushed back behind his ears, but it hung loose. He hadn't bothered to shave, and he looked so sexy with that scruff around his face. I kind of wondered if he remembered that I liked guys with beards. He had to, because he always complained that facial hair was so itchy. He eyed me up and down with a smile.

"You look good," he commented.

"It's not too much? You didn't tell me where we're going," I nagged and poked him in the chest.

He winked. "It's a secret! You ready to go?"

I flipped off the light switch, grabbed my coat, purse, and locked my door behind me. He slyly slid his hand in mine, like I wouldn't have noticed, and I laced my small fingers in-between his larger ones. I knew I was short, but he seemed to always remind me with his hulking figure. I did always have a thing for tall boys. He ended up taking me to a nice little Thai place, he knew I loved Thai food. Pad Thai and crispy tofu here I come!

He pulled out my chair, like a perfect gentleman. I laughed to myself, he was being way too nice right now. I settled into my seat to look at the menu. "We're definitely way over dressed for this place," I mused.

He smiled over the menu at me and glanced around. He loosened his tie. "Yeah, I guess. I debated taking you somewhere nicer, but I know how much you like Thai food. We could go somewhere else?"

I waved him off. "This is perfect. Good choice."

A waiter came over to take our orders. Noah kept pushing his hair behind his ear, so I knew he was nervous. I reached a hand across the table and placed it over his big one. "Hey, why do you seem so nervous? It's just me."

He squeezed my hand back and then let it go. "Sorry."

"How many Canadian sorry's am I going to get tonight?" I joked.

He laughed. "Oh, you think you're so funny, eh?"

"Um, I *know* I am funny," I told him with a grin. I teased him about the 'eh's' and 'sorry's' but secretly I loved them.

He smiled at me, and it went all the way to his eyes. When he looked at me, I felt like he was looking into my soul. I had been with my husband for a long time, but I think it was okay for me to date again and to find happiness. He wouldn't have wanted me to die alone and without someone, right? But was that person Noah? When I looked at him it felt right, but I couldn't tell for sure. What if I was making a mistake?

"So…I think you're still waiting on an answer from me," I began.

He smiled at me from over his glass. "It's no rush," he assured me.

I shook my head. "I don't want you to think that I don't want this," I explained and gestured between the two of us.

He cocked his head at me. "What are you saying?"

I swallowed, but I steeled myself and made myself look into his ocean-blue eyes. "Noah, I very much would like to date you."

He smiled big at that, and I smiled back. We were silent

for a moment, the two of us just eating our food and relaxing in each other's company. I loved spending time with him, and now that we had both laid out our feelings, I felt like I could relax.

I broke the silence, by admitting, "I never did the dating thing."

"What do you mean?" he asked after he took a drink of his water.

"I met Jason in college. I don't think anyone has ever asked me out to dinner before."

He scrunched up his face at me. "That's not true! What about that guy you met at one of our games?"

I groaned. "Don't remind me."

"Where did he end up taking you?"

"Just some run-of-the-mill Italian place. It was fine, this is better."

"Are you picky about Italian because of your family?" he asked, clearly thinking about my brother Frankie.

The question threw me off, but he was actually onto something there. The Italian place that guy had taken me to was beyond mediocre. Like I could have cooked better, and the cooking gene seemed to have passed me over.

I nodded. "Yeah, I guess I am. Glad you didn't pick Italian."

He grinned. He was so cute when he did that.

After dinner, we ended up back in my condo, where I kicked off my boots in relief. Those had been killing me all night. Noah took off his own shoes and left them at my front door. He shed his suit jacket and flopped his large frame onto my couch. His hands reached up to loosen the tie around his neck. My mouth watered at the sight of him, he looked so deliciously sexy just then. How had we only slept together once? I was definitely changing that tonight.

I had to go into my kitchen just to cool myself off.

"You want a drink?" I called to him.

"Sure!" he yelled back from the living room.

I pulled two beers from my fridge and walked back into my living room. I handed him his beer and sat on the couch beside him, curling my feet underneath me. I cracked open my own beer and started drinking from it. I put a hand behind my neck and sighed.

"What's that for?" he asked.

"Hmm? Oh, that was like a sigh of contentment. Can't I be content?" I asked. I took another large gulp of my drink, and then set it down on the coffee table.

There was a twinkle in his eyes. "Nothing wrong with that. Now, get over here and kiss me."

I pouted. "I thought I was the boss lady?"

He grinned, but I yelped when his strong arms slung me over his thick thighs so I was straddling him. He cupped my jaw in his hand and slanted his mouth against mine. His other hand roamed down my back, slithering to land on my ass, while we kissed aggressively. I nipped at his lip, and his eyes shot open in surprise at the dominant gesture. His blue eyes were wide with both shock and desire. I left hot kisses down his jaw until I was nuzzling into his neck. I licked and sucked at the soft flesh while he moaned quietly beneath me. He guided my mouth back to his, and I parted my lips when his tongue glided across the seam. I moaned into his mouth, our tongues in a war with each other while I was pulling his tie off and starting to undo his top button. He swore under his breath before he scooped me up into his arms and took me to my bedroom.

I was frantically undoing the buttons of his shirt and pulling it from his pants while he searched my back for the zipper of my dress.

"It's on the side," I told him.

"Oh! Sneaky."

"Easier to put on."

I didn't think he really cared about that, because in a flash it was pooling at my ankles. We were both standing there in my bedroom in our underthings, our chests heavy and our faces red from the passion. He licked his lips as he eyed me up and down, his gaze lingering on my ass which was bare from the lacy thong I was wearing. I couldn't help myself, the way he looked at me made me feel so desired. He pulled me towards him, one hand firm on the back of my neck and the other bit into my ass-cheek as he kissed me hard. His kisses were urgent, like he was trying to claim me as his own. I wanted to let him, I wanted to let this man brand me with those talented lips. His eyes snapped open when he realized I had slid his boxers to his feet and my hand was already working on him. He was hard and thick in my hand and desire was wrapping around me at the thought of what we were about to do.

He ran his hand down my face, and his thumb glided across my bottom lip. "Oh, you're a bad girl," he announced in that husky voice of his.

I think it was his bedroom voice, because he literally never sounded like that at any other time. I also think he knew what it did to me.

"Shut up, I'm the boss lady," I growled.

He grinned. "Yes, you are, and I fucking love it."

I kind of loved that, so I couldn't help myself but drop down to my knees and show him just how much I liked to be in charge.

CHAPTER SIXTEEN

NOAH

This woman was going to be the death of me. Hard stop. When I slid her dress to the floor to reveal the sexy black underwear she was wearing, I nearly came right then and there. Then she made it even harder, no pun intended, by sinking down onto her knees and sliding my cock in between her plump red lips. She grinned up as me as she glided me deeper inside her mouth and I loosely grabbed her hair in my fist which only seemed to encourage her. I don't know if it was her or me who was moaning now.

Oh fuck, she was going to leave me deceased. I closed my eyes as I felt her hot mouth and her tongue licking and sucking on me. I definitely had fantasies of this before, but I didn't think I would be towering over her, while this petite woman was on her knees pleasuring me like there was no tomorrow. I wanted her so bad, that I had to make her stop, or else I was going to come in her mouth, and as hot as that would have been, I didn't want it to stop there.

"Why did you make me stop?" she asked confused. I

pulled her up on her feet so she was eye-level with me, or rather chest level. I always forgot that I was almost a foot taller than her.

"My turn," I said as I found the clasp on her bra and slid it off. Then I grabbed the thin string of her throng and dragged it slowly down her legs. My hands grazed across the pale skin on her lean body, lingering on the outside of her shapely thighs.

"What?" she asked confused, but I lifted her up and threw her onto the bed.

Her eyes were wide with desire at my display of aggressiveness. I pinned her arms above her head on the bed and kissed the inside of her wrist where her quill tattoo was. I trailed my mouth down her arms and landed on the side of her neck. I kissed her there slowly until I heard her sigh in content beneath me. I ran my hand down her chest to cup her breasts, twirling a calloused finger across the hard bud of her nipple.

"Noah..."

"Mmmhmm," I murmured against her skin.

I trailed my mouth further down her body, using my mouth and tongue to lick and suck at her flesh before situating myself between her thighs. I placed soft kisses against her thighs and parted her legs with my hands while she whimpered in anticipation. I parted her with my thumb and flicked my tongue out for that first delicious lick across her most sensitive area. She moaned softly and I loved that I made that sound come out of her pretty little mouth.

I lifted my head up when she couldn't stop giggling.

"I'm sorry!" she laughed. "Your beard's so ticklish!"

I rubbed my face on her thighs and she continued to laugh. "Oh, do you not like beards?" I asked.

She leaned up onto her elbows, and I got an eyeful of

her boobs. God she looked so sexy from down here. "Noah! Are you growing a beard because I told you beards were hot?"

"No," I lied into her thigh and started kissing up towards her center again. "Is it too annoying?"

"No," she sighed and laid back as my tongue flicked inside her again and I added a finger into the mix. "I like the way it feels on my thighs."

And then her hands were touching the top of my head, her fingers sliding through my hair while I gave her what I knew she craved. I loved doing this for a woman, and I felt more confident this time because I knew the noises she was making were not fake. I set my hands firmly on her thighs, pressing them into the mattress while I continue to lick and kiss her in the spot she craved the most.

"Don't stop," she begged.

I leaned up with a grin at her. "Beg me," I demanded.

She smiled down at me and then just shoved my face back down into her pussy. "Do what you're told, Kennedy."

"Yes, Ma'am," I muffled into her thigh.

She was laughing above me. "Man, you really are a giver."

"Mmmhmm, now let me give you my tongue some more."

I definitely liked a lady who knew what she wanted and took it. Dinah was very good at doing that, and her demanding nature was so sexy to me. This pocket-sized woman was playful and dominant, and I loved being able to please her. I did as she asked, lapping at her center in soft, slow strokes. She whimpered and it turned me on more, that I focused on her clit until her orgasm rolled through her a few minutes later. My inner caveman was beating at his chest, because I got to do that to her. I climbed up on the bed and laid down beside her.

She was lying on her back with her eyes closed. I kissed her on the corner of her mouth, and one green eye lazily opened. "Now, there's the look of contentment I was hoping for," I teased.

Both eyes were open now. "How could anyone ever tell you that you were bad at that?" she asked with a dreamy sigh.

I shrugged and my fingers danced across her chest. "I don't know, especially since I love doing that."

"Wait, for real?" she asked with a hint of surprise in her voice.

"Hell yeah! I love going down on a woman. I love tasting you and feeling you come apart on my tongue. Feeling your legs quaking against my head. It's so fucking sexy."

"Oh my god! Finding a man that actually enjoys that is hard," she explained. "It's the same for me. Going down on you really turned me on too."

My hand ghosted across her chest and she leaned into it shamelessly. I kissed her neck. "That's the sexiest thing you have ever said to me," I whispered into her ear.

"You don't mind that I'm demanding in bed?" she asked.

I shook my head with a big grin. "Dinah, I love when you tell me what to do. I like a woman in charge who knows what she wants."

She leaned over to kiss me passionately again and then she was straddling me. She fumbled around in the bedside table before finding a condom, rolling it onto my hard length and then climbed on top. I helped her by positioning myself at her entrance and then she slid down onto me in a deliciously slow manner. Her hands pressed hard on my chest and she looked determined, so I let her ride me as hard and fast as she wanted. Her nails scratched down my chest and I grabbed her ass which seemed to just make her get more into it. Maybe I was a bit submissive, but Dinah seemed to be the type of woman who thrived on it and loved being in charge. I had to admit there was a nice view from down here too, so I was one hundred percent here for this tiny woman being on top and in charge of things.

I sat up in bed after a little bit, so we could be face-to-face to ride out our orgasms while clutching each other.

"Noah," she moaned in ecstasy into my neck and gripped my shoulders.

I held onto her hips tightly and thrusted fast up into her as she rocked on top of me. My own orgasm hit me square in the chest while she was moaning into my ear.

I came back down to earth with my chest heavy like I had just spent it skating lines. My hand was still tangled up in her dark tresses, her long hair wrapped tightly around my fist. Sex with her the second time was even better and it made me glad I could make her happy like this.

I unwrapped her hair from around my fist and caressed her cheek. I kissed her softly. "Dinah..." I panted out of breath.

"Noah...holy fuck," she agreed.

She disentangled herself from off my lap and I shamelessly watched her firm ass bend over to pick up her discarded clothes. I laid on the bed to catch my breath, after disposing of the condom in the trashcan underneath the bedside table.

"Hey, I kind of want to get a shower," she announced.

"Okay."

She was standing in the doorway of her en suite bathroom, naked and looking sexy with her teeth digging into her bottom lip. Her lipstick was half-smeared off, her chest was burned red from my beard, and her hair was all disheveled, but that tiny woman was sexy as fuck to me in this moment.

"Are you coming?" she asked in a way that said, 'fuck me in the shower, Noah.'

I looked up at her in surprise and ran a hand through my sweaty hair. I grabbed a condom from the bedside table just in case.

Later while Dinah was blow-drying her hair, I laid back in her bed clad in just my boxers waiting for her to be done. I was in such bliss, I didn't even realize it was so late. I looked at my phone and checked my schedule for upcoming games. Practice tomorrow, and then a 1:00 pm game Saturday from home, off on Sunday, Monday was a travel day for a Tuesday game in Chicago. From Chicago, we headed to Toronto for a Thursday night game, home on Saturday, and in New York on Sunday. I wondered if she would come to the game on Saturday, but I knew she had been procrastinating on her book, and I didn't want to get in the way.

My phone buzzed and I saw a text from TJ.

TJ: *How'd it go?*

ME: *Yeah, we're on the same page.*

TJ: *AND???*

ME: *I guess we're dating now.*

TJ: *Bro!!! Don't fuck this up, I want to still be friends with her.*

I shook my head at him and put my phone back on the nightstand. Dinah came out of her bathroom still not dressed, but her hair was now silky straight like it always was. I watched her ass move as she walked over to the dresser. She dug around in her dresser before putting on some clothes to sleep in. She was looking at her phone absent-mindedly while she slid into clean clothes. I heard her scoffing, "Ugh! What a dick."

"TJ?" I guessed.

She rolled her eyes.

"He's just trying to get a rise out of you."

"I know!" she called after me as she headed back into the bathroom. I heard her brushing her teeth and it reminded me that I probably should get my own bedtime routine going. I already had a spare toothbrush here, but I needed real clothes to sleep in and not just my boxers.

I climbed out of bed and started putting my pants back on.

She spat in the sink and asked, "Are you leaving?"

I was mid-button, and the disappointed look on her face nearly crushed me. "I want to go wash up. You want me to stay over tonight?"

"You don't have to."

"But..." I tried to goad her.

She ran a hand through her now dried dark hair and didn't want to look at me. I crossed over to her and lifted her chin to look at me. I bent down and kissed her quickly. "You like having me in your bed, eh?" I asked.

"Well, duh."

"That's not what I meant."

She blushed. "I do like waking up beside you. But you don't have to stay."

"What if I come back over?" I asked.

"Noah, it's fine. You don't have to stay."

"But, I want to," I urged and pulled her to my chest. Her head went immediately to the spot against my heart, and I ran a hand over her now smooth hair. "I'll be back."

"Use your spare key, I might be asleep when you get back," she admitted.

"You have to work tomorrow, right?" I asked.

"Yeah, but it's my half-day work from home day."

I pulled away from her and kissed the top of her head. "Okay, I'll be back."

Dinah was sliding into her bed when I left her place with my shirt hanging loosely on my chest and my suit jacket in my hand. Thankfully TJ was in his bedroom with the door closed, or else he would have just razzed me for my appearance. When I got into my bedroom and was changing into clothes for bed, I realized why he had his door closed.

Huh, good for him.

Just to be an ass I texted him.

ME: *GET SOME!*

I threw some clothes for tomorrow into a bag and went back over to Dinah's. The light was off in her bedroom, but I saw she was still on her phone. I dropped the bag on the floor, and went into her bathroom to brush my teeth. I thought it was too soon to ask about leaving clothes here, plus I literally lived next door so it wasn't that hard to just go next door and change. That was, of course, if she wanted me to continue staying the night with her. But since we were now dating, I didn't think that was going to be a problem.

I slid into bed and she was off her phone, but not asleep yet. She was on her side, and I went to the other side of the bed. I laid my arm across her and pulled her tight against my chest. I breathed in the hair at the base of her neck, and she laughed.

"Stop breathing on me!" she exclaimed.

I kissed her neck. "Ah, you like it."

"Jerk."

I kissed her again and smiled against her neck when she laughed. She turned around so she was facing me and she pulled me down to her to kiss her. I never dreamed that I would get to kiss her as much as I was currently doing. I don't think she understood the crazy things that she did to me.

She pulled away. "Goodnight, Noah."

"Night, Dinah."

She shifted position again so she was on her side, and I pulled her close to me again. In a moment, her quiet breathing filled the room and I knew that she had finally fallen asleep. I wanted this moment to last forever. I wanted to be here in her bed, holding her tight for as long as I could. I couldn't believe my luck that Dinah Lace not only wanted me as much as I wanted her, but she was totally okay with actually dating me. Now, I just needed to get her to fall in love with me as hard as I had fallen in love with her. I honestly still thought it was a dream. I drifted off to sleep with probably the dumbest grin on my face.

❄

I woke up the next morning on my back, and Dinah's small frame was curled into me, her head leaning on my arm. I slowly slid myself out of her bed as carefully as I could, and put her head back on her pillow. She stirred, but didn't wake, so I went into the kitchen to start a pot of coffee. I've known Dinah long enough to know to not fucking talk to her until she had her morning coffee. Her words, not mine.

Dinah was one of those people who liked to grind her own coffee, and she usually kept the freshly ground stuff in a plastic container in her kitchen cabinet. Luckily there was some already ground, so I didn't have to wake her up with the sound of her super loud old coffee grinder. I should look into getting her a new one, she always complained about how much this one sucked. What did it say about me that my first thought was to get the woman I was dating a practical gift that she actually wanted?

I shook my head to myself and started the coffee maker. I opened the fridge and inspected her groceries. I didn't know how this woman was alive, but something told me maybe her insane brothers were more than just overprotective. She complained more than once about how her brother Frankie 'mommed' her too much. Her fridge was practically empty, but she had some eggs at least, so I cracked them into a pan and started making breakfast. I was buttering toast when I heard her feet pitter-patter across the tile in her kitchen behind me.

I turned to her with a smile and she had her hands on her hips. "Um, excuse me? What are you doing?" she asked but she was grinning.

I took the plates over to her kitchen table, but didn't answer her. She got herself a cup of coffee and joined me at her table. She took a sip of coffee like a nicotine addict took a drag off a cigarette.

I poked her in the arm. "You're an addict."

"Hush!" she remarked, but had a twinkle in her eyes.

"Did you just hush me?"

"Shut up! Did you seriously make me breakfast?"

I shrugged. "It's just eggs & toast."

She glanced over at her fridge. "I'm honestly surprised I even had that in there. Sometimes Frankie brings me food. You really didn't have to."

We were quiet for a moment as she dug her fork into her eggs and drank her coffee. She was still sluggish and sleepy, which just made her look even cuter. In my wildest dreams, I never thought we would get here. When I met her she had been happily married, so there was no shot in hell. I had to admit I did feel a little guilty being with her even though I knew her husband was gone. I liked to think we still would have been friends if he was still around. I wasn't the kind of guy that was going to try to get a woman to cheat, so thinking of the what-ifs was kind of a waste. After everything she went through, all that loss, she deserved to be happy and I wanted to be the man who could give that to her.

She looked at me curiously from over her cup of coffee. "You okay?" she asked.

I nodded and smiled at her. "Fine, just thinking."

"You had your brooding face on. Are you sure?"

I smiled at her again and leaned over to kiss her cheek. "I'm fine."

She narrowed her eyes and I knew she didn't believe me. I pulled away, and we ate breakfast in silence. I took her plate when she was finished, despite her protests that she could get it. She finished her coffee and joined me at the sink, wrapping her arms around my waist from behind and leaning up on her tip-toes to kiss my shoulder.

"It's kind of sexy when a man does housework," she joked with a wink.

I turned around to kiss her then, long and tender. She pulled away abruptly, and I cocked my head in question.

She sighed heavily. "If you continue to kiss me like that, I will never start working."

I grinned and bopped her on the nose. "Oh, that's my evil plan."

"It's working! I just want to rip your clothes off you right now."

"You still going to work from home today?" I asked, trying to ignore that last part. Although, my cock didn't get the memo, as it was lifting up in interest right now.

She nodded. "You have practice today?"

"Yeah, I should probably go see if TJ's gonna leave without me. I think he thinks I moved out."

"Did he have a girl over last night?"

I nodded.

"He's just ploughing through all of Philadelphia isn't he?"

I tried not to laugh. "Um, I guess? I'm starting to worry about him."

She cocked her head at me. "How so?"

I shrugged. "I worry he's going to wake up so utterly alone one day because he didn't allow himself to find love."

Her green eyes softened and were shiny with her admiration of my words. "Aw, Noah!" she cooed.

I kissed her cheek. "I just want him to be happy."

She patted me on the arm. "He'll figure it out. By the way, thanks for dinner last night, you totally didn't need to pay."

I slid my arms down her frame to rest onto her waist, and I smiled as she shivered at my touch. "Just let me," I insisted.

She made a face, which I silenced with another kiss. So that was how we ended up in her bed again, writhing together in a mess of kisses and tangled sweaty limbs. So much so that afterwards she jumped out of bed and got dressed in a hurry.

"What's the rush?" I asked with a laugh.

"I have a conference call in thirty minutes! Oh, boy, you're trouble for me!" she exclaimed. But she leaned down and kissed me again. "I got to go."

She disappeared behind her office door, and I leaned back on her bed with a sigh of contentment. I wasn't really planning for that one, but I was by no means complaining. I showered in her bathroom and got dressed in the clothes I brought over last night. I flopped down on the bed and checked my phone. I had a message from TJ.

TJ: *HA HA. I thought you weren't coming home.*
ME: *I just needed to get some things.*
TJ: *Are you legit moving in next door?*
ME: *NO!*
TJ: *haha, yeah right. You're whipped already.*
ME: *I'm not complaining.*
TJ: *gross.*

I laughed at him and set my phone down. It was probably time for me to slip out since Dinah had to get work done and I needed to get my ass to practice. I got up from the bed and walked into her living room. I saw her office door was ajar and she waved me in. She was still on the phone, but she must have had it on mute.

"Do you need to head out?" she asked.

"Yeah, I have practice." I bent down to kiss her cheek. "I'll see you later."

"Okay. I had a good time last night."

"You want to do it again?"

She grinned from ear-to-ear. "Oh most definitely."

At practice I was all smiles, so much so that my teammates wouldn't stop giving me shit about it. TJ hit me in the leg with his stick, but I skated around it and went through the puck carrying drills. I was even smiling when I completely fucked up on a shot on Metzy.

Metzy pulled his cage off his head and gave me a confused look. "What's up with you today?"

"He's lovesick!" TJ called.

I gave him the finger, and the guys laughed. Hallsy clapped me on the back. "It's a good look on you, I'm glad to see you happy."

And I was happy, so disgustingly happy. I was sure that past me would have wanted to punch present me in the face.

CHAPTER SEVENTEEN

DINAH

After I finished work for the day, I spent the rest of it working on my edits. I was so close to getting all these done. I just needed that extra push, but by the end of the day I had burnt myself out. So when Noah asked me if he could come over, I jumped at the chance. We sat on my couch watching tv, and I put my feet in his lap. Without me having to ask him, he started rubbing my feet.

"Babe! I can't have possibly whipped you that much already," I mused.

He glared at me and tickled the bottom of my feet, to which I squealed. It made him grin at me. "Don't be mean," he teased.

I stuck my tongue out at him and took a sip of my beer. He had an afternoon game tomorrow, so he wasn't drinking, and probably wanted to go to sleep early. I was probably going to stay up and play video games to keep my mind off of the book I really needed to finish edits on.

"Did you want me to come to your game tomorrow?" I asked suddenly.

"Of course I do."

"Okay."

He gave me a quizzical look. "Did you finish your edits yet?"

I looked away from him and drank more of my beer.

"D!"

I gave him the finger. "Stay out of it."

"Then, no, I don't want you to come. I think you should finish your edits first."

I groaned and leaned my head back against the couch. "You suck."

He poked my arm. "You know you need to do it."

I shifted position on the couch so now my head was laying in his lap. I pouted, "FINE!"

He smiled down at me and stroked my hair. I was pretty sure I purred at that, his long fingers threading through my hair had this calming effect on me. He tweaked my nose. "You're cute when you're all pouty."

I gave him the finger again.

"Ah, there's my girl," he said with a laugh and continued to stroke my hair.

I never thought that things would feel so easy with someone who wasn't Jason. I never really had anyone but him, but I always cherished that I could be myself around Noah. I valued his friendship so much, and now that we were trying this dating thing, I was happy, but really scared. If I fucked this up with him, if I drove him away, I didn't think I would ever forgive myself. I didn't want to lose my best friend.

His big hand ran down my cheek. "Hey, why are you giving me that look?"

I snapped away from my thoughts and smiled up at him. "What?"

He narrowed his eyes. "Were you spacing?"

"Just thinking," I answered and leaned up to kiss him. He kissed me back, but broke it quickly. "Hey! What's that?" I asked, insulted that he was depriving me of those good kisses.

He cradled me in his arms, and was giving me this amused look. "I don't know...I think I need to hold back my kisses until you finish your edits."

I sprung up and tickled underneath his arms until he laughed so hard he let me go. "MEAN!" I squealed, and we both noticed that I was back to straddling his hips. "Does this mean I don't get to take you into my bedroom and have my way with you?"

He shifted beneath me, and the hardness of his erection pressing against me told me why.

I grinned evilly and ground myself against him.

"NOPE!" he teased and tried to shift away from me.

I kissed his neck. "Uh huh, sure, you can't last," I whispered in his ear.

He pushed me off him and down onto the couch. "Nuh uh. You can have your way with me after you finish your edits."

"Please, Noah!" I whined with a pout. "Give me that good dicking."

He squeezed his eyes shut. "Christ, lovey, don't tempt me."

I laughed and returned back to my place on the other side of the couch. I took a swig of my beer, but I was still smiling. My phone buzzed on the coffee table and I picked it up to see it was TJ.

TJ: *Hey, need to talk.*

ME: *Okay...*

TJ: *Sorry, realized Kens' over there. I don't want to interrupt.*

ME: *Not interrupting. What's up?*

He didn't answer my text because then he was at the door. Noah cocked an eyebrow at me.

"It's TJ," I explained.

His brow furrowed a little bit more, but he stood up to open the door to see his roommate standing there.

TJ walked in and he looked really upset. He flopped down on the couch next to me. "Ugh! I don't know what to do! D, help me understand women!"

Noah looked amused and sat on the other end of the couch. I gave him a questioning look, but he just shrugged his shoulders. "Oh, honey, tell me what's wrong," I insisted.

"Taylor broke up with me," he explained. His hand went to the bridge of his nose and he rubbed it. "Oh, man," he turned to Noah. "Am I being a total cockblock? Dude, sorry."

I laughed. "TJ, you're good. Apparently I'm not getting any until I finish the edits on my book."

Noah's face was beet red at that. He just shook his head at me in disbelief, but TJ laughed. "That shit won't last."

"I know, right? Anyway, who's Taylor? And why is this the first time I'm hearing about her?" I asked, changing the subject.

"I was casually seeing her," TJ explained

"Isn't that a good thing, that she broke up with you?" Noah interjected.

TJ gave him a weird look. "We wanted different things, at least I thought I did."

"Oh no, Noah! I think our robot TJ caught feelings, what do we do?" I joked.

"Not funny!" TJ exclaimed.

Noah was trying to hold back his laughter, but I maintained my composure. TJ was kind of hopeless, he said he didn't do relationships, but I had a feeling that wasn't really true. Something told me there was a reason why he did a lot of casual hookups. I remembered his sister saying off-hand that she figured out she was bisexual when TJ's high school girlfriend kissed her on a dare when they were all drunk at a party. I had to wonder if that had something to do with it, but I never really felt like it was my place to ask.

"TJ, how do you feel about this girl?" I asked him.

He shrugged. "I honestly don't know, but I'm really upset that she broke up with me."

"Maybe you should give it a couple days, see how you feel," I suggested.

He nodded. "I just miss her already."

I squeezed his shoulder. "Oh, honey, I think you're in love."

TJ ran his hand down his face. "I...don't...no...that..."

Noah was smirking. "I told you it would creep up on you. One day you'll just be sitting there laughing, and then the next you'll notice how the light hits her face whenever she smiles and how you feel all warm inside when you're with her. That's love."

It took me a couple more sips of beer to realize that Noah was talking about me. No way, we had just started dating. We were a little handsy and smitten with each other now, but it was too soon for him to be so in love with me. But when he smiled at me, it made my heart melt, and I started to wonder if maybe I loved him too. My brother Eddie had said Noah was in love with me, so maybe it wasn't too soon for Noah, but it was for me.

TJ was still sitting there with his head in his hands. "I

still feel like I don't know what to do."

"What does your heart say?" I asked him.

He just shrugged.

"If you miss this girl already, what does that tell you?" I asked.

"That the sex was really good?"

I shook my head. "You clearly have feelings for this girl!"

He narrowed his eyes at me. "I don't fall in love with people, that's not me."

I patted him on the back. "It'll be okay, you'll figure it out."

"Maybe you should just talk to her," Noah suggested. "Tell her how you feel. Also groveling helps."

Noah rolled his eyes at me over the top of TJ's head. I just smiled, but tried to not make it obvious to TJ. TJ glanced back and forth between the two of us and glared at me. "You two are insufferable together."

I stuck my tongue out at him and downed the rest of my beer. "You need a beer?" I asked him.

TJ shook his head, but ran his hands down his face. "Nah, we have an afternoon game tomorrow, I should get to bed. Thanks for listening to me."

I hugged him. "Hey, you know anytime."

He nodded and stood up. Noah stood up with him, but then he bent over and gave me a quick kiss. "I'm going to go sleep in my own bed tonight," he explained.

I pouted, but I knew he needed to be refreshed for his game tomorrow, and if he slept over tonight I wasn't going to let him get a lot of sleep. "Good luck tomorrow!" I told him.

He smiled. "Finish your edits."

"Text me when you get back, okay?" I asked.

He nodded and walked out the door with TJ. I stood up

to lock the door behind them. I sat down back on my couch and shot off a text to TJ's twin sister, Rox.

ME: *Hey...any chance you have spoken to your other half?*

ROX: *Lisa??*

ROX: *She broke up with me.*

ME: *WAIT...What? CALL ME!*

Within seconds my phone was ringing with Rox's name on the screen. "Are you okay?" I asked her.

She sighed on the other end. "Not sure, D, she cheated on me."

Rox sounded so dejected. I wasn't that close with TJ's sister, but we talked here and there. She was one of the coolest chicks I knew, so fearless. She didn't visit a lot, but that's mostly because her and Benny hate each other and there was so much drama with them. Although, I really suspected it was just both of them trying to deny their feelings. I think Benny had a thing for her, and he said all the wrong things to her. Plus, I've noticed her checking him out when she thought no one was looking.

"Wait..." I trailed off. "Weren't you living together?"

"Yup. She kicked me out," she explained.

My heart ached for this woman. Rox and her girlfriend had been together for three years and they had been best friends before that. That had got to hurt.

"Oh, Rox, I'm so sorry. Is there anything I can do?" I asked.

"Nah. I'm couch surfing. Although..."

"What?"

She sighed. "I applied for a job with the team on a whim."

"What team?"

"Dinah, with the Bulldogs. I doubt I'll get it, but I kind

of need to just get out of St. Catharines."

"Oh, honey, I'm so sorry to hear about that. Let me know if there's anything I can do to help."

"I—" she cut herself off and I swore I heard her crying on the other end. "Thanks, D, that's really nice, but I'm sure I'll be fine. Now, were you talking about my brother when you meant my other half?"

I laughed at how quickly she changed the subject. "Yeah! Has he talked to you about Taylor?"

She scoffed on the other end. "Yes, he's a dummy. My brother, love that douche to death, but he's very afraid of getting hurt. His ex in high school put him through the wringer. I love Natalie, she's one of my good friends now, but she wasn't the nicest person in high school. I think Tristan's still nursing some wounds from it."

"Aw, poor guy," I lamented.

She laughed. "I'm sure he'll be okay."

I laughed. "You two are close, huh?"

"Can confirm. Don't tell Noah, but I'm pretty sure I'm Tristan's best friend."

"That's okay," I told her, "I'm pretty sure I'm Noah's best friend."

"Speaking of which, you and Noah Kennedy, eh?" she teased.

"You know, all of you jerks could have told me he had a thing for me sooner!"

She laughed that throaty laugh of hers. "Well, where's the fun in that?"

I hung up with Rox after a little bit, and more than anything I just wanted to turn my game console on and melt my brain with video games, but I felt like I needed to do something else. With a sigh I locked myself into my office and worked on edits until two in the morning.

CHAPTER EIGHTEEN

NOAH

TJ laughed at me as we walked into our condo next door. "There's no way you're seriously going to withhold sex, right?"

I shrugged. "Maybe."

He continued to laugh. "No man would ever do that."

I went into our kitchen and grabbed a drink of water. TJ stood across the kitchen island giving me a funny look. "Oh, I have a feeling she'll finish her edits by tomorrow," I told him with a grin.

He made a grossed out face. "File that under things I didn't need to know about our neighbor."

I gave him a quizzical look. "This from the guy who wanted to know what the sex was like."

TJ shook his head. "I was just teasing you. I'm not sure I want to know. Like what if you tell me D's into whips and chains? I would never be able to look at her with a straight face again."

I took a drink of my water, and then set it down on the

island. I cocked an eyebrow at him in amusement. "Maybe she is. Nothing wrong with that."

He blanched. "Nope! I don't want to know!"

"So I thought you were done with Taylor?"

He shrugged. "I don't know, maybe D's right."

"You know we can talk about these things right? I'm sorry if I've not been—"

He waved me away with his hand. "It's fine. I just wanted to hear it from D, you know her being an older woman and all. Fuck, Roxie basically told me the same thing."

I nodded at the mention of his twin sister. They were pretty close and talked after every game, especially if we lost. For a guy who came off as the fun-loving party guy, he was surprisingly co-dependent.

TJ leaned against the island and gave me a serious look now. "You think we're going to make the playoffs?" he asked.

He looked as nervous as I felt whenever I thought about it. The team had been doing bad all season, but with a coaching firing, things had gotten shaken up and maybe, just maybe we could squeeze into the playoffs. I finished my water and put the empty glass in the sink. "I don't know," I admitted to him with a sigh. "It's been a rough year."

"But we're on a hot streak," he agreed, but he didn't look that confident.

I nodded. "Have to take it game-by-game."

He nodded in agreement. "D going to come tomorrow?"

I shook my head.

"Really? I figured you'd want your girlfriend cheering you on."

"She has to finish edits on her book," I explained.

TJ shook his head. "Man, you two are weird."

He headed to his bedroom, and I trudged along into my own. I flopped my six-foot-two frame onto my bed with a sigh. It wasn't the same not having a small woman cradled underneath my big arm. God, maybe she was right and I was whipped. The smile spread across my face. I didn't care if I was whipped, I knew that being with her made me happy.

I couldn't help myself by pulling out my phone and texting her.

ME: *I miss you already*

DINAH: *Aw!*

DINAH: *What has it been like five whole minutes? I literally live next door.*

ME: *Work on your book!*

DINAH: *Oh yeah, what will I get if I do?*

ME: *You know.*

DINAH: *use your words.*

ME: *I prefer to use my tongue.*

DINAH: *OH MY GOD! Noah Kennedy, who knew you were such a dirty boy?*

ME: *You did! And you love it.*

DINAH: *Fuck yeah I do!*

DINAH: *Go to bed, good luck tomorrow.*

ME: *Thanks. Good night!*

I put my phone down on my nightstand and plugged it in, making sure my alarm was set. TJ would have probably barged in tomorrow even if I slept through my alarm. It was nice to have my teammate as my roommate, because we were always backing each other up. TJ was my bud, and I knew no matter what he would always have my back, just like I would always have his.

I drifted off to sleep thinking about Dinah and how

happy she made me. Before I knew it, my alarm was blaring in my ear and it was time to get ready for work.

TJ came into the open door when I had finished getting dressed for our morning skate. "You almost ready?" he asked.

I pushed a chunk of my hair behind my ear and nodded. "Yeah, bud. I'm good."

"You want me to drive?" he asked, holding up his keys.

"I can," I offered.

We walked out together and down to my car in the underground parking garage in our complex. I got into the driver's seat and started the engine. "You planning to go out after the game?" I asked TJ as I left our complex and headed to the arena.

"Nah. Think Riley and Hallsy might come over, have some drinks."

"I'd be down with that. What's Benny up to?"

TJ rolled his eyes. "Back with Stephanie again. Who knows, he might show up."

I sighed. Benny had been going out with this girl all season, she was sweet and they looked happy but Benny said he didn't ever want to get married, and she seemed like the type who was ready to settle down and have kids. I think they just wanted different things, which was a bummer, but it's hard when you and your partner just weren't on the same page. I wondered if it was a conversation that Dinah and I should have, but I thought it was too early to be having those conversations. Plus, I knew even if things went well between us and down the line we decided to settle down with each other permanently, kids were not on the table for us. At least not biologically, and I didn't want to bring that up with her. I was there that night when the doctors told her she probably couldn't have children, and I hugged her while she cried about it.

Fuck, to lose your spouse and then find out you lost the only piece left of him weeks later, it had been rough for her. I partly wondered if doing this thing with her was right. Part of me wondered if when she kissed me was she thinking of him. Fuck, that made me feel like a complete asshole.

I was kind of pumped for the game today, but still really nervous. This season hadn't been the best, but with the new system and the new coach, we were on a hot streak. Home games were always fun, but also extra nervous for me because I wanted to play my best, and wanted to give our cheering fans what they craved — a win. We needed a win for sure. Afternoon games were also fun, because then you had the rest of the night to yourself.

"So, things serious between you and Dinah?" TJ asked as we turned onto Broad Street.

I scratched the bridge of my nose and shrugged. "I want them to be. We agreed to date."

"Kens, I know you love her and have for a while, but just..." he trailed off.

"What?"

He sighed. "I love both of you, but Dinah's older, she's been through a lot. You're the first guy she's dated since her husband, don't expect her to fall in love with you immediately."

"Okay..."

"I know you were talking about her last night when you were talking about what love's like."

Shit. He had noticed that? Which meant maybe Dinah did too, but I hadn't noticed her feel uncomfortable, if anything she seemed to smile warmly at me when I said it.

I bit my lip. "You think she noticed?"

I pulled into the private parking lot for the players. "Not sure. I just don't want you to get hurt," TJ warned. For all the talk of TJ being the fun, party guy without a care in the world, sometimes he was surprisingly honest about how he worried about his friends.

"Aw, T, you really do have feelings!" I teased.

He punched me in the arm. "Don't tell anyone! Come on, let's go win this thing!"

At least that I could agree with him on.

❄

I sat on the bench in the dressing room with my earbuds in and my eyes closed. I didn't have a lot of weird rituals like other players, I mostly just had to put on all my gear in a certain order — socks, shin pads, pants, shoulders pads, elbow pads, and then my jersey. The only other thing I did to get myself in the zone was listen to music and shut out all my teammates. TJ was convinced that as soon as I put my earbuds in I didn't talk to anyone, and if that was true, I never really did it on purpose. I usually didn't check my phone that much before or during games, but I wanted to see if I heard from Dinah.

DINAH: *Good luck today, I'll be rooting for you*
ME: *Thanks, lovey. Good luck writing today.*
DINAH: *Ugh don't remind me, this is going terribly already.*

I smiled to myself and put my phone back in my cubby hole. When I looked up Girard who was sitting across from me at his spot gave me a cursory look. "You never check your phone before a game," he commented.

I shrugged, but TJ slapped me on the back and announced. "My man's lovesick!"

I shoved him away, but I was smiling. "I'm not!

Girard smirked. "Still?"

I laced up my skates and just shrugged my shoulders. I stood up and followed TJ down the tunnel. The music was loud and I heard the sounds of cheering coming from all the fans in the arena today. It felt good to hear that, and I felt pretty good about today's game. I hopped onto the ice, flying across it on my skates around the zone, laughing at some joke Hallsy made. Metzy was stretching out on the ice, talking to the Pittsburgh Miners' goaltender about something. I did a few practice shots at the net, feeling good at hearing the thwack of the puck against the netting.

I was on the starting line tonight, and I fist-bumped the flag bearer who was standing next to me during the National Anthem. He seemed a little star-struck. It was so weird to me, because it wasn't like I was that much older than him. I mean, yeah, it was a lot of years, but I was still a young kid in this league. I still had a lot of playing on the ice. It made me wonder if one day Dinah was going to wake up and realize just what an immature kid I was and dump me. I hoped she didn't think I thought she was too old for me, because none of that shit had ever mattered to me.

Girard started it off by taking the face-off at center ice, but he lost and the puck was turned over in the neutral zone. I pumped my legs chasing after the Pittsburgh leftwinger who was heading into our offensive zone and straight for Metzy's five-hole. I slammed the winger with the puck into the boards and tried to swipe the puck from underneath his skates. His teammate swiped it from me and tried to get the one-timer in, but luckily for me TJ was always on my line and knocked the puck back into the neutral zone. I chased after the puck to get to the blue line and TJ passed it to me so we could head into Pittsburgh's zone. I didn't think, I just did, and I swung my arm back with my stick and lobbed the puck into the back of their net.

I raised my arms in cheer, hearing the roar of the crowd and the goal horn blaring. TJ skated over to me and gave me a big hug, while Girard clapped me on the back. Out of breath, and my chest heaving, I skated over to the bench and climbed over it in a lazy fashion. I slid down on the bench as the next set of players were changing up the shift. TJ handed me some smelling salts which I took with a hard shake of my head. He laughed and I felt our assistant coach tap me on the helmet. I chewed on my mouth guard while I watched the action on the ice.

The Pittsburgh Miners kind of sucked this year, but we didn't really have room to talk as our team wasn't doing too well this year either. I had asked Dinah once if she thought we could get it together to make the playoffs. She had only laughed and said I didn't want to hear her answer. She was probably right.

TJ nudged me, and I realized we were back on the ice together. Fuck, I needed to get my head in the game and not think about my sexy writer girlfriend. I took the face-off but got kicked out for going too soon, so Hallsy stepped into the circle. We kept possession of the puck, and we were getting good shots in, but Pittsburgh's net minder was a brick wall tonight. It was like he saw me out on the ice again and closed up shop. We chipped away at the puck and tried our best to get another goal, but then Hallsy iced the puck and we were back in our zone.

I saw one of Pittsburgh's players get a clean shot off the net, so I dove to block it and fell hard on the ice. Out of the corner of my eye, I saw the black puck at the side of my head, and then for just a second everything went black.

I heard TJ and the team's physician Doctor Franklin calling my name and asking me if I could get up. The right side of my head was pounding and Doc was holding a towel against it. I smelled the metallic, coppery scent of blood, and it took me a while to realize it was my own. TJ was asking if I could get up, I nodded and struggled to get off the ice. He and the doctor helped me skate over to the tunnel while I held the now bloodied rag on my head. TJ went back to the bench, while Doctor Franklin urged me back to the dressing room so he could assess the damage. I was in pain, but I didn't feel like the wind got knocked out of me, but they probably wanted to check on concussion syndrome.

I sat on the medic bench while the doctor tended to my wounds. "Is it bad?" I asked.

He inspected me. "I think you'll live."

"Har har har," I spat.

He started pulling out some stitches from his kit and pulled at the cartilage on my ear. "Looks like it's just your ear, it bled a lot, but I think you're okay."

"Can I go back in?"

He frowned. "I want to keep you here for a bit, just to make sure you're good. What's your pain level?"

I chewed my bottom lip. That was a good question, because I honestly didn't know, also as a hockey player, I had a high tolerance for pain.

"Kennedy," he warned. "We want to make sure you don't have a concussion. You took a flying puck to the face."

I nodded, but didn't say anything while he started stitching up my ear. This sucked big time. My head did hurt a lot, but I wasn't sure if that meant concussion or just the fact that I got hit with a flying piece of rubber at a high speed. When he was done he told me to sit tight for a bit. I heard the sound of the first intermission starting and my teammates coming back into the dressing room. I wanted to know what the score of the game was, I wanted to know if I had blocked that shot, because if those fuckers actually scored a goal, I was going to be pissed.

Eventually TJ came in to ask me how it was going and told me the score. "2-1, us," he explained.

I hung my head. "I don't think I'm coming back to the game. I blocked that shot though, right?"

He barked out a laugh. "Yeah, you did, with your thick skull."

I gave him the finger before he just laughed again and headed back out for the start of the second period.

CHAPTER NINETEEN

DINAH

I knew not to bother Noah that much during his game. I totally didn't want to mess with his rituals or mess up his game head, or whatever the hell he called it. I wished him luck before the start of the game and continued working on my edits. I had worked all night after he and TJ left my condo last night, and I was getting a lot done today with no cute boy around to distract me. I was feeling really good about where this book was heading. My editor was so right, I did need to completely re-write this one part.

I had the game on mute and kept on checking the score periodically, but I didn't really know what had happened in the game. The game was almost over by the time that I felt like I was ready to submit this back to my editor. Big picture edits were the hardest parts, so once we got there I would get to the line edits and that would be much easier. I knew I was supposed to feel better now, but I didn't yet. I had the pressure to always do better when it came to my writing.

I submitted to my editor, tweeted out some more about pre-ordering of the new book and then sat back on my couch to watch the last five minutes of the game. I cranked up the volume and jumped when TJ scored the game-winning goal, but then my brow furrowed during his end of the game interview talking about Noah leaving the game early.

I texted Noah quickly.

ME: *What happened?!? Are you okay?*

NOAH: *You didn't see?*

ME: *NO....had the game on mute while I worked on my book.*

NOAH: *Took a puck to the face.*

ME: *NO! My poor baby!*

NOAH: *Oh, I'm your baby now?*

ME: *Shush! Are you okay?*

NOAH: *Yeah...we can talk later. They still want to check me out.*

I stared at my phone in disbelief and then searched twitter to see if I could find a playback. It looked really bad, like concussion bad. FUCK. I didn't know what else to say, so I set my phone down on the coffee table and took my rage out on video games.

My phone buzzed on the coffee table, but I ignored it as I mashed buttons on my controller and killed this insane boss I had been trying to beat for what seemed like forever. I cheered when I finally beat it and saw my phone was rattling across the table some more. I jumped at seeing that Noah was calling me.

"Hey," I answered.

"Hey, sorry if I was short with you," he apologized.

"It's fine."

He sighed on the other line. "They told me I need to take it easy, but they don't think I have a concussion."

"That's good, right?" I asked.

"Yeah, I'm just frustrated."

"Why don't you come over and I'll make you dinner?"

He was silent on the other line for a minute. "Did you just offer to make me dinner? You don't cook." I heard the laughter in his voice.

"I can cook, I'm just lazy. You seem upset, and I want to cheer you up."

"That would actually be really nice. I'll see you in a bit."

I hung up with him. Why did I offer to make him dinner? That was SO not me. I texted Chloe.

ME: *I just offered to make a man dinner, what's wrong with me?*

CHLOE: *HAHAHAHAHAHA*

CHLOE: *HAHAHAHAHAHA*

ME: *CHLOE!!!*

CHLOE: *Oh, honey! I think that means you love him.*

I stared down at my phone for a couple minutes. No, I didn't think that was right. Could I? Could I really love Noah? I mean I always said I did before we crossed from the friendship zone to the dating zone. I cared about him very much, I knew that, but loved him? I wasn't sure about that. I thought it was way too early in this thing to be tossing around that word. At the same time, I wasn't really much of a cook, so why did I offer to make my new boyfriend dinner? I shook my head to see if I could physically shake all the unsure thoughts out of my head.

I went into my kitchen and started putting something together. I didn't have much in the way of dinner stuff in my apartment. Jason had always done the cooking, so for the most part I ended up eating for one which was mostly salads. Or whenever my brothers felt sorry for me, they would bring me food. Mostly it was Frankie. It was a sad existence, but it had never felt that sad to me before.

I looked in my cupboards, and had to settle on some burrito bowls. I pulled out the rice cooker and started the rice, while I opened a can of pinto beans to heat them up on the stove. Luckily I had some ground beef in the freezer that I was able to heat up on the stove as well.

I was dicing tomatoes, when there was a knock on the door. I had given TJ and Noah a spare key to my place years ago for emergencies, so Noah could have just let himself in. It was kind of nice that he respected my boundaries. He was definitely something else.

I walked over to the door and was not surprised to find Noah's towering frame standing in front of me. He bent down to kiss me, his hands going to my waist and lifting me closer to him. I was pretty sure I squealed like a giddy teenager, because I felt the smile spreading across his lips while he kissed me.

"Hey, put me down! I need to finish dinner," I insisted.

He put me down and I rushed into the kitchen to turn the meat. The rice cooker popped up, and I realized I timed this all wrong. Noah's strong arms wrapped around my waist. "What can I do to help?" he whispered in my ear. Did he know how sexy it was when he did that?

I turned off the burner for the beans, and stirred the meat a little more, it still needed a few minutes. "Hmm, can you just unplug the rice cooker? Maybe set the table?" I asked while my hands were busy with other tasks.

"I can't believe you actually made me dinner," he mused as he pulled away and did as I asked.

There was something so sexy about a man that helped

out in the kitchen. Noah was setting the table, putting out the bowl of cheese, tomatoes, and diced spinach when I finished up the meat. I turned off the burner and moved it to a plate. I took it over to my kitchen table, where Noah had done a pretty good job of setting everything up.

I wiped my hands on a hand towel, and grabbed a beer from the fridge. "You want a beer?" I asked.

"Sure."

I pulled another one from out of the fridge and poured both of them in glasses. I walked over to the table and handed him his glass. I set my beer at my place at the table, but before I could sit down, his hands grabbed my waist and pulled me down into his lap.

"Hey!" I exclaimed.

His big hand wrapped around the back of my neck and pulled me into a long and slow kiss. He smiled when he pulled away. "Hey, yourself," he breathed.

My hand grazed his cheek and I saw the blood and metallic stitches on his ear. "Aw, babe, that looks bad."

He jerked his head away from my hand. "It hurts, but I'll be okay."

I narrowed my eyes at him. "Don't go being all old-school hockey tough guy on me, okay?"

He gripped my waist harder, and pushed my hair behind my ear. "I'm fine, it was just a nick, really. It just hurts, but I'm okay. It's cute that you're so worried."

"Of course I'm worried!" I squealed.

The smile stayed put on his face, but he finally let me go. I got up and sat in my own seat, even though when he kissed me like that, the last thing I wanted to do was just sit across from him. I doled out the food into my bowl. I hadn't really eaten a big breakfast, and got too wrapped up in my writing to eat lunch, so I was pretty hungry. Noah must have been pretty hungry after his game too, even though it seemed like he hadn't gotten to play all that much.

"This is nice," he murmured after a little while.

I shoved more food in my mouth and nodded. "Tell me about the game," I urged.

He shrugged. "It was going okay, I scored the first goal of the game, but then I blocked a puck with my face."

I smirked. "Did you make the save?"

He tipped his head back and laughed. "Yeah, I did."

I took a sip of my beer. "Well...I think you have job security now."

"What do you mean?"

"Philly will probably hire you as their penalty kill coach when you retire."

He laughed again and just shook his head.

I shrugged. I knew it was true. We in Philly liked the down and dirty, do whatever it took hockey guys. Noah had quickly become one of those since he was drafted by the team when he was a mere eighteen years old. God, he made me feel old.

He cocked his head at me, and I realized he had asked me something and I hadn't answered him. "Lovey?" he asked.

I smiled back at him. "Sorry," I apologized and gave him a sheepish look.

He put his hand over mine. "What are you thinking about?"

I shook my head. "It's nothing."

He squeezed my hand. "Tell me."

I sighed and took another long sip of my beer. "I forget how young you are sometimes. Sometimes I think I'm too old for you."

His mouth turned down into a frown. "You know that doesn't matter to me, right?"

I ran a hand through my hair. "I know."

"It doesn't," he urged.

I nodded, and waved him off. I knew when I looked at him that age didn't mean shit to him. I just couldn't help thinking about it. Age gaps could make things difficult, but our friendship before all this had never felt weird. So why was I so worried about it now?

We finished up and Noah started clearing up the plates to wash up. "Hey, you don't have to do that," I told him.

He shook his head. "You made dinner, let me help do the dishes."

I laughed.

"What?" he yelled in response over the sound of the water running in the sink.

"A man who wants to clean is seriously the sexiest thing ever," I explained as I brought more dishes back into the kitchen. I put away the leftovers while he rinsed off dishes and put them in my dishwasher.

I watched him scrub the stainless steel pan I had cooked the ground beef in.

"Eh, you might want to just let that one sit for a bit," I suggested.

"If you insist, but whatever will we do while we wait?" he asked sarcastically with a wicked grin.

"Oh, I can think of something," I grinned back.

In no time I found myself in his arms, my legs wrapped around his waist and he was carrying me back to my bedroom. A girl could seriously get used to this.

CHAPTER TWENTY

NOAH

I pulled Dinah tightly against my naked chest and drew circles on the small of her back. I took her hand in mine and kissed the tiny quill tattoo on her wrist. She let out a girlish giggle from my beard tickling her sensitive skin. I felt her lips form a smile as she kissed my shoulder. I kissed the top of her head.

"Tell me about your day," I whispered into her hair.

She looked up at me with squinty eyes. "It was boring, all I did was edit."

I kissed her nose. "Tell me. I want to hear about it."

Her brow furrowed. "You do?"

I smiled down at her. "Of course I do, did you finish it?"

She nodded. "Yeah, I did. Sent it off to my editor, it's why I really only got to catch the last five minutes of the game. Sorry I couldn't be there."

I ran my hand through her long hair, and stroked it gently. "I didn't want to keep you, I know how important your writing is. It must be hard to have two jobs. I wonder if I'm too much of a distraction."

She twisted in my arms so she was facing me now. "You are a distraction!"

I frowned.

She kissed me softly. "A good one."

I held her tightly. "Good." She started to squirm out of my arms and I laughed. "Where do you think you're going?"

"I want to take a shower."

I sighed dramatically and released her. My phone buzzed on the nightstand and I saw several texts from TJ.

TJ: *Boys are going to come over and get lit, you in?*

TJ: *Or are you too busy with your lady tonight?*

TJ: *Dude, are you alive?*

I had to laugh at that last one and I started typing away a response, but before I could Dinah was out of the shower and was rummaging through her drawers for clean clothes.

"TJ just asked if I chained you to my bed," she announced with amusement.

I smiled. "Well...if that's what you want..."

She laughed as she got dressed. "Uh...I don't know about that, but I don't want to keep you from your friends."

I cocked my head at her and slid out of the bed. I put my boxers back on and walked across the room towards her. I pushed her damp hair out of the way and kissed her neck. "You're not keeping me from my friends. Besides I think any of them would be doing the same if they were in my position."

"Hmm...Oh! Do you know if Mia's coming?" she asked and then tore off into the next room towards her office.

I pulled on the rest of my clothes and followed her in there. She was pulling a hardback of her first book off her shelf and writing something in the front cover. She looked up at the sound of my footsteps and set her pen down. "I told Mia I would get her a signed copy of my book for her little sister."

"That's really nice of you."

"Gotta keep my readers," she said with a happy sigh.

"I don't know, I would assume so. Let me text Hallsy," I reassured her and pulled out my phone to ask. I nodded once he confirmed that he was bringing his girlfriend over.

She set the book down and walked back into her bathroom to brush out her hair. I leaned against the doorway. I saw her smile through the mirror at me as she brushed out her hair and started plugging in the blow-dryer.

"Are you waiting for me?" she asked. "I might be a little bit."

I scratched the back of my neck. "I can wait if you want."

"You go on ahead, I'll see you over there."

I nodded and bent down to kiss her cheek. A red blush smeared across her pale face, and it made me just want to kiss her some more. She was so cute when she blushed like that, and I still couldn't believe my luck that I got to do that to her.

I walked next door into my own condo and TJ called to me, "HE LIVES!"

I gave him the finger and walked into the kitchen where Riley and a tall redheaded woman were standing next to each other talking in hushed whispers. She had bright red hair and was dressed casually in a Philadelphia Bulldogs jersey and jeans. Riley perked up when he saw me.

"Hey, Noah!" he called.

We shook hands and that's when I noticed the silver ring on his left hand. Had he always worn that? He put a hand out to gesture to the woman next to him. "Fiona, this is one of my teammates, Noah Kennedy."

She put her hand out to me and I shook it, she was also wearing a silver ring on her left hand. I cocked my head at Riley in confusion. Wait, was Riley married? How did I miss that one? Wait, didn't he say he was going to ask out Dinah not that long ago? Was he just fucking with me then?

"Fi's fine," she said with a smile and let my hand go.

"Noah, this is my wife, Fiona," Riley stated.

I cocked an eyebrow at him. "I'm sorry, did you just say your wife?"

They both shrugged and then she sighed. "It's a long story. We're newly married."

"Uh..." I trailed off.

I didn't know what I just walked into, but I was trying to walk out of my kitchen to get away from it. Hallsy and Mia came in just in the nick of time to save me from the awkwardness. What the fuck was that? Riley was married to some random woman I had never met before. He had gone to Vegas for a friend's wedding not that long ago. Oh, man, what did he get himself into? I took that as my cue to sneak out of the kitchen to start a game of beer pong with TJ.

"You meet Riley's new wife?" he asked while setting up the cups.

I scrunched up my nose and looked at him with a confused face. "Yeah, man. What the actual fuck?"

TJ laughed. "Man, I do NOT know."

"Was Riley even dating her?"

TJ shrugged. "I've met her before, but I was under the distinct impression they were just friends. Their moms are besties or some shit."

"Weird..." I trailed off and sipped on my beer thoughtfully. Riley getting married made no sense to me.

"Where's your old lady?" TJ asked.

"Don't call her that," I snapped.

TJ held his hands up. "It's just an expression. Nothing about her being older than you. That doesn't bother you, right?"

I shook my head. "No, but I think it bothers her."

"Nobody gives a shit about that, so don't worry about it."

At the sound of the door opening, I looked up to see Dinah walk inside. Before she saw me, she glanced across the room and saw Riley's new wife. A look of recognition crossed her face and she went over to her and the two women hugged. They spoke animatedly with each other, like they knew each other. It gave Riley the chance to stride over to us.

"What was that about?" TJ asked, pointing at my girlfriend and Riley's wife.

Riley hung his head. "It's a long story," he explained.

I took a swig of beer. "We've got time. Also, how does she know Dinah?"

"Ah, writers, publishing tends to be a small circle," Riley explained and ran a hand through his short blonde hair in frustration.

Huh. We both ended up with women who write, interesting. Dinah waved at me and I waved back, but she didn't come over to me.

"So tell us!" TJ urged.

Riley sighed. "It's complicated."

"Then tell us, man!" I urged.

"Ugh, fine. She's my best friend."

"So you just decided one day to get married?" TJ asked.

Riley shook his head. "Nope, that would make sense. No, she was engaged to someone else."

TJ and I shared a confused look, so Riley pressed on, "He left her at the altar."

"What an asshole!" I exclaimed.

He nodded. "Yup. I was pissed. She was with that douche-canoe for five years!"

"So what, you just married her instead?" TJ asked.

Riley laughed. "Pretty much."

Riley shook his head some more, but his gaze lingered back to Fiona who was laughing with my girlfriend and doing shots. I recognized something in the look in Riley's eye. "You love her," I stated.

He turned away suddenly with a fearful look in his eye. "What?"

TJ looked back and forth between the two of us.

I nodded to the redhead across the way in my kitchen. "That's why you did it, because you've been in love with her all this time."

He hung his head and ran a hand down his face. "Shit, man, I do. Is it that obvious?"

I nodded my head. "Yup."

"Then what's the problem?" TJ asked.

Riley's gaze lingered on Fiona, and she seemed to catch his eye, there was something there, but I wasn't sure what it was.

"She wanted a divorce," he started to explain.

"Shit," TJ swore.

Riley shrugged his shoulders. "She thought we made a mistake getting married like that on a whim. I'm trying to persuade her to just stick it out, let's see if we can do this."

TJ elbowed him in the ribs and I laughed too. Good for Riley.

"What does she want?" I ask.

"She doesn't know, but she agreed to this 'arrangement' I guess. She wants me to convince her that this will work out between us," he explained. "I'm just tired of the single life. Tired of women who can't handle our grueling schedule. Fi gets it."

I patted him on the back. "Sorry, man."

He shrugged. "It was really stupid, but I just wanted to save her. And yeah, maybe a part of me wanted to see if she could love me the way I love her. I've been in love with her since high school."

"Ri, was she your first?" I asked.

"Yeah..." he trailed off.

I took another big sip of my drink, and glanced over at Dinah laughing with Fiona. Dinah's eyes sparkled and I was sure then that she had sunk her claws deep into me, and I would let her do anything she wanted to me. I got the wistful look on Riley's face, because I felt the same way every time I looked at that pint-sized brunette.

"She doesn't have a clue how you feel, does she?" I asked.

"Nope!" he exclaimed, but then sighed and changed the subject. "How's the ear?" he asked me.

I fingered the stitches on my ear and showed him and he winced. "It's okay. No concussion, but they told me to take it easy. I think I'm going to get benched though for our next game."

He clapped my shoulder. "Maybe not!"

I grumbled, and I had a feeling the medical team was going to be a little cautious on this one, even though I really just wanted to be back out on the ice.

CHAPTER TWENTY-ONE

DINAH

I grinned at Fi and we knocked back a shot together. It was such a small world that Riley of all people would know Fiona Gallagher and end up marrying her. I couldn't believe the insane story she just told me. The publishing world was a bit small, so a lot of us in the YA world knew each other. I loved Fi's sci-fi books, but I didn't think I would have ever been a good sci-fi writer.

"So what are you gonna do?" I asked her.

She shrugged and then winced as the shot burned down her throat. "He wants to stick it out. I agreed to try it for a couple months, but I don't know. Maybe it was a dumb idea?"

I rested my hand on my chin to think. Her situation was weird, but when I glanced over and watched Riley and Noah playing beer pong together, I saw the way he looked at her. "This sounds like the plot of a romance novel," I mused.

She tipped back her head and laughed. "Shit, girl, you're right."

I smiled. "Course, I am!"

She nudged me as she caught me staring across the room at my boyfriend. Noah caught my gaze and his lips turned up in a smile before his attention went back to the game. Fi was pouring another round of shots for us, and Mia had walked back into the kitchen to do them with us.

"Missed you at the game today!" Mia cried when I handed her the book for her sister. She hugged me tight.

"I had to get work done. Noah insisted," I explained with a smile.

"Ugh, they are so sickeningly cute," Mia groaned to Fi with an eye roll.

Fi smiled. "So, Noah's your boy, huh?"

I smiled back at her.

The three of us clicked our shot glasses together and took it together. I didn't usually drink this much, but I was celebrating finally having finished my big picture edits. Plus, Fi looked stressed like she needed this too. I wondered if she was also on deadline, I kind of recognized that stressed out writer look on her face.

"You think he's a bit young for me, don't you?" I asked Fi.

Mia twirled her blonde hair around her finger and rolled her eyes at me. "Who, Noah? D, no one cares about that shit."

Fi grinned and pointed at Mia. "She's got a point."

I frowned, but didn't say anything else because Noah came into the kitchen to grab a beer out of the fridge. He eyed the vodka bottle in front of the three of us and the lined up shot glasses. "You okay, lovey?"

My heart nearly melted when he called me that. God,

he was so cute. I felt Fi pinching my side teasingly. Already I liked this brazen girl and I had a feeling her and Riley were going to make it. She seemed perfect for him. I batted her away with my hand, and smiled up at Noah. "Good. Just celebrating finishing those edits," I explained.

He leaned down to my height and kissed my cheek. "I'm proud of you."

I shooed him away.

He smiled and pulled away but very slowly. He was such a tease.

"Damn," Fi breathed. "That boy loves you."

Mia was nodding her head in agreement, but then she walked away when Hallsy came over. He wrapped an arm around her and said something in her ear that made her laugh. It made me smile to see two people who got together when they were just kids still so in love.

"So when can I get my hands on your book?" Fi asked.

I was shocked. "You want to read it?"

She gave me a confused look. "I love YA contemporary, of course! I don't know if I'll ever write in it, but it's like my favorite thing to read."

I laughed. "Oh my god, I feel the same way about sci-fi! When's the last book in your trilogy coming out?"

She groaned. "Just handed in the first draft. Riley's been begging me to read it. I think it's a pile of garbage."

"It's a first draft!"

She nodded. "I know. I lost a lot of time with my wedding, but like the night before we came back I got inspired and Riley basically told me to go write. It was really nice of him. My ex would always complain I was more into my book than into him."

I grinned at her. "Noah's really supportive of my

writing too. He forbid me from coming to the game today because he knew I needed to get work done."

She put a hand on her heart. "Oh my god, girl! Did you build that man in a factory?"

I shrugged with a smile on my lips. "I've thought the same thing. He's such a good guy."

Then her eyes got a sparkle to them and she suggested, "We should challenge each other to write in the other's genre. Maybe for NaNoWRiMO!"

"Oh! That's an awesome idea!"

We clinked water glasses and lapsed into silence. I knew Fi was local, so we ran into each other at book events, but I had no idea that she knew Aaron Riley! I leaned across the kitchen island and saw Noah and TJ high-fiving, clearly they had won their game of beer pong against Riley and Metzy. Noah was grinning wide and TJ was laughing with his full body like he always did.

Riley crossed the room to come over to talk to Fi, and she teased him about losing. I side-eyed him as his hand came around her waist and he pulled her into his side. Yeah, they might have gotten married on whim and for a dumb reason, but the chemistry nearly sizzled off of them. Those two were so in it for the long haul, but I didn't think they realized it yet.

I decided to get out of the way and go into the living room. I flopped down onto the couch, and wasn't that surprised when Noah sunk into it next to me. He put an arm around me from behind the back of the couch and I slid down to nestle into his side. There was a buzzing in my head from all the shots I had done, it made my chest feel all warm and fuzzy.

I hadn't even realized I had closed my eyes until Noah asked, "You tired, lovey?"

I shook my head and slowly opened my eyes. "It's just the alcohol."

He chuckled, and scratched a hand through his growing beard. "How many shots did you have?"

I shrugged. "Too many!"

He squeezed my shoulder and pulled me closer. TJ came over to us and started chatting Noah up about how the team was doing. Talking about special teams and their penalty kill, most of which I agreed with, but my head was buzzing so I didn't feel like agreeing with him.

TJ kicked my foot. "Hey, you alive?"

I shook my head. "Nope. I is dead."

"Some writer you are," he mused with a laugh.

I stuck out my tongue.

I felt Noah's laugh bubbling up and vibrating in his chest next to me, and TJ just shook his head. "You two are so sickeningly cute."

I smiled. "That's what Mia said."

Noah's smile was sheepish, and I got the feeling it made him a little embarrassed. Huh. Then he scratched his beard with his fingernails and just smiled wider and pulled me into his lap.

I laughed and leaned my head in the crook of his neck.

TJ made a gagging face. "Disgusting!"

Mia who was standing behind him talking with Hallsy shot us a grin. "Aw, they're so cute. You're just jealous, T!" she teased.

TJ shook his head.

Huh. I wondered if TJ was still broken up about that girl he had told us about the other night. He hadn't said anything since, and I hadn't seen any girl around here tonight hanging off his every word.

As the night went on Noah and I mingled with

everyone else, and I helped him clean up as people started filing out. TJ had already passed out on the couch. I put a pillow under his head and a throw blanket on top of him.

"Aw, don't baby him," Noah scolded me.

I grinned as I looked over at him. "I can't help but 'mom' him a little."

He frowned a little at my choice of words. I walked into the kitchen and started helping with the dishes. "Oh, come on, don't do that," he groaned.

"Just let me."

His warm presence came up behind me, his big hands running down my back and then up my arms. He pushed my hair away from my right shoulder and bent to kiss my neck. I leaned into it and probably purred a little bit too. "Come on, let's just get to bed, you look really tired."

"I am really tired," I agreed.

I wiped my hands on the hand towel at the sink, and let him pull me toward his bedroom. It was different being in Noah's bed with him, but I felt bad being here and bothering TJ if I had my whole condo to myself. Noah gave me one of his t-shirts to sleep in and I curled into his side on his bed.

"I think I like your bed better," he announced.

I looked up at him. "Me too. Plus, I don't have a roommate."

"Ah, TJ doesn't care."

I glared at him. "I don't think he wants to hear us having sex. Bad enough I live next door."

He laughed and kissed my temple. I snuggled more into his chest. He stroked my hair and asked, "Are you too tired?"

"I think your cock might fall off if we have sex again," I joked.

He pushed me down onto my back and leaned over me, kissing me long and hard. His kisses were aggressive and hungry, kissing me like he needed our lips fused together in order to breathe.

"Is that a challenge?" he asked with a devilish grin on his face.

I slipped my hands up behind his neck and threaded them through his hair. "Um…"

All thoughts seeped out of my brain when he started kissing my neck and his hands were slowly pushing my shirt up my torso. He was smooth as shit, and I kind of loved it. I felt the smile on his lips as he covered my body with kisses that sent tingles down my spine.

Noah's cock did not, in fact, fall off.

Despite my best efforts to really put it to work.

CHAPTER TWENTY-TWO

NOAH

We finally had a day off with no practice and I wanted to spend every waking hour of my free time with Dinah in my arms, but I knew she had her own obligations. This whole relationship thing was tough work with my crazy schedule, but I would sacrifice my sleep if it meant I got to see the woman I loved. She tirelessly worked her nine-to-five and then worked on her writing, so I wanted to be respectful of her time.

When I woke up and she wasn't in my bed with me, I had to admit I was a little disappointed. I got up out of bed, pulled a pair of sweatpants on and walked out into the kitchen. The smell of coffee and something cooking wafted in from the kitchen. I smiled when I saw Dinah at our stove making eggs and laughing at something TJ had said. TJ was slumped on the bar stool in front of the island, with his head on the cool surface. Dinah gave him a glass of water.

I crossed the room and kissed her in greeting.

She plated some eggs and toast and handed them to me. "Here. Coffee's ready too."

I cocked my eyebrow at her strained smile. "You okay, lovey?"

She nodded and put a hand on her temple. "Yeah, just a slight headache. I'm fine. Remind me to never drink with Fiona Gallagher ever again. She's worse than Rox, which I thought was impossible."

TJ laughed. "My sister even drinks me under the table, so I hope those two never meet."

Dinah looked like she was thinking really hard, then she sighed and asked TJ, "Have you talked to your sister lately?"

He nodded. "Yeah, we talked. I never liked that Lisa girl, even when they were just friends."

I poured myself a cup of coffee and took a seat next to TJ. I didn't ask what they were talking about, but I could hazard a guess. TJ had never liked his twin sister's girlfriend, and it sounded like maybe the two were done. I would have thought he would have been happy about it, but he seemed kind of sad about it. There was an empty plate next to him and he was nursing his water like his life depended on it. I smirked, served him right for getting so drunk last night.

"You know, I think I could deal with hearing you two fuck so much if I get breakfast in the morning," TJ said wryly.

I nearly choked on my sip of coffee, but Dinah just barked out a loud and long laugh. I loved her laugh, it was such a loud sound to come out of the mouth of such a small woman.

Dinah turned off the burner and got her own plate and cup of coffee, before sitting down in the seat next to me. "That sounds fake, but okay," she commented.

TJ groaned and felt his head. "Ugh, I feel like death."

"Maybe you shouldn't have drank so much last night," Dinah teased.

He dropped his head to the surface of the island again and gave her the finger. I playfully punched him in the arm. "Hey, that's my girlfriend!" I joked like I was insulted.

Dinah's cheeks flushed pink at the mention. I guess I had never really said the G-word in front of her before, but the blush turned into a bright smile, so I knew it wasn't unwelcome. TJ slumped out of his chair and announced he was taking a shower.

Dinah and I ate our breakfast together in a comfortable silence for a few moments. "I have the day off today, we should do something," I suggested.

"Like what?" she asked and took a huge gulp of her coffee.

I shook my head. "Not sure yet. I just want to take you out again."

She waved me off with her hand. "Noah, you don't have to do that with me."

I slipped my hand into hers and gripped it tight. "I know, but I want to. Let's go out and do something!"

She nodded finally in agreement after some more coaxing. "Okay, okay," she conceded with a bright smile. "But I need to get some work done. Maybe in a few hours?"

"Perfect."

She went to go start cleaning up the dishes, but I shooed her out of the kitchen. She kissed me goodbye and headed next door to get some writing done. I took out my phone and started making a plan for what to do today. I looked up and saw TJ staring at me.

"What?" I asked.

He had this funny look on his face, that I couldn't really place. "You really love her, don't you?"

"Yeah..."

"Huh."

"What does 'huh' mean?" I asked, slightly offended.

He shook his head. "It's good to see you happy. For the record, I think she loves you too, but she doesn't know it yet."

With that little revelation he walked away. Sometimes that guy made no sense. His weird mood reminded me that I wanted to know what was going on with his sister. I scrolled through my contact list until I found Rox's name. I shot off a text to her.

ME: *You ok?*

I watched the three dots starting to type across my screen for a little bit and finally her answer came.

ROX: *No.*

ME: *You want to talk about it?*

ROX: *Ugh. Noah, could you please be more Canadian?*

ME: *You can't say that when you're also Canadian! Seriously, Rox, if you want to talk about it, I'm here.*

ROX: *I'll be okay.*

ME: *Aw, Rox! I'm so sorry.*

ROX: *Yeah...me too. Breakups suck.*

I ran a hand through my hair and sighed. TJ's twin sister was funny and had a foul-mouth, but she also cared so deeply about the people around her. She would go to war for her twin brother, and I knew the two were close. Especially since her and their parents didn't see eye-to-eye since she came out as bisexual. I can't say I understood what that was like, but I knew Rox needed to know that she had support in her friends. I'd always be the guy who wore his heart on his sleeve and was there for my friends, so it bummed me out that she was going through this tough time. Roxanne Desjardins was a cool chick, and she didn't deserve the grief that she put up with.

ME: *Let's grab a drink next time we play Toronto?*
ROX: *You're ON!*

❄

"You have got to be fucking kidding me!" Dinah exclaimed while I bent down in front of her to make sure her skates were tight enough.

I smiled up at her. "Nope!"

"Babe! You skate for a living, you can't seriously want to take me ice skating?" she moaned in exasperation.

I sat on the bench next to her and laced up my own skates. I kissed her on the cheek. "You always said you wanted to go ice skating, so I'm going to teach you."

Her face softened at that. "You actually listen to the things I say?"

I frowned at her. "Of course I do."

She smiled at that. "God, you're such a sweet baby angel."

I grimaced. I didn't know about that one, but I did know the only thing I wanted in this world was to make this woman happy. "Maybe…however it's like a sin for a diehard Philadelphia Bulldogs fan to not know how to ice skate."

She sighed at me but just shook her head with a laugh.

I stood up, took her hand in mine and led her out onto the ice. I felt her nails gripping into my arm as she cautiously took to the ice. I smiled and let her grip me. There was something about this strong independent woman holding onto me for dear life that was kind of hot. What did that say about me?

She soon got her bearings on the ice and her grip on my arm softened after a slow lap around it. Her hand finally shifted down to lace her fingers through mine. Her hand felt so small in my large one, and I was always afraid that I was going to break her if I wasn't too careful. She would freaking hate that if I ever voiced those words aloud.

"What are you thinking about?" she asked, suddenly pulling me away from my thoughts.

Our feet skated in time together around the rink and I looked down at her small frame with a smile. "I'm just happy with you."

"Me too."

My thumb rubbed over her hand where we were connected and we skated on a little more. She seemed to have warmed up to being on the ice. For someone who said they didn't know how to skate, she had done surprisingly well out here with me. I also had been super slow on it, steadying her with my hands and skating backwards in front of her to teach her how to be on the ice by herself. A lot of the boys on the team said taking a girl skating was a bad date, especially if you were a hockey player, but I think she kind of loved it. All I ever wanted to do was make her happy. I still couldn't believe that she was here with me and we weren't just friends anymore. I couldn't believe a woman like her actually wanted to be with a dumb jock like me.

We skated for a little while longer, but then we both got tired and decided to call it quits. We unlaced our skates, returning the rental pair for her, and I put my own back into my gear bag. We made plans to get lunch at the vegan fast food place she liked over in Rittenhouse Square. It was unseasonably warm for March, so we ate in the park across the street, sitting on the ledge of the fountain.

"So vegan food? You're not vegan," I commented just as she took a huge bite of her burger.

She shook her head and I waited for her to swallow. "I was vegetarian for like eight years."

I furrowed my brow. "I didn't know that."

"It never really came up in conversation."

"What changed?" I asked.

She looked down at the ground with a frown. "When I found out I was pregnant. I wanted to make sure my nutrition was right. That was right before...well you know."

I grabbed her hand and rubbed the pad of my thumb across her palm comfortingly. I knew it was hard for her to talk about the miscarriage and how it would affect the rest of her life. My heart had broken for her that day in the hospital. The doctor had wrongfully assumed I was her husband because she was still wearing her wedding ring, so he just blurted out in front of me that she probably couldn't have kids. It broke her, and all I could do was hold her and tell her it was going to be okay.

"You don't have to talk about it if you don't want," I reassured her.

She looked at me with what looked like relief. "Noah, I can't have kids."

"Lovey, I know that."

She was shaking her head. "No, you have to understand that I will never be able to have kids."

I squinted at her. "How about we cross that bridge when we get there, okay? None of that matters to me anyway," I tried to reassure her.

She waved me off with her hand. "Forget it. I'm ruining this awesome day you planned!"

I smiled at her and took a bite of my own food. For vegan food, it was actually pretty decent, and it was nice being able to have a day with her to myself. With my schedule, whether it was training, practicing, or traveling for games, it could be hard to maintain a relationship. I had always been a relationship guy. Sure I had some meaningless hookups when I first entered the league, but I always preferred to have a partner in my life. Meaningless hookups were great when you were eighteen and horny, but not so great when the loneliness sunk in. The more time I spent with Dinah, the more I realized I was hopelessly in love with her, and I wasn't sure yet if she felt the same about me.

She cocked her head at me, studying me. "This has been a really nice day. Thanks for forcing me to learn how to ice skate."

"I'm glad you enjoyed it. TJ nagged me saying it's bad date idea."

Her little nose scrunched up. "Why would he say that?"

I shrugged. "I guess because we're hockey players? I just wanted to do something with you that was fun since I had the day off."

"It was nice. Don't doubt yourself," she told me with a smile. Her hand trailed down my arm to grab my hand. Her touch lit me on fire every time.

"I'm glad you enjoyed it."

"What's your week like?" she asked.

I chewed my bottom lip thinking about the coming week of games. "We travel tomorrow, I should be home on Friday."

"Hmm," she commented and went back to eating.

I sighed. "I'm sorry my schedule's crazy."

She shook her head. "It's okay, I understand."

I took her hand in mine, rubbing my big thumb on the pad of it. "It doesn't mean I don't want to spend every waking hour with you."

Her eyes softened at that. "I want that too."

"Can we do something on Friday? We could go to dinner?" I asked.

She frowned. "Can't. I'm sorry."

"Oh. What do you mean, you can't?"

She sighed. "I have a family thing. My parents are in town and it's my niece's birthday."

"Oh. When is it?"

She was looking at me like I had a death wish. "Why?"

I squeezed her hand. "Do you want me to come with you?"

She continued to stare at me for a really long time. Then she squinted at me as if she was thinking real hard. "Are you sure you aren't concussed?"

I laughed. "What?"

"You've met my family, they're certifiable. You want to voluntarily spend your free Friday night with them?" she asked.

Her eyes were wide with fear for me. Her family wasn't *that* bad, they were just protective.

"Yes, lovey, I do."

Her smile was wide then so I leaned over and pulled her face to mine to kiss her right there in Rittenhouse Square Park. It was the perfect moment, and the perfect place to finally tell her that I loved her. I just didn't know if it was the right time. For me it had been agony not telling her how I really felt, but I had years of pining over this incredible woman. For her, this thing had really just started, and I wasn't entirely sure she was over her husband yet.

When I pulled away, she smiled but held my face in her hands, her small hand running down the length of my jaw and pushing the hair out of my face. "Do you want me to come to the game next Saturday?"

I must have looked like the Joker with how wide the grin spread across my face. "God, I love you, yes, please come to my game on Saturday."

She pulled her hands away and leaned back away from me with an unsure look on her face.

FUCK!

"Noah? Did you just say what I think you said?" she finally asked after a few uncomfortable seconds passed between us.

I ran a hand through my hair, but couldn't look at her now. "Um...you don't have to say it back, but I've loved you for a long time, and I just had to tell you."

She turned my face so I was looking her in the eyes. She had this intense look on her face, that I would say she only really reserved for the bedroom. Whoa.

"Noah Kennedy, you don't tell a woman you love her and then turn away from her."

My lips quirked up into a grin.

She didn't let me get another word in though, and just kissed me again. "I think it's time to get out of here," she whispered in my ear.

I wasn't one to say no to that, but it didn't escape my notice that she didn't say she loved me back.

CHAPTER TWENTY-THREE

DINAH

Noah had been on the road for a couple days, which was fine because it allowed me some time to process the fact that he told me he loved me. It was such an off-hand comment, but when he told me I felt my heart squeeze in my chest. I wasn't sure if I loved him yet. I wanted to, but it felt so awkward him saying it to me and me not being sure if I was ready to say it back to him. He said that I didn't have to say it back, but I saw the hurt on his face when I didn't. It was kind of why we had rushed back to my place to hop into bed together. Being with him was great, but I knew I was holding myself back because I was so scared that I would lose him just like I lost Jason. I didn't think I could bear it.

I spent the time while he was gone, working on the first draft of my third book, in between my day job and line edits for book two. I knew I was drowning myself in my work just so I didn't have to think about if I loved Noah. It had gotten so bad that Frankie and Tony had stopped by to make sure I was okay. When Frankie saw my empty fridge he began to mother hen me until I let him buy me groceries.

The truth was, I really missed Noah when he was gone, and my heart did a little jump every time I got a text from him. Even more on those occasions when he video chatted with me to say goodnight. The team was in a downward slump again, which honestly, as a fan I wasn't surprised. As Noah's girlfriend I felt like I wasn't supposed to tell him they were playing like hot garbage and turning over the puck too much. Normally, I wouldn't have cared, but I thought I already hurt his feelings by not telling him that I loved him. I also didn't want to be *that* girlfriend, and sometimes he just needed one who would support him.

Sometimes I thought maybe he was just too perfect. What man wanted to actually subject himself to the scrutiny of The Mezzanetti family? Tonight was my niece Abbie's eighth birthday party at my brother Frankie's house in South Philly. I didn't think Noah knew what he was getting himself into. He had texted me earlier that he was back in town but was busy with some team stuff. Probably reviewing game tape and having team meetings, so I was planning to meet him back at my condo before we headed over. I ended up sneaking out of work a little early, because after 4:30 PM on a Friday afternoon nothing ever really got done.

I dropped my purse at the door and headed into my bedroom where I inspected my clothes. I was still in work clothes, so I changed into a pair of skinny jeans and a striped long-sleeve shirt. I was inspecting how it looked in my mirror when I heard the knock on my door. With a smile I headed to my front door and was happy to see Noah standing there. I jumped into his arms, wrapping my arms and legs around him while I kissed him fiercely.

He chuckled and kicked the door shut. "Oh someone missed me," he mused when he broke the kiss.

I rested my forehead against his and my hands clung to the back of his neck. "Oh most definitely."

His hands lingered on my ass. "Damn, you look good in those jeans," he admitted and gave me a little squeeze.

I squealed with laughter and slid out of his arms. I gave him a questioning look. "You really think so? I was afraid my family was gonna make some comment about my weight in this outfit."

His face was a cloudy torment. "I don't understand. You're pretty thin."

I sighed. "I didn't used to be, and my family likes to comment on it."

He grumbled and muttered something under his breath but I didn't try to ask him to repeat it.

"Are you sure you want to deal with my family tonight?" I asked instead.

"Lovey, I'm positive."

I noticed he had a gift bag in his hand. "What's that?" I asked.

"Oh! You said Abbie's favorite Bulldog is Benny, so I got him to sign a puck for me."

My heart flipped over in my chest and then did a little dance. That was so sweet, of both of them really. Benny was definitely a soft-hearted man like Noah. He just hid it a little better.

"You didn't have to do that! Fuck, now you're showing me up."

He laughed. "I can not give it to her if you want?"

I shook my head. "No, it's perfect. Let's go!"

He helped me into my jacket and we left my condo. I had offered to drive, but since he had an afternoon game tomorrow he didn't want to drink anyway. Which was good because my family tended to drive me to drink. We drove into South Philly where my brother Frankie lived. Nerves were building up inside my chest while Noah found a parking spot.

He rested his hand on my thigh and my whole body felt like it got shocked at his touch. He gave me a shy smile. "Why are you nervous?" he asked.

"I haven't introduced my family to a boyfriend in like eight years. I met Jason in college."

Noah kissed me softly and tucked a piece of hair behind my ear. "I'm your boyfriend, eh?"

I smiled at his little Canadian inflection. God, could he be cuter? "You know you are."

"I've never heard you say it out loud."

"Well, you are. Come on, let's get this over with!" I urged with a groan.

We got out of the car and he slid his hand into mine. The warmth of it made me feel steady, centered even. I knocked on the door and was greeted by my sister-in-law Sofia with a big hug, her curly dark hair flying haphazardly into my face. I had to disentangle myself from Noah's hand just to let the woman engulf me.

"Hi, Sof," I greeted her.

The older woman pulled away from me and then her brown eyes glazed over Noah's towering form behind me. "And who's this?" she asked.

Sofia wasn't big on sports, even though my brother, her husband, was a diehard Bulldogs fan. So it did slightly surprise me that she didn't recognize Noah. However, he did look a bit different up on skates and with the number 13 on his back then in the real world.

"My boyfriend, Noah."

"Oh, D, he's tall, like really tall, and handsome," she mused and I held in my laughter at Noah's blush.

"Yes, he is," I agreed.

"Come in, come in," she gestured to us and shuffled us through the door of her home.

I shoved our gifts into her hands and then a blur of pink threw itself at me. "Aunt D!" my niece screeched at me and clung to my waist.

"Hey kiddo! Happy birthday!"

"You came!" she exclaimed and hugged me tighter. I loved being the fun Aunt.

"Of course I did!"

She was staring intently up at Noah who just waved and smiled at her. "Aunt D, how do you know Noah Kennedy from the hockey team?"

I mouthed 'sorry' at him but he waved me off. He bent down to Abbie's height. "Hi, Abbie. Can I tell you a secret?"

She nodded enthusiastically, but she was still hugging my leg.

"Your Aunt D's my new girlfriend. But it's our secret, okay?"

She nodded, but then one of her friends asked her to play and they were darting down into the basement. I couldn't help but notice that she had a big smile on her face though. Noah helped me out of my jacket and I hung it on the coatrack along with his own.

"You're good with kids," I said to him.

He shrugged. "Kids are easy to talk to."

I tried not to focus on the fact that Noah would never have that if he stayed with me.

I walked further into the house, tugging Noah along with my hand in his. He didn't seem to mind and he squeezed my hand in reassurance which made me feel comforted. Noah opened a bottle of beer for me and I was just taking a sip of it when we got ambushed by my brothers. Frankie was standing there in his dumb 'Kiss the Cook' apron his greying hair looking like it had multiplied, Tony had his 'swole' arms crossed over his chest, but my brother Eddie just stood there in his trademark leather jacket looking amused.

"Kennedy," Frankie started evenly.

"Don't start," I warned and leveled the three of them with a death glare.

Tony ignored me and pushed a finger into Noah's chest. "Yo man, what's your intention with our sister?"

I pushed Tony's meaty hand away and gave him the finger. "To fuck my brains out, obviously. And he does that very well. Fuck off, man."

Frankie hid a smile behind his hand and Eddie's shoulders were shaking hard to hide his laugh. Tony was kind of a meathead, and the tough-big brother act always annoyed me. He pulled the same shit on Jason, who had just rolled his eyes at him. Tony puffed out his chest, trying to be all alpha-male. Like Noah couldn't take him down a peg in a heartbeat. Noah was not a fighter, which I was glad about because I worried about fighting and its impacts on concussions. I have seen him in the rare fight, though, and he could snap my annoying-ass brother in half.

"Answer the question, man!" Tony demanded.

"Don't!" I warned just as Noah was opening his mouth. "Tony, will you just leave my boyfriend alone? Stop the overprotective older brother bullshit."

"Boyfriend, huh?" Frankie asked amused.

Eddie was smiling too. "Good for you, D."

"Boys!" my mother's sharp voice called out. "Leave your sister alone."

I sighed.

"You're on your own!" Eddie joked and dashed off.

Coward.

Mom walked over to us and gave Noah a big hug. He had to hunch down to her height, but he was a good sport. "Noah! It's good to see you again," she beamed at him. She turned to me and hugged me tightly too.

Noah was a saint. He humored her while she peppered him with questions about what we were doing. In terms of, 'How long have you been dating? Is it serious?' I drank my beer a little too quickly getting more and more annoyed while my mom started waxing poetic about wedding bells and new grand-babies.

"Mom!" I finally snapped. "Will you stop?"

"Honestly, Dinah, I'm just asking because you're not getting any younger. You don't get pregnant now you might miss your chance."

Noah reached a hand out to me and squeezed mine. He knew that I had never told my family that I couldn't have kids. Tears were pricking at my eyes but I refused to let them fall. I downed my beer and went to grab another. If it wasn't for Noah I might not be here gritting my teeth to fight off snapping at my mother. I had never told my family that I couldn't have kids. My mom was too traditional, too much into the fact that women should find a good man and have kids with him.

I almost died during my miscarriage because I was hemorrhaging and I didn't know it. They had to perform surgery on me, and there was some scarring. The doctors had told me if I really wanted a kid, I could try IVF, but it was costly and unlikely. They gave me a one percent chance of bringing another pregnancy to term. I had since made my peace with it, but I didn't like to talk about it. My life could be fulfilled without a husband or children in it, but I was not bringing that conversation up with my family. No wonder Eddie was scared to tell them that his business partner was his boyfriend. They just wouldn't understand.

"I need some air," I made an excuse and went outside with my beer.

Noah looked like he wanted to follow me but then my Dad had walked over and I knew he was going to drill Noah about the Bulldogs. In the backyard, I slunk against the wall and drank my beer slowly. I blinked the tears down my face thinking that I was finally alone.

"Hey, what's wrong?" I smelt the cigarette before I heard Eddie's voice asking the question.

FUCK!

I wiped my tears away. "Nothing," I lied.

Eddie stubbed out his cigarette and pulled me into his chest, wrapping his arms around me like a good older brother. "Come on, tell me," he urged.

Sobs racked my chest and I let it soak onto my brother's leather jacket. "Shit, I'm sorry."

"Hey, seriously, what's wrong? Why isn't your boyfriend out here consoling you? Did you get in a fight already?"

I shook my head. "Dad trapped him in a hockey conversation."

Eddie laughed sarcastically. "Poor guy."

"He's a fucking Canadian saint, I swear!"

"Must be if he puts up with you."

"Ass!"

He stuck his tongue out at me and I gave him my middle finger. "He's good to you, though, right?"

"So good. Like I think I built him in a factory, Eds."

He rolled his eyes at that. "So, why the fuck are you out here crying?"

I sighed. "Mom was going on and on about if we were going to get married and how we should do it soon if we want to have kids before my eggs shriveled up."

"So? Just ignore her."

"Eddie...I can't have kids."

Eddie looked down at me with a shocked and concerned look. "What do you mean?"

"I had a miscarriage right after Jason died. It was really bad, I almost bled to death, but Noah found me in the stairwell and took me to the hospital. I basically owe him my life."

"Okay, so lots of women have miscarriages and go on to have kids later."

I shook my head. "I had to have surgery and there was scarring. They suggested IVF being an option, but the likelihood of it being successful are slim. Like one percent. Basically I'm infertile."

"Okay...that's not the end of the world."

I laughed. "Have you met our mother?"

He laughed too. "You should just tell her. Get it over with so she'll give it a rest."

I leveled him with a raised eyebrow. "Like how you told them about you and Alex?"

"Noah was there for you when it happened? He knows?" he asked, changing the subject.

I nodded.

"Fuck, sis. That man loves you."

"I do," came Noah's voice from the back door. My gaze shifted over to him and I swiped my fingers across my face to wipe away the salty tears. "You okay?" he asked.

Eddie looked between us and slunk away suddenly.

Noah put his hands on my shoulders to steady me. "Your family doesn't know you can't have kids."

"Nope."

"Oh, Dinah, I'm sorry," he said softly. His hand grazed across my cheek, wiping away the last of the tears I had let fall.

"I'm sorry for abandoning you to deal with my dad."

"I was more concerned about if you were okay."

I looked up into his blue eyes and they were a storm of torment. Eddie was right, this man did love me and I was too much of a coward to say it back to him. "Be honest with me, do you want children?"

He balked. "What?"

"Noah, I can't have kids. Even if I tried to do IVF, it likely won't work. I could go through another painful miscarriage like before."

"Lovey," he whispered and ran his hand down my cheek. He caressed me there and I leaned into the warmth of his hand. "I care about you. You not being able to have kids isn't a deal breaker for me. Okay?"

"Noah, if you want kids down the line—"

He cut me off by bending his head and capturing my lips in a soft kiss. I melted into him and pushed my fears to the side.

CHAPTER TWENTY-FOUR

NOAH

I sat at the kitchen table and watched in amusement at Dinah's brothers, Tony and Eddie, arguing about football. Every few minutes they asked for my opinion, but I played the dumb Canadian hockey player line so I didn't have to get involved. I glanced across the room, spying Dinah sitting on the floor in the living room playing with her niece.

My heart was breaking for the woman I loved. Finding her during her miscarriage had been the scariest thing I ever had to deal with. I thought she had died, so I could only imagine the scars she still dealt with. It also made me mad that she thought because she couldn't biologically have a kid that would be a deal breaker for me. I wasn't even sure I wanted kids, but if I did, there were other options. There were surrogates and there was adoption, and holy fuck I was getting too far ahead of myself. I wanted to just take her home and hold her until she felt better about this. But today

I was playing the good boyfriend and dealing with her insane family.

I beamed at the thought that she finally admitted I was her boyfriend. It filled me with this warm feeling in the center of my chest. I felt a hand on my shoulder and I looked up to see Dinah's oldest brother Frankie standing in front of me. Frankie, the oldest of the Mezzanetti siblings, was a little stoic, but he also seemed to keep his brothers in line. Especially Tony, that guy had such an aggressive personality. I half-wondered if that was all an act though. Eddie was more reserved, sitting back in the shadows with a sarcastic remark here or there. I think I understood where Dinah got it from.

"Hey, man," I greeted Frankie.

Frankie ran a hand through his greying hair and nodded his head towards his sister. "You really love my sister, huh?"

"That obvious?"

He nodded with a smile. "Saw it when she brought you into my shop. You're a good guy, don't fuck it up."

With that he walked away, leaving me a little confused at his words. Unlike Tony, who had threatened "if you break her heart, I'll break your face" the words from Frankie rang more like, "I like you and want you both to be happy." Huh. Maybe her brothers just put on that Italian tough-guy act.

I didn't have time to think about it because Dinah was walking over to me now with a smile on her face. I smiled back at her and pulled her onto my lap. She curled into me, resting her head in the crook of my neck while we listened to her brothers debate. I was starting to come to the conclusion that Eddie was arguing with Tony just for the sake of arguing.

She lifted up her head to glare at her brothers. "Will you two give it a rest?"

Eddie smirked at her. "It's like you don't even know us."

Tony was glaring at me, probably because my hand was wrapped around Dinah's waist dangerously close to her ass. I wanted to say I wouldn't be a completely overprotective brother with my little sister Maddie, but I also knew I already scared off her last boyfriend when I visited home last summer. I wondered if she was still mad at me about that.

"What are you thinking about?" Dinah asked me.

"Maddie."

"Your sister?"

I nodded. "Did I tell you I scared off her boyfriend last summer?"

Dinah barked out a laugh and looked at me in disbelief. "You? I just can't picture it."

I shrugged. "He wasn't good enough for her."

Tony leveled me with a stare, as if studying me then he just nodded and returned back to arguing with Eddie. Dinah was giggling into my neck and it tickled so much, but I loved it. "What was that about?" I whispered.

"I think you've been approved," she explained.

I laughed too. "I think Frankie already gave me the approval."

She kissed my neck softly and her breath was hot in my ear. "I think we should get out of here."

"You sure?"

She nodded and slid off my lap. "Yeah, you have a one o'clock game tomorrow anyway. Wait, stay there. It takes like a half hour to say goodbye to everyone in this family."

I stared as she took off to make her rounds to her family, but was a bit confused on why she hadn't asked me to join her. Although, the way her dad had trapped me in a conversation on how I needed to just shoot the puck, maybe I was being rewarded. Eddie and Tony had stopped their fight because Eddie had walked away to talk to one of their cousins. I watched from my spot as Dinah said goodbye to her cousins, her brother Frankie, and his wife Sofia. I stood up when she returned back to me and took her hand.

"You didn't take that long," I joked.

She grimaced. "My mom wanted to say goodbye to you."

I laughed. "Oh come on, your family isn't that bad. They're just very protective of you."

She grumbled and dragged me towards where her parents were sitting. Her niece was in her dad's lap, and he tickled her until she laughed. Dinah had a pained look on her face, and I knew she was just thinking about one of the worst days of her life.

I bent down to hug her mom. "Mrs. Mezzanetti, thanks for having me."

She waved her hand at me as if to dismiss me. Her dark eyes were shining as she looked between me and her daughter. "Anytime, Noah. We're so glad you two sorted this out."

I eyed her in question.

She laughed. "Oh, honey, we knew when you showed up for Jason's funeral that you only had eyes for our Dinah."

Dinah was blushing. "Mom," she whined.

I squeezed her hand. I held my hand out to her dad. "Sir, thanks for having me."

Her dad shook it firmly. "You be good to our girl, okay?"

"Yes, sir."

"Dad..." she whined. "He's so good to me, like you don't even know. Stop worrying."

I squeezed her hand again and smiled at her.

Her mom was beaming again and turned to me. "Maybe you can convince her that she needs to seriously think about getting on the baby train."

"Hon," her dad warned.

Dinah was balling her hands into fists. "Mom, stop."

I squeezed her hand again to tell her to calm down.

Her mom just shrugged her shoulders. "What? You need to really think about it."

"What's there to think about?" Dinah snapped back. "I can't fucking have kids."

My heart broke to see the tears welling up in my girlfriend's eyes. Her mom's face went ashen. "Oh, Dinah. Why didn't you tell us?"

"Let's go," Dinah snapped at me. "Now!"

"D," her dad called. "I'm sorry! Calm down, let's talk about it."

"I don't want to talk about it. Just please, stop asking me about when you're getting grandkids from me. Please," my girlfriend was begging and it broke my heart even more.

"You could always adopt," her mom offered.

"Mom...please," she urged.

"Come on, lovey, let's get you home, eh?" I asked, trying to diffuse the situation entirely.

I helped her back into her jacket. We walked out of her brother's place and I got her into the car. She was now in a fit of crying, and I didn't blame her, but I hated seeing her this way. I felt completely helpless, because there was literally nothing I could do to fix this problem for her. Other than hold her and let her cry on my shoulder.

I was getting into the driver's side when I heard someone call my name. Her dad was walking over to me and he clapped me on the shoulder. "I'm sorry about that. Dinah never told us."

"I know. It was hard for her."

He eyed me. "Was it..." he started to ask and let the question hang.

I shook my head. "It happened after Jason's death."

Her dad hung his head. "She okay?"

I nodded. "I was the one who found her."

"Fuck..." he swore and drawled the word out.

I just nodded in agreement, there wasn't much to really say about it. "I better get her home."

"Not your fault, son. But thanks for being there for her."

We shook hands and then I got back into the car. Dinah was wiping tears from her eyes, but I knew she didn't want me to make a fuss. This was hard for her. When we got back to our complex, she unlocked the door to her place, and I followed her inside. She went into the kitchen and grabbed a glass of water. I leaned up against the counter and watched her rummage around in her kitchen. Dinah wasn't a girl that I think men would call 'hot', but to me she was the most beautiful girl in the world, even when she was scowling at me for being a creep and watching her drink water.

I crossed over to her and lifted her up onto the counter so we were eye-level. She laughed, but wrapped her delicate hands around the back of my neck. I bent my head and kissed her lips softly. I pulled back to just look at her.

"Hi," I breathed at her.

"Hi yourself!" she joked. Her hands were starting to play with my hair, her fingernails caressing my scalp and it felt so good. I had to bite my tongue just so I didn't give her the satisfaction of my moan.

"You okay?" I asked.

She nodded. "I'm glad I finally told them, but it just sucked."

"I know, lovey. Sorry it had to be that way."

"Me too. I might have overreacted with my mom."

I held my forefinger and thumb together. "Just a bit."

"Thanks for putting up with me."

"I'm good to you, eh?" I joked, hoping changing the subject would distract her.

She tweaked my nose. "Don't be a little shit, you know you are."

"How good?"

"So good!" she exclaimed and had a wide smile plastered across her face.

"Oh, yeah?" I teased some more. "You want me to demonstrate how good I am some more?"

She laughed and kissed the side of my neck. "Boy, you know it."

She yelped in surprise as I lifted her up into my arms and led her into her bedroom.

CHAPTER TWENTY-FIVE

DINAH

The Bulldogs had a later game today, and I was tagging along with Fi, who I had been talking to more now that we had really connected. It was nice to have a fellow writer friend, especially one who was also new to this whole hockey WAG lifestyle. I wasn't really sure if she and Riley were going to make their marriage work, but I was really pulling for them. I totally and shamelessly shipped it. I couldn't believe she didn't see how much he loved her. I've known Aaron Riley for a couple years, and I have never seen him look at a woman the way he looked at Fiona Gallagher. Riley had always come off to me as the king of casual hookups, never one to settle down, but as soon as he brought his new wife to TJ and Noah's, I knew why he was like that. Holy hell, he loved that woman something fierce. He would pull down all the stars from the sky if she only asked him to. It made me want to slap her silly, because she looked at him in the exact same way when he wasn't looking.

I had woken up early this morning so I could get some writing done before Noah had to leave for the arena. Since it was an early game, there was no morning skate, so in lieu of his pre-game nap he slept in a little later than usual. I hadn't been lying to my family last night when I told them Noah was good to me. I let him be very good to me last night after putting up with them too. Especially all the drama when I finally blurted out the secret I had been keeping from them.

I jumped at the tap on my shoulder.

Noah looked at me apologetically. "Sorry, lovey."

I took my headset off my head and placed it on my desk. My eyes tracked over him, taking in the royal blue suit he was wearing. His dark hair was slicked back still wet from the shower. He looked so good in that suit.

"Are you heading out?" I asked.

"Yeah, got to get to the arena. Make sure you remember to eat lunch, okay? I know you get too in the zone sometimes and forget," he told me with a stern look in his eyes.

"I'm grabbing lunch with Fi before the game, remember?" I chided.

He lifted my chin up with his finger and he knelt down to my height to kiss me softly. "I forgot. You'll come to the game, right?"

I placed both hands on the side of his face. "I promised I would. Go on, then."

His hand slid into my hair, his nails raking across the back of my scalp and I might have purred at the sensation of it. He kissed me again, long and hard this time.

"Babe, go!" I insisted and practically pushed him away.

He laughed, but finally left. I turned back to my computer and set a timer so I didn't get so lost that I forgot to go meet Fi. By the time the alarm sounded on my phone,

I hadn't really gotten that much done. I ended up just rereading all the chapters I had already written, before getting to the place I had last left off. Which meant I was really stuck and I was just procrastinating by rereading and revising without actually doing any real work.

With a sigh, I closed my laptop and headed into my bedroom to figure out what to wear. I mean I knew what to wear, it was a hockey game. I wasn't sure if I wanted to go with the jersey that had Noah's last name on the back or one of my old school Patrick O'Sullivan jerseys. Or just a Bulldog shirt. I stood in front of my closet with my finger on my lips in contemplation, when my phone buzzed in my hand. I rolled my eyes at Fi's name on the screen.

"Hi, Fi," I gritted out.

"We're still meeting right?" she asked.

"I'm not late..."

"No! I just know us writers can be flaky."

I barked out a laugh. "Yeah, I'm just trying to decide which jersey to wear."

"Um...Kennedy, no?"

"Hey! I've been a fan of this team since birth, I did have a tiny crush on Patrick O'Sullivan back in the day. He's probably why I like hockey."

"Holy shit, Sully! That's crazy to me that a guy like that's still playing hockey in his forties!"

"I know, right? He's like ancient in hockey terms."

She laughed on the other end.

I fingered the Kennedy jersey in my closet. "Okay, Kennedy jersey it is. I'll see you soon."

"K!"

I laughed as I hung up with her. I think her and Rox would get along great. Hell, she was kind of Rox's type, but I was team Filey all the way. I wore the black Kennedy jersey and a pair of black skinny jeans. I ended up Ubering to the Mexican restaurant in South Philly instead of driving, and figured Fi and I would figure out how we wanted to get to the arena later. I had met Fi a couple times at various book cons and such, but this was the first time we actually hung out. Getting to know her at the party last weekend had been a lot of fun.

I slid into the seat across from her, and she looked up from her beer with a smile. "You made it!" she greeted.

"I did!" I grinned back at her. "Was stuck in a pile of edits."

She grimaced. "Ugh, I feel you girl. What book number are you on?"

I took a bite of the chips on the table, until a waiter came by and I gave him my order. "Two and three. Two is on deadline and supposed to come out this summer, and three is on draft one."

She nodded her head in understanding. "Book three is coming out for me this summer. I don't know what I'm going to write after this trilogy's over."

"Maybe you should try your hand at something different," I suggested.

She seemed to ponder this, but I noticed she was studying her beer a little too much.

I eyed the silver band that was still around the finger on her left hand. "How are things with Riley?" I asked.

"Um...well you know they've been on the road, so kind of weird?"

"Did you miss him?" I asked with a raised eyebrow.

She gulped down the rest of her beer and sighed. "Yeah, I think I really did."

"So what's the problem?"

She shrugged. "I feel like he'll just get bored with me, I

don't see a guy like that wanting to settle down with one woman. Especially not with me."

She kind of had a point. I always used to think that Riley was the kind of guy who hit it and quit it with a lot of beautiful women. He seemed like a total fuckboy who didn't 'do relationships' but I was pretty certain the woman sitting across from me was the reason why. I had a suspicion that she was the reason he had a lot of casual hookups. No wonder he offered to marry her after her ex left her at the altar. He just wanted to be her knight in shining armor.

Fi shook her head. "What's new with you?" She must have seen the grimace come across my face, because she placed a hand on mine. "Hey, are you okay?"

I drank a third of my beer. "Um...Noah told me he loved me."

"That's good, right?"

I rubbed the back of my neck. "I didn't say it back."

Her mouth formed a little 'O.' I just nodded. "Well..." she began and then didn't know what to say. "Well...fuck."

"Yup," I agreed.

"Do you not love him?" she finally asked, looking at me with kind eyes. No judgment, she was telling me that I could tell her whatever was on my mind here.

I shrugged. "I don't know. It feels too early for me, I really want to. I think I might."

"Then what's the problem?"

I couldn't answer right away because our food came and we got busy chowing down. Once we both came up for air, and I was on my second beer, I felt like I could tell her the real reason. "I feel like I'm betraying my late husband," I confessed with a long-drawn out sigh.

"Oh, Dinah! Just because he's not around doesn't mean you need to act like you're dead."

"I just...I never thought I would love again after he died."

She narrowed her eyes at me. "If that's the only reason, then I have to call bullshit on that."

I shook my head at her and downed the rest of my beer. She was looking at me expectantly, as I finished off my second beer. The thing was, she was so right. I was being difficult for no reason. I had been avoiding going out with anyone since my husband's death, but Noah, was the first person I really felt like I could be myself around. Noah was sweet, and I loved being with him, just like he loved spending all his waking moments of free time with me. I think it was time to finally tell him that I felt the same way.

"Come on!" Fi urged. "Let's get over to the stadium."

We paid our bill and took a UBER over to the stadium.

Mia practically squealed when she saw us. "Oh my god, you made it!" she exclaimed.

"Hi, Mia," I told her with a smile as she hugged me tight and then did the same to Fi.

I looked to the ice and saw the boys coming out of the tunnel for warm-ups. My heart swelled when I saw a helmet-less Noah skating around the zone and slapping pucks into the net. He must have seen me because he slapped the glass with his stick as he skated past it. I smiled to myself, and felt Fi poking my side.

"See!" she exclaimed.

Mia looked between the two of us, her blonde hair waving back and forth. "What?" she asked confused.

Fi rolled her eyes. "Dinah's unsure if she loves Noah or not, but look at her face!"

Mia joined Fi with the eye rolling and I gave them both a scowl and my middle finger. They both laughed. "Okay, girl, you need to spill," Mia urged.

I sighed and ran a shaky hand through my hair. "Noah told me he loved me."

"Awww!" Mia cooed, but when she saw my face, her expression darkened. "What happened? Why do you look like he kicked your puppy?"

"I didn't say it back," I explained with a grimace.

Mia gave me a pointed look. "Why not?"

I shrugged. "I'm not sure I'm ready for that yet, but maybe I do?"

Fi was poking me again. "She's just being difficult."

Mia nodded. "Yeah! Every time I look at you I can see the love coming off both of you. Just tell him how you feel."

I bit my lip. I knew they were both right. Seeing Noah out on the ice where he belonged and the warmth that spread across my chest when I looked at him, proved it. I still felt a little guilty about it though, but I knew I shouldn't.

I changed the subject so we could stop talking about my insecure love issues. Fi went to go get us another beer, even though I probably didn't need a third beer. I felt nervous as the puck dropped and I watched Girard win the first face-off. He passed it up the blue line to Riley who stick-handled it out of the neutral zone. The team passed it back and forth, but only got a few shots on goal before it was turned over and Chicago got possession of the puck. I saw Noah hopping on the ice during the shift change, and my heart raced while I watched him take to the ice with such speed and determination that it made my heart soar with pride. God, he was good at this sport, and I loved watching him slicing into the ice on his skates and dominating his opponents. He was still considered a rookie to some, but this was just the start of what was clearly going to be a successful NHL career.

He skated alongside Hallsy, passing the puck up the blue line, when he was slammed hard into the boards from the opposing defenseman. Noah was a big man so he could take a hit, and hockey was a physical game. As a fan, I was used to the fast paced hard-hitting nature of the sport. It was what made things so exciting, but my nerves were firing off on all cylinders when I saw that Noah was having trouble getting up off the ice. My head thrummed in panic, but I remembered to breathe when he shook himself off and got up on his skates. TJ took the face-off in their opponent's zone, but lost the puck again. I heard the boos from the crowd, and I was right there with them. The boys really needed to get another win out of this shittastic season. I was rooting for them, but I was also a Philly fan, I had grown up used to disappointment.

I watched the play go back-and-forth down each end of the ice. I looked for where the players went, not necessarily where the puck was going. I cheered when Noah lobbed a messy wraparound goal into Chicago's net, and then booed with the rest of the crowd when Chicago's coach challenged it for offside.

"Offside, my ass," I seethed out loud, which just made Fi laugh and spill some of her beer.

We booed together when the officials called off the goal. The anger swelled up inside me for Noah. I practically felt the frustration that he felt. I saw him on the bench shaking his head and using smelling salts with TJ.

I was cheering with everyone else when Hallsy had the puck and passed it to Noah. Noah took the quick wrister, but then he was slammed into the glass and he didn't get up this time. The guy who hit him, held his hand up for the officials and they whistled the play dead. TJ skated over to the guy and was getting into his face. Atta boy. Noah still hadn't gotten up and Hallsy was bent over him, trying to talk to him. A hush of silence rung out across the stadium, with every Bulldogs' fan holding in a breath, just waiting for Noah Kennedy to get his ass up off the ice. A lump formed in my throat when I saw the trainer come up to talk to Noah. Slowly he got up on his skates with help from Hallsy, while TJ and the other player were being pushed away from each other by the refs. Noah seemed slow on his skates, and he needed help getting to the bench.

All the blood rushed to my head when I saw him being taken down the tunnel and he didn't come back for the game. In a flash, my mind went to that awful night when I couldn't get a hold of Jason. I paced in our condo wondering why he wasn't home from work yet. No text, no call, no nothing. I was angry, thinking he was cheating, until I got the call from the hospital that he was in an accident and he hadn't survived. Watching Noah get slammed into the boards like that unearthed all those old feelings, and I knew that I couldn't start anything serious with him. The thought of losing him too was too much.

"I can't do this," I admitted aloud and started gathering my things.

"D!" Fi called after me.

I just shook my head, called an Uber, and got the fuck out of there. As soon as I got home, I texted Noah that I couldn't do this with him and turned my phone off. It was an asshole move, but I couldn't have my heart break again.

CHAPTER TWENTY-SIX

NOAH

Having your bell rung during a game was the absolute worst, especially when you knew your girlfriend came to watch you play and you were afraid you messed everything up by telling her you loved her too soon. I had to sit out the rest of the game and have the doctors test me for a concussion. They were worried about me, but I passed the baseline test, so it was all right. In between periods Coach LaVoie came to see me.

"How's the head?" he asked.

I shrugged. "Got my bell rung a little, but I think I'm okay."

He narrowed his eyes at me. "Are you sure?"

I just shrugged, because honestly who knew when it came to head injuries. I felt fine right now with the adrenaline of being in the zone and then tomorrow I could be in a fog.

"We're going to scratch you for a few games, just to make sure you're okay."

I groaned. "Come on, I can play."

"Don't argue," he said before walking away.

This freaking blew.

LaVoie ended his career early because of concussions back in the day, so maybe he was just extra cautious when it came to his players. I was too pissed to even look at my phone until I hitched a ride with TJ back to our shared condo. What I saw on my phone hurt worse than my head.

DINAH: *I'm sorry, Noah. I can't do this.*

"What the fuck?" I yelled out loud.

TJ raised an eyebrow at me and cut his eyes back to the road. I threw my phone down on the floor below me. This was NOT freaking happening right now. Why? I clenched and unclenched my fists throughout the whole ride home. My heart felt like an empty black hole inside my chest, filling itself with rage. I couldn't even look at Dinah's door, instead just barreled inside our condo.

TJ went into the kitchen, poured a shot of vodka and handed it to me. "Here," he said shoving it towards me. "You need this."

I took it without answering him. I downed the hatch and exhaled, running a shaky hand down my face. I had a shit game and now my girlfriend decided to end it for reasons that seemed unknown to me. What in the actual fuck? I was too angry to even respond to her text and she hadn't sent anything further. I didn't understand what I had done wrong. Because I told her I loved her? If it was too soon for her, that was fine for me, but to just break up with me?

TJ looked up from his phone. "You want to talk about it?" he asked cautiously.

"No," I huffed.

TJ clapped me on the shoulder. "Okay, well we're on

the road again for the next week, so how about you just focus on games?"

"I'm scratched for a few games."

TJ winced. "Sorry, man."

I poured out another shot and made him do one with me. I slammed the glass back down on the table. "Did you know?"

"Know what?"

"That she was gonna break up with me?" I asked with a sigh.

TJ shook his head. "No. I thought things were going really well between you. What happened?"

I shrugged, but I think I knew what had happened. I scared her away by telling her I loved her, but I couldn't take it back. Even though my heart felt like it was ripped in two right now, I knew that I loved her with every fiber of my being. I loved that woman so fiercely, but she would never see me in that light. She did the smart thing by breaking up with me instead of stringing me along. But damn to do it over text when I was having a shittastic game, that was kind of cold. I never thought of Dinah as being a cold person. She was a little flaky at times and got into her own head, but never a cold-hearted person.

TJ continued to stare at me for some time and I just stared off into space with my own thoughts. He cocked his head at me. "Kens, are you okay?"

I shook my head. "Not in the fucking slightest."

"Are you sure she broke up with you?"

I pulled out my phone and showed him the text message. His brow furrowed and he shook his head. "This doesn't seem like her. Were you guys fighting?"

I scratched the back of my head and took my phone

back from him. "No...I mean things have been awkward between us since I told her I loved her."

His eyes widened.

"What?"

He cringed. "Maybe she wasn't ready for that."

"I didn't expect her to say it back, I told her that."

"Did you respond?"

I shook my head.

"Don't. Give it a day and sleep on it."

I left my phone on the counter, and just headed to bed. It wasn't that late, but I felt like the moon was crushing down on my world and I was spinning out of control. All I wanted to do was sleep and not think about anything, but my bed was cold without the small woman I loved curled up into my side. I spent the night staring at the ceiling just thinking of everything I did wrong to make her turn away from me.

TJ woke me up in the morning, as we had a travel day before the next week of games. We had back-to-back games in Anaheim and San Jose, then in Tampa, before returning for a home game Saturday afternoon. I was going to travel with the team, but coach didn't want me to play in California. So I went to morning skate, let the medical staff fuss over me, watched video, and went to all the meetings, but I wasn't really there. I wasn't myself and everyone was worried that it was a concussion, but I finally had to admit it was just heartbreak.

"I'm fine," I seethed at the team's doctor. "It's not my head, it's my heart."

He nodded his head and clapped me on the back. "You'll get through it, there's always another girl."

After the game in San Jose, I went out with the boys for drinks, but I felt my phone burning a hole in my pocket. I pulled it out and stared at the screen at that sentence some more. I didn't want to respond at all, but I had to know why. I had to know what I did to make her just end it all in a snap decision.

ME: *Why?*

I saw the dots typing, then they stopped. That went on for a little bit, but stopped again. I shoved my phone back into my pocket and guzzled down my beer. I flagged down the waitress for another and pretty much gulped that one down quickly too.

Riley eyed me with worry. "Kennedy..."

I gripped the glass hard in my hand, so hard I thought I was going to break it. "I'm fine."

He leaned back in his chair and took his phone out too. He was typing something and looked up at me with a worried glance. The silver ring on his finger glinted underneath the low bar lights.

"Ri, are you seriously still married?" I asked.

"Yeah, man, wooing my wife takes time," he explained.

"Why aren't you in like an open marriage or some shit?" TJ asked.

Riley balked at that and gave him a dirty look. "I DON'T cheat."

TJ stood up to go talk to the cute Asian girl he had bought a drink for earlier, leaving Riley and I to stew in our lady drama. Riley turned to me and said, "I asked Fi to check in with your girl, she can't figure out why D just up and broke up with you either."

"Appreciate it, man. I think I scared her away," I admitted honestly as I took another swig of my beer.

He raised an eyebrow. "You told her you love her, didn't you?"

I nodded.

Riley scratched his jaw. "I don't think that's why she broke up with you though. I've hit on her multiple times throughout the years, and she's only had eyes for you."

"I just don't understand."

"She was there when you took that big hit, maybe it scared her. Maybe it made her think about all she went through with her husband dying?"

I stared at him for a really long time.

He just shrugged at me.

"Holy fuck, I think you're right."

He laughed. "Women, man. They certainly make our lives...interesting."

I finished my beer. "Complicated more like it."

We clinked beer glasses. "That's for sure."

❄

It had been two weeks since Dinah had broken up with me via text, and I was a miserable fucker. So when we lost yet another game, and were now officially out of the playoffs, I didn't even have a reaction. I just went through the post-game motions in a fog, but luckily I didn't have to talk to the media today. It was safe to say we all needed to go to the bar and get a bit drunk. I was heartbroken, and I needed to be drunk right now. TJ was happy to oblige.

I grabbed a beer at the bar with Benny. His brown skin shone under the bar lights, his hair perfectly styled which turned a lot of heads from the women in the bar. He was kind of a pretty-boy and women always noticed him. Also, at six-foot-four, the giant tended to turn heads. He was wearing a burden on his shoulders though, so I think he needed this too.

"You okay, man?" he asked me.

I just grunted.

He chuckled. "Okay...you know if you need to talk I'm here, right?"

I nodded.

He sighed and ran a hand down his neatly trimmed beard. "Listen, I think I get how you feel right now."

"Oh?" I asked, curious, but also not really because I found what was in the bottom of my beer to be super fascinating.

"Yeah. Stephanie and I just aren't working out. I think we're going to break-up."

I frowned. "I'm sorry to hear that."

He shrugged. "We just want different things. Great girl, but I'm not the marrying type."

"Is that what she wanted?"

He nodded. "Yeah, the whole marriage, kids, the white picket fence, she wanted all that shit and I have never wanted any of that stuff. A partner would be great, but marriage? Kids? That's a hard no."

"Hmm..." I trailed off lost in my own thoughts.

This conversation sounded very familiar to me. Someone else had told me pretty much the same exact thing. A Canadian girl who pretended she hated Benny's guts, but secretly checked him out when he wasn't looking. That was interesting.

"So is it over?" I asked.

He shrugged. "Not yet, but I think it's on the way. Great girl, it just sucks when you want different things."

I didn't really know what to say, but I guess it didn't matter because I saw his mouth drop open slightly at something behind my head. I turned around, and just laughed at him straight up gawking at the curvy blonde who had walked into the bar and was hugging TJ tightly.

Roxanne Desjardins.

What was she doing in Philly?

Benny's eyes swept over her form, almost zooming in on her ample chest. It probably didn't help that Rox was wearing a low-cut top and jeans that fit her perfectly. Not that I was looking. Rox was just my friend, but she was an attractive girl. I nudged him, but it was too late, her eyes crossed the room to us and she pinned Benny with a death glare. It was so hard, if looks could kill, Benny would be a pile of dust right now. She gave him the finger and Benny turned away to scowl into his beer all grumbly.

"Benny!" I exclaimed and punched him in the arm.

"What?" he grumbled, annoyed at me.

I shook my head. "You have to stop foaming at the mouth around her. And maybe fucking apologize for what you said to her the last time!"

He grumbled and tossed back his drink. "I did apologize. She's made it clear that she rather make-out with a skunk than ever have a normal conversation with me."

I just shook my head at him again, because he didn't see the way Rox's eyes scanned across his body when his back was turned to her. I didn't know if *she* knew she did it. Someone definitely needed to knock some sense into those two. This man was so in love with her, he was hopeless. Benny looked as miserable as I felt, but I left his side to go greet Rox. She was probably the only other person that knew what I was going through right now.

"Noah!" she greeted with a smile.

I hugged her tightly. "Hi, Rox. What are you doing in Philly?"

Her gaze slid across to her brother, and the twins shared some sort of telepathic conversation. "I had some time off, so I figured it was time to come visit."

The smile plastered across her face was fake, but I didn't know if it was for my benefit or hers. Rox was an attractive girl, but I was pretty sure TJ would straight murder me if I ever showed an interest in his sister. Some guys took the code very seriously. She was a like a sister to me too anyway.

"Let's get a drink!" she exclaimed, and led me over to the bar. Benny was still at the bar staring into his drink, but Rox side-stepped him to go towards the other end of it. She ordered shots for us to take.

"Rox, come on," I complained.

She grinned wickedly and handed me the shot. "I think we both need this."

We clinked glasses and downed the hatch. Maybe it would be okay to just bury myself in being with my friends and having a good time. I could ignore my heart as it broke each day that I wasn't with Dinah. I ordered another round. In hindsight, it was probably a bad idea because Rox could drink me under the table. She could probably drink all the guys under the table.

Rox and I settled into the bar stools and she casually put a hand on my shoulder. "You okay?" she asked.

I shook my head. "Not in the fucking slightest."

She gave me a small smile in sympathy.

"What about you?"

"Fucking terrible," she admitted.

I took her hand and gave it a little squeeze. "I'm sorry about what happened with you and Lisa. You want to talk about it?"

She sighed. "Not really. She cheated on me. Three years down the drain like that, and then kicked me out."

Anger coiled itself around my chest. "What?"

She waved a finger at me. "Do NOT tell my brother that last part. I'm fine."

I could tell by that last part that she was definitely not fine, but if there was anything I learned from living with TJ, it was that the Desjardins were the most stubborn people on the planet. I put my hands out as if to surrender. Rox knew her secrets were safe with me, because I wasn't one to go telling everyone.

She fixed me with a pointed glare. "So what happened? I really liked you and Dinah together. The height difference is kind of comical, but you two always made sense to me."

I just shrugged and opened my mouth but the words wouldn't come.

"What?" she asked confused.

"I have no idea," I admitted. "She came to a game, I took a bad hit to the boards and then she broke it off via text."

She put an arm around my shoulder. "Noah, I'm so sorry. Maybe I can talk to her?"

I shook my head. "I don't know, she's not really talking to anyone. I'm about ready to go track down her brothers that's how bad it is."

Her eyes widened. "You've met her brothers?"

I nodded. "They're a bit much, but I think they really love her."

She laughed. "That's for sure. Her brother Tony hit on me aggressively last time I came to visit. Eddie's cool though, I might get a tattoo from him."

I laughed and eyed the maple leaf tattoo on the inside of her wrist.

Rox seemed to be pondering something, her black manicured fingernail tapping against her plum-colored lipstick. "Noah, I love you and I feel for you, but I don't think this is about you."

I gave her a confused look.

She sighed and ran a hand through her hair in frustration. "I think whatever reason Dinah broke up with you, it might not be about you. It might be about her issues with her dead husband. I think maybe you just need to give her some time."

CHAPTER TWENTY-SEVEN

DINAH

"I need to take a sick day," I called into work. I wasn't really sick, I just needed a mental health day.

"Are you okay?" My boss Stacey asked with concern in her voice. I sighed as I laid on my couch still in my pajamas. I thought I had covered the phone, but she heard it. "I get it, it's the anniversary of Jason's death, that must be really hard for you."

I closed my eyes. No wonder I had decided to just call it quits on Noah like a fucking asshole. I called quits with a really good guy, because I was scared of losing Noah like I had lost Jason. It had been a couple weeks since I had done it, and I still felt sick to my stomach. He had wanted to know why, and I couldn't even tell him. I would have to wait to talk to him when he got home from his road trip, if he would even speak to me.

"I'm ahead of deadline, but call me if you need anything."

"I understand. You guys pulled me out of the gutter after my divorce. Take the day, we'll see you on Monday."

I hung up my phone and just sighed some more, dropping my head onto the arm of the couch in defeat. I turned in my final edits on my second novel, and now I just wanted to wallow in my sorrow. Losing my husband had been really hard, and everything that came after it had been the worst thing that ever happened to me. But watching Noah get slammed into the boards like that had broken me. It was like everything about Jason's death came crashing back down over me. I was helpless and I couldn't find a way out of it. I had messed up big time, and if I was Noah I wouldn't have forgiven me either. I wasn't even sure if I could win him back.

My phone buzzed on my chest where I had dropped it. I saw Fi's name scrolling across my screen. "Hey," I answered.

"What are you doing?" she asked briskly without any real introduction.

"Um...wallowing?"

"Why the fuck did you break up with Noah?" she demanded.

"Hi, Fiona, it's nice to hear from you too."

"At least you finally answered me this time."

I sighed. "I'm sorry."

"Riley has been getting on my shit about sorting this out, because Noah's a sweet baby angel and you have gutted this boy's poor heart!"

I picked at a loose thread on my throw blanket. "I know."

She sighed on the other line. "Fuck, I'm coming over."

"Why?"

"We're getting drunk and are going to figure this shit out!"

She hung up before I could protest. I was still hungover from last night from getting drunk with my brother Tony. Who was also nursing a broken heart, which I only found out when I had to finally admit to my family that I wasn't calling them back because Noah and I had broken up. Tony came over with a bottle of wine that we polished off in no time. I threw my phone on the floor and just flopped back on the couch. I had made my own bed and now I had to lie it in. In no time, Fiona was at my condo, with a bottle of whiskey. I let her in reluctantly, and she immediately made me a drink.

She shoved the glass into my hand and I took it. It wasn't like this woman was giving me a choice. We clinked glasses and both of us took a huge gulp.

She looked pointedly at me. "Okay, what the fuck?" she finally asked.

I just shrugged.

She was still glaring at me. "Do you know how up my ass my husband has been to get you and Noah back together?"

My eyebrow raised at her phrasing. "Um, I didn't really need to know that about your sex life."

She gave me the finger. "You know what I mean."

I sighed and took a large sip of my drink. "I'm sorry."

She placed a hand on my arm. "What happened? You were all ready to tell him how you felt and then you freaked out when you saw him take that bad hit."

I downed the rest of my drink, hoping I didn't have to answer her question. She crossed her arms and tapped her foot on the tile of my kitchen floor impatiently.

I ran a hand through my messy hair. "I just...I had flashbacks about Jason dying and feeling so hopeless. I just couldn't go through that again."

Fi put a hand to her heart and then she pulled me into a hug. "Oh, honey. You can't sacrifice your happiness just because you're afraid of what's gonna happen."

"I know, I know," I agreed and ran a hand through my hair in frustration. "I just don't think Noah's gonna give me the time of day."

"You did kind of break his heart," she agreed.

She poured another drink and we slunk into the chairs at my island counter. "We're quite a pair, eh?" I asked with a laugh.

She smirked but nodded in agreement. "I think Noah will listen to you. I think he was really hurt you wouldn't even tell him why."

I ran a hand down my face. "God, I really fucked up."

I looked at my phone and saw a text from TJ.

TJ: *OMG! Will you two just talk to each other? I am sick of this.*

I furrowed my brow and started texting him back.

ME: *What do you mean?*

TJ: *Can you please just get back together, already? You're both annoying when you're not together.*

ME: *I really FUCKED up.*

TJ: *Then un-fuck it up, girl! I miss hanging out with you and I'm not allowed to hang out with you if you and Noah aren't together.*

ME: *Says who?*

TJ: *BRO CODE, girl!*

TJ: *Just apologize.*

TJ: *And then get it in, because he's annoying when he's not getting laid on the reg!*

I put my phone down and laughed out loud. Fi gave me

a quizzical look, and I just shook my head. I needed to figure out what I was going to do to get Noah to talk to me again. He wanted to know why, and I could tell him that but I didn't know if doing it via text was a good idea.

Fi and I spent the day brainstorming, and drinking a lot of whiskey, which in hindsight was probably a bad idea. I didn't even like whiskey! At the end of the day she was lying on my couch moaning about her issues with her weird marriage of convenience, while I was lying on the floor below her trying to text Noah without making it appear that I was drunk as fuck.

"Why don't you just tell Riley you love him, you weirdo," I finally told her.

She leaned down to look at me with a confused look. "Are you high?"

I stuck my tongue out at her. "No, just drizzunk!"

She eyed me texting on my phone. "Are you texting Noah?"

"Trying to! Your drunk ass keeps on interrupting!" I exclaimed and glared at her. "Why did you bring over a bottle of whiskey during the day? This was a bad idea!"

She laughed and leaned back on the couch again. "I feel like this is the experience that makes us best friends! Two strong-willed writing women who ended up with hockey players. What are the odds?"

I shook my head at her and looked back at my phone where there were just a bunch of question marks from Noah. Oh fuck. I looked down at my phone to see I actually had hit send on it. Oh no!

ME: *heyyy....we nedz to talkkkk whennn you get.........*
NOAH: *um...okay?*
ME: *Supperrrr*
NOAH:*????*

NOAH: *Are you drunk?*
ME: *no?????????????*
NOAH: *What do you mean no? Like you don't know??*
NOAH:*????????????*

"Oh, fuck!" I exclaimed, but Fi just erupted into laughter. I put my phone down so I wouldn't continue to make a fool out of myself. "Now he's never gonna take me seriously!"

"Oh, that shit doesn't matter! Riley has never taken me seriously, but somehow his dumb-ass decided to marry me. Still don't know why!" she laughed.

"Girl!"

"What?"

"That dumb-ass loves you, that's why."

She leaned down at me. "What are you smoking? No, Riley's just a good guy. There's just no way. He can't."

I gave her a dirty look. "How does that equal, 'hey let me marry my best friend who was left at the altar?' No! He married you because he wanted to be your knight in shining armor and hoped that maybe you would fall in love with him in the process."

She was shaking her head at me slowly. "No. No way!"

"Why else would he want to stay married to you? And loyal to you?" I asked her, but she was still shaking her head. "TJ said he doesn't even look at other women when they go out anymore."

Her eyes darted back and forth as if she was thinking about this a little too hard. "No, I don't believe you."

"Yeah, girl!"

"But..." she trailed off and sat up on my couch. I sat up from my position on my floor and stared her down. "Ohhhh!! How are we both so dense when it comes to these hockey boys?"

I shrugged, but had to turn away when my phone buzzed across the table. Noah's name came across the screen, but Fi jumped at it and answered it for me. Oh no, this was not good.

"Uh huh," she said into the phone. "Hey, is my husband with you?" she was quiet for a minute while she listened to Noah saying something on the other line.

Then she handed the phone to me. I heard the laughter in Noah's voice. "Hey," he said.

"Hey," I said back. "We need to talk."

He cleared his throat. "Yeah, I gathered that, but maybe we can do it when you're not completely hammered?"

"Okay. When do you get home?" I asked quietly. God, even though I was drunk as a skunk, I had missed his voice. I missed him so much, and I had been so foolish for just up and ending it over text. I didn't even let him respond before I blurted out, "I'm sorry."

"I know, lovey," he said quietly. "We're on the way back, but we have an afternoon game tomorrow."

"Oh."

He sighed on the other line. "I don't think you and Fiona should hang out together, you two seem to get up to bad things together."

"Noah..." I cried.

He sighed again, and that just made my tears fall more, because I really fucked up with this amazing man.

"Lovey, we'll talk about this later, I promise."

❄

I woke up the next morning with my head pounding and my mouth felt like the Sahara desert. I slowly opened my eyes and I felt like I was still spinning even though I was lying down in my bed. I tried to move, but there was a large forearm wrapped around my waist. I blinked for a second, that was a familiar muscular arm. I shifted around in my bed and squinted at my alarm clock, it was 3 AM.

What the fuck?

I managed to slide out of the bed, and downed the entire glass of water that was sitting on the bedside table next to me. My head was still pounding when I padded into my bathroom. I honestly didn't remember anything after talking to Noah on the phone.

I glanced back into my bedroom and saw his sleeping form in my bed. His six-foot-two frame was stretched out across the length of the bed. He was shirtless and I watched for a moment the rise and fall of his chest as he slept. I shut the bathroom door behind me and splashed water on my face. I felt like complete and utter death and I thought I might vomit. I was never drinking with Fi ever again. She might be slightly worse than Rox, and I didn't think that was possible. I brushed my teeth, but still felt like hot garbage, so I decided to hop in the shower. I didn't even wash my hair, I just wanted to feel the water on my hot skin. I haven't felt this hungover since—oh the last anniversary of my husband's death. I guess I was predictable.

I wrapped a towel around my body when I got out, trying to squeeze all the water out of my long hair. It was too late, or rather too early to try to blow dry it, but the damp feeling of my hair actually made me feel good. The shower maybe helped by a percentage, but I still felt like complete and utter shit. I tip-toed back into my bedroom and changed into a different pair of pajamas, trying to be as quiet as possible, so I didn't wake up Noah.

I still couldn't remember why he was here. Did we talk last night? I was still really thirsty, so I went into my kitchen to get another glass of water, and ended up drinking two glasses right at the sink. I needed sleep, but now I had so many questions that I wanted answers to. I didn't want to wake Noah though because he had a game today. What the fuck was he doing here? Did we have sex last night? No, Noah was very good on the consent thing and if I was blackout drunk he wouldn't have done anything like that.

I filled up another glass of water and returned to my bed. I slid into it, hoping not to wake Noah, but he turned over and his strong arms gripped my waist. "What time is it?" he murmured all cute and sleepily. God, I loved this man so much, and I just wanted to tell him and fix the mess I had created.

"Late...or early, go back to sleep," I whispered.

"Why's your hair wet?" he asked, his face nuzzled into the crook of my neck.

If I didn't feel like absolute death I would have been pulling him on top of me now, or getting down on my knees to show him just how sorry I was.

"Go back to sleep," I ordered and I shifted onto my side to stop the spins.

He pulled me close to his chest. I had really missed this, just being with him and having him hold me. He stroked my hair, and I felt like I came undone. "Noah..."

"Hmm?"

"I'm sorry."

"I know, lovey. We'll talk about it later."

"Did we..." I trailed off and let the question hang in the air.

He seemed to get what I was asking. He laughed. "Oh, you definitely wanted to, but you were very drunk when I came over here."

I cringed. "I'm sorry. I would like to blame Fi for bringing over that bottle of whiskey, but—"

"I know," he cut me off. He knew what yesterday was, and I wasn't sure if that made it hurt more. "We'll talk about it later, okay? Let's just get some sleep before I have to wake up for morning skate."

"I feel like absolute garbage," I admitted.

He laughed again, his breath tickling the back of my neck. "You were very drunk last night."

I groaned.

He stroked my hair some more, and it relaxed me so much that I found myself falling back into the black hole of hungover sleep. I was out so hard, that I didn't even hear when he left.

CHAPTER TWENTY-EIGHT

NOAH

I laced up my skates and had my earbuds in at my cubby, when Riley tapped his stick against my shin guards. I took out the earbuds and looked up at him expectantly. He smirked at me and shook his head. "Our women are quite the pair, huh?" he asked.

I shook my head with a laugh. "I don't think they're allowed to hang out."

He started taping up his stick for like the fifteenth time today. Like most guys, Riley had weird pre-game rituals and one of his was taping his stick up way too many times. "Yeah, we both know that won't stop those two strong-willed women."

"True," I agreed.

I was really hoping to fix things with Dinah, and I wasn't about to do that last night when she was hammered. I had figured out why she wanted to call it quits, but I also wanted to call her out on being such a coward. Last night wasn't the time to get into it with her, especially when I knew she was blackout drunk and wouldn't remember anything. Like how she didn't remember that she told me she loved me last night. I knew the saying, 'Drunk words are sober thoughts,' but I wanted to hear it from her when she actually remembered it. Right now I had to focus on this game, and afterward I would figure this thing out with the woman I loved.

The crowd was getting loud, the music pumping loud in the arena. It was go time! TJ and I did our pre-game hand shake before stepping out of the dressing room and onto the ice. I glided across on my skates with ease, feeling the excitement of the crowd on home ice filling me with the desire to help bring home the win. I wasn't on the starting line today, so I took my place on the bench in between TJ and Hallsy. We fist-bumped each other with our gloves and hunkered down to get into the zone.

I watched from the bench as our captain took the starting face-off, and then lost the puck. I chewed on my mouth guard in anticipation. We were officially out of the playoffs, so in the grand scheme of things this game didn't matter, but I still wanted to bring it my all. It was hard not to doubt yourself when you were on the ice in front of cheering fans or had to listen to the media constantly criticize you. It could be draining, but at the same time there was nothing better than being out there on the ice with your stick in hand chasing after the puck.

I hopped over the bench during the change up, sliding across the ice to get into position on the face-off in our opponent's zone. Riley iced the puck to get it away from the other team, but now we had to win the face-off and get possession of the puck. It was still scoreless, and we had a lot of hockey still to play, so I was optimistic when I put my stick on the ice and focused on the play. Of course the other team got the puck and tried to one-time it into our net, but Metzy had those silky hands and caught it in his glove. I wished we had called up Metzy earlier, I could only imagine what our goaltending would have been like if we had him all season.

I took the face-off and won, stick-handling the puck down the ice and passing it to TJ once I got past the blue line. He took it to the corner, but got slammed into the boards, allowing the other team to scrap for the puck while we had it in their zone. I skated over to the center of the zone lining myself up for the open pass, but it never came. We turned it over again, and we were hustling down back into our own zone to get the puck back. I nearly threw my stick in frustration when the other team got the first goal in.

I skated back to the bench for the change up in between the stoppage of play and took my seat on the bench. My chest was heaving, and I felt the adrenaline pumping. I didn't doubt my playing, I mean I knew there was always room for improvement, but it just wasn't our year. This game didn't even matter, but I still wanted to give it my all.

We tried to bring the game back, but after sixty minutes of play and a five minute overtime, The New York Gladiators beat us 4-3. It was such a close game, but it didn't matter. We were already out of the playoffs. I just wanted to hop on the bike to cool down, hit the showers and get the fuck out of there, but of course since I had a goal and assist in the game, I had to talk to the media. I knew it was important, but I also was just so frustrated with how this season was ending for us.

"Now that you're out of the playoffs, what do you do going into these last games of the season?" one of them asked me, pointing their phone into my face.

I ran a hand through my sweaty hair in frustration. "I

think right now we just need to focus on our playing, taking every game at a time. Just focus on doing what we do best."

"Thanks, Kennedy," they told me, and I was finally free. I pretty much raced out of there to get my cool down on the bike. TJ was getting off the bike when I got there.

"I'll meet you at home?" he asked.

I shrugged and hopped onto the bike, my legs starting to spin in circles on it. "Not sure yet."

He cocked his head at me. "You square everything away with D last night?"

I shook my head. "She was blackout drunk, so no. Gonna try to talk to her tonight."

He clapped me on the back. "Good luck, man!"

Then he was out of there to take his shower and head out. A couple of the boys were going to grab drinks after, but my mind was running on the woman that lived next door to me. All I wanted to do was get through my post-game stuff I always did and then finally have a chance to fix this awkwardness between us. It was all I could think about while spinning on the bike and when I was in the shower. My brain was hooked on what I could do to keep Dinah, and how much of a miserable fucker I had been without her.

I changed back into my suit, straightened my tie, and smoothed back my long hair. It was getting a little too long, and I probably needed to cut it again soon, but Dinah was kind of into it. A tingle went down my spine just thinking about how good it felt when she threaded her small hand into it, or pulled on it when I had her tangled up in her sheets. I felt a tightness in my pants just thinking about it, and tried to push the thoughts out of my head. I could think about that later, right now I needed to be thinking about my heart and what I wanted to say to her.

I was a mess of tangled thoughts driving back to my condo. I had driven home on autopilot and ended up sitting in my car in the parking garage for a bit before working up the nerve to go upstairs. I looked at my phone and saw a string of texts. I hadn't looked at my phone since I left for the arena.

DINAH: *I feel like death.*

DINAH: *But maybe you should come over after your game?*

DINAH: *I think we need to talk about everything, now that I'm sober.*

Good, she wanted to talk, but it still made me feel a little nervous. I started typing back to her.

ME: *Is now good?*

I saw the three dots typing.

DINAH: *Yes.*

I finally got out of my car and took the elevator up to our floor. I knocked on the door to her condo. She slowly opened the door. Her eyes lit up when she saw it was me leaning against the door.

"You want something to drink?" she asked.

I raised an eyebrow. "You want a drink after last night?"

She laughed. "You know, hair of the dog and all that shit, right?"

I laughed. "Sure. Beer me woman!"

She laughed but went into the kitchen to get me a beer anyway. I settled down on her couch and thanked her when she handed it to me. I cracked it open and drank a little bit.

"So..." she began.

"I'm sorry if I put pressure on you by telling you I loved you. I knew it was too soon for you."

She shook her head. "It wasn't that. It was watching you take that hit."

I opened my mouth to speak but she held up a hand to silence me.

"I felt everything about Jason's death come tumbling back onto me. I felt helpless, and I didn't want to go through that again."

I took another gulp of my beer. "I'm sorry, I've kind of been in love with you for a while, but I knew it wasn't the same for you."

She put a hand on my arm. "I just got really scared when you took that hit. When you didn't get up..." she trailed off and squeezed her eyes shut at the thought.

"You're a hockey fan, you know what the game's like."

She nodded. "I know, I know. I was being irrational."

"I know it must have been really hard to lose Jason, he was a good man."

"I didn't think I would ever find love again," she admitted.

She turned away from me and wouldn't look at me. I put my beer on the coffee table and pulled her toward me, my hand lifted her chin up, making her look me in the eye. "What are you saying?"

Her eyes were shiny like she was about to cry. Aw, fuck, I've dried her tears a lot in the past couple years, but I never wanted to be the reason for it. I never wanted to make her cry.

"I was going to tell you I loved you that night, but then you got hit and I was just thinking about how I couldn't go through losing you too," she finally choked out.

"So you just decided to break up with me instead?"

"I'm sorry," she cried, and I felt like an asshole at the tears welling up in her eyes.

I drummed my fingers on my leg. "You really hurt me when you broke up with me like that."

"Noah, I was an asshole. I'm sorry."

I frowned at the tears falling down her face. Fuck, I hated when women cried, but I really hated when this particular one cried. I pulled her small frame close to me, my arm around her back and her head on my chest. I stroked her hair. "It's okay," I soothed.

She looked up at me and wiped her eyes. "Do you forgive me?"

"Of course, lovey."

"Do you still love me?" she asked. "Even after I hurt you?"

I looked down at her and pulled her face up to meet my lips. I put every ounce of feeling into the kiss. I sighed in content when her hands slid into my hair and she opened her mouth to me so our tongues could battle. Her kisses tasted like all my dreams come true. I loved feeling her tongue against mine and hearing the soft murmur of her moans. God, I loved this tiny fierce woman so much.

I pushed her back against the couch and was hovering over her without having broken the kiss. She pulled away to catch her breath. Her smile reached all the way to her eyes and she was laughing. "I forgot how much I missed your kisses."

I leaned down and kissed her neck, smiling against her soft skin when she whimpered beneath me. "Mmmhmm, me too," I whispered into her ear.

My hands traveled all over her body as we hungrily kissed each other senseless. I had missed her, not just because of the physical attraction, but just being with her and talking with her. When I got that break-up text from her I was heartbroken.

I pulled back to look at her and she smiled up at me. "Are we back together now?" I asked.

"You still want me?" she asked.

"Of course. Dinah, I love you."

"But I hurt you," she argued. "Why would you still want to be with me?"

I pulled her hand onto my chest so she felt my heart beat. "You might have broken my heart, but you can mend it too. Feel how it beats when I'm with you?"

She nodded.

"You're my heart, my home, and my love."

"Noah, I'm so sorry. You're such a good man, it's one of the reasons I love you, but I don't deserve you."

I smiled her. "You love me, eh?"

She nodded her head. "I love you so much, and I know I was stupid. I was scared of losing you like I lost Jason. I was trying to protect my heart."

"Promise me something?"

"Anything."

"You tell me if you get scared again, okay? And talk to me about it before ghosting me?"

She didn't say anything instead she just kissed me fiercely. I loved the way she gripped my shirt and pushed my suit jacket off of me. I shimmied out of it and threw it over the back of the couch. I groaned, I was so hard it kind of hurt. She yanked my tie off and started working on the buttons of my shirt, pulling it out from beneath my dress pants. She unzipped my pants and reached inside, her small hand finding my cock and pulling that out too.

"D..." I moaned as she stroked my cock lightly. Then she was on her knees in front of me. "What are you doing?"

"Apologizing," she told me and gave me a wicked grin before she dipped her head down to lick me from root to tip.

Fuckkkkk....

I bunched her hair up in my hand and spread my legs to

give her more room. "Fuck, yes..." I moaned while she licked and sucked on me. I tipped my head back and closed my eyes while she used her mouth to please me.

"Lovey, you need to stop," I growled at her seconds later. If she kept doing that I was going to come immediately.

She gave me a pouty look from the floor. "Why?"

"Because I'm gonna blow my load down your throat!"

She laughed. "That's the point, babe! Let me show you how sorry I am."

I smiled at her and tucked myself back into my pants. I crooked a finger at her. "C'mere you."

She straddled my thighs and then yelped when I stood up and carried her into her bedroom. I deposited her on the bed with a smirk. She tore off the jersey she was wearing and threw it to the floor while I shed myself of the rest of my clothes. When I crawled into the bed with her, I felt like my cock was going to explode the exact second she touched it again. Especially since she shed the rest of her clothes herself, and was now lying in her bed naked and waiting for me.

I rolled on top of her, taking her face in my hands and slanting my mouth on hers. Her tiny hands slid into my hair, her fingers threading there and pulling while we kissed open-mouthed and hungry for each other.

"I love you," I told her in-between kisses.

"I love you too," she moaned as my hands started to travel south.

My mouth marked a path across her skin, tumbling down her neck, until I was licking and sucking at her breasts. I smiled into her soft skin as she arched up into me, my one hand toyed with her nipple while my tongue darted out across the other one.

"Noah, please..." she begged, whimpering like she was in pain. All I wanted to do was alleviate that pain — with my mouth.

I kissed down her stomach, and when I looked up, her eyes were heavy-lidded with lust. "Tell me what you need, lovey."

"Fuck, Noah, please!" she cried out when I glided a finger inside her.

I kissed her thighs, spreading them while I kissed the tender flesh. "I missed you so much. I think I know what you need."

"Mmm, keep doing that," she moaned as she closed her eyes.

I slid a second finger inside her, while I bent my mouth to her clit. I flicked my tongue across it, in tiny teasing licks while I thrusted with my fingers inside her at the same time. I moaned into her, loving the noises she was making and how her nails raked across my scalp.

"No," she moaned.

I lifted my head in question. "No?"

She was biting her lip and looking all pouty. "No, I want you inside me right now. I need you Noah, please."

I chuckled. "You're the boss lady, I'll give you whatever you want."

Her smile was a thousand-watt at that. "C'mere you."

I removed my hand, grabbed a condom from her bedside table and slid it on. I nestled myself between her legs, teasing her with my cock until she thrust her hips up in frustration. I sank into her hot heat and smiled when she wrapped her legs around me tightly. I thrusted inside her, running my hands through her hair and kissing her every so often.

Her hands pushed onto my chest in a hard shove. "Ugh, get off, you're going too slow."

I laughed. "What?"

I slid out of her with a groan, but then her small hands were pushing me down onto my back. She straddled me, reached down to grip my hardness below her and sank down onto it in a swift motion. Oh fuck yes, I loved when she was in control. She rode me slowly, bracing her hands on my chest, which allowed me to explore her with my own hands. I traced down her throat, past the valley of her breasts, only to stop there to squeeze them lightly, which made her laugh. I skated my hand down her belly, until I hit the place where we were joined. She rocked on top of me and the view was spectacular. I plumped a finger on her swollen clit and she cried out in ecstasy.

"Oh, you're a bad boy," she growled at me.

I grinned and met her thrust for thrust. "You like it."

"Mmmhmm," she moaned.

She leaned over my chest and kissed my neck. I pressed my hand onto her spot, and moaned at both the sensation of her mouth on my skin and her grinding against me. She cried out seconds before I felt my own orgasm rack my entire body.

I fucking loved make-up sex.

CHAPTER TWENTY-NINE

DINAH

I groaned into Noah's neck and he laughed, but wrapped his arms around me. We were still joined, but I needed to catch my breath. I glanced down at him and smiled at his chest heaving just as much as mine. He reached a hand up and pushed a sweaty lock of my hair behind my ear. His thumb brushed across my cheek and I leaned my face into his hand. These small moments with this man were what I wanted most. It didn't matter to me that I was eight years his senior, or that I couldn't have kids, none of those things had ever mattered to Noah.

"Fuck, Noah," I breathed out and got off of him to lay next to him.

"Sorry if that was too fast."

I shook my head. "No, it was good."

We cleaned ourselves up and I changed into a pair of comfy pajamas. I jumped back into bed with a sigh. Noah was trying to gather his clothes that were scattered across my apartment. "It's true what I said," I called after him.

"What?" he yelled from the other room and then came back into the bedroom with his suit jacket in his arm and started to put his dress shirt back on. "What's true?"

"That I love you too."

A smile spread across his face. "You better."

I eyed him as he put his clothes back on. "You know, I can clear a drawer for you so you don't have to keep on going back over to your place if you want to stay here."

He eyed me cautiously. "Are you sure? I literally live next door."

I weighed his words carefully, maybe that was too soon for him. I mean, we had broken up and were just back together, maybe clearing a drawer for his things would be weird for him. I didn't want things to be weird between us. I looked at my phone to distract myself and chewed on my fingernail.

Noah crossed the room to my bed and sat on the edge of it next to me. He ran a hand up my torso and caressed my cheek until he ran his long fingers into my messy hair. He kissed me tenderly, and pulled away so suddenly that I barely felt the kiss. His thumb rubbed against my cheek and I leaned into it, loving the feeling of him touching me, even in such a chaste gentle caress.

"Only if that's what you want," he finally said.

I nodded.

He smiled and kissed me on the forehead. "Okay, I'll be back."

I sighed and snuggled down into my bed, hearing my front door close. I felt content, like a warm fuzzy feeling had washed over my body. I had been such a fool, a scared fool, when I ended things with Noah. I was glad he was able to forgive me, even though I didn't think I deserved it. I closed my eyes in contentment and checked my phone when it buzzed across my bedside table next to me.

FI: *So????*

I smiled at her text message. Fi had been right getting hammered together had bonded us.

My fingers flew across my phone typing a message back to her.

ME: *We're back together.*

FI: *YAY! I'm so glad for you. Riley has been complaining about your boy for a while.*

ME: *Sorry to bring you into my drama.*

FI: *No worries, us writer girls have to stick together!*

ME: *True, now stop torturing YOUR man and tell him you love him and want to have his babies.*

FI: *I do not!*

FI: *well...maybe just not the babies part.*

ME: *HAHA! You're still lying, girl!*

FI: *Fuck, you're right. I want to have little red-headed babies with him.*

ME: *Aw! You'd have such cute babies. Details!*

FI: *LATER!!*

I smiled and put my phone down. I got myself out of bed and went over to my dresser. The truth was, I had cleared out a drawer for Noah a while ago, but with me completely freaking out I had never told him about it. It felt like it was a big step in our relationship. It wasn't, 'Hey, move in with me,' but it was close to that. I liked when he stayed here and slept in my bed with me. He made me feel safe when he was with me.

I walked into the kitchen to grab the now warm beer I had been drinking when Noah came over. I took a sip of it and scrunched up my face at the warmness of it, but I drank it anyway and headed into my office. My fingers were itching to work on this new book, so I started working on the new scene that I needed to get out of my head. Writing was weird for me, sometimes I just had to power through to get through a scene, other times it felt like if I didn't write about a certain thing at that very moment I would explode. This was kind of one of the former unfortunately, which was common for me when starting a new story.

I nearly jumped when I felt strong hands slip around my shoulders. I tilted my head up to look at Noah. I glanced at the clock on my laptop, and it had been about an hour since I had come into my office. "Hey, how long have you been here?" I asked.

He rubbed my shoulders and I relaxed into his strong hands. "A bit."

I involuntarily moaned, and when I opened my eyes to look up at him, he was smirking. "You should have come in sooner. It's pretty late."

"I didn't want to interrupt."

My heart swelled in my chest. The fact that he was so respectful of my writing time made me love him even more. "You should have, because I'm getting nowhere with this."

I pulled away from him and pushed my chair from out behind the desk. Noah was wearing a pair of sleeping pants, and nothing else, and even though I was super tired, it still made my mouth water. This man made me think crazy things all the time.

I slid into the bed beside Noah and he pulled me against his hard chest. He wrapped an arm around my waist as I got comfortable. I had really missed him being here beside me. There was definitely something nice about having a man in bed next to me. Especially a man who really cared about me, and fought through my own insecurities to be with me.

I really never thought that I would find someone to love after Jason's death, but maybe it was okay to find love even after death. I had loved Jason with all my heart, but his sister was right, he wouldn't want me to be unhappy. Feeling Noah's arms around me while I drifted off to sleep, it finally felt like my life was clicking into place.

EPILOGUE

TWO MONTHS LATER

NOAH

"Never thought I would see the day," TJ mused next to me and took a pull off his beer.

I smiled at him and did the same. The boys had given me grief about moving in with Dinah after only dating for two months, but there was nowhere else I would rather be. Tonight all our friends were gathered here for a housewarming party. But when I saw Fiona Gallagher and Aaron Riley walk in the front door, I knew it was really to celebrate that those two women had both released their next books. My chest swelled with pride that my girlfriend had released her book and she was almost done with book three. She worked so damn hard, and I was amazed at how she did it all.

"Honestly, T? Me neither," I finally answered my best bud.

"Hey, can you do me a favor this summer?" he asked,

but he was looking across the room into the dining room where his twin sister Roxanne was staring out the window.

I had barely recognized her today, with her signature bleach blonde hair now dyed closer to her natural color. It definitely suited her much better, but I was a smart enough man to know to not comment on a woman's looks.

I noticed Benny's drunken ass sidled up beside her. Oh no, that probably spelled bad news. Since I moved in here last week, Benny had moved next door after his eventual break-up with Stephanie finally happened. That man really was lazy and needed to learn how to find a place for himself. But TJ had offered up the spare room that used to be my bedroom, so it all worked out.

"Sure, man."

"Can you make sure those two don't kill each other this summer?" he asked and pointed across the room at the two in question.

I laughed and just nodded because Riley walked over to us. We greeted him and shot the shit for a little bit until we all saw Rox storming off and TJ went to go chase after his twin. Benny and Rox living next door together this summer was certainly going to be interesting. I gave the six-foot-four winger a sad smile because he looked so defeated. I was one hundred percent sure that Benny was in love with TJ's sister, but he would never admit it. I had even tried to coax it out of him earlier today, but he denied it again. Poor guy, he always said the wrong things to her and it was why she hated him. Although, I think hate and love could be a fine line, because I saw the way her eyes grazed across his body too.

I laughed and made a comment about it to Riley, who didn't seem at all convinced. The girls joined us in the kitchen soon after, forcing the conversation dead. I pulled

Dinah into my side, wrapping my arm around her waist. God, it felt so perfect being here with her.

"You know it's weird to have a house warming party when you literally just walked all your shit over," Fi teased.

I shrugged. "House warming? I thought we were celebrating your book launches."

"Both, babe," Dinah insisted.

Riley laughed and looked between the two women. "I'm still uneasy about the two of you being all buddy-buddy."

"Well...good thing it's not about you!" his wife teased back at him.

I'm not sure what happened between Riley and Fiona after her and Dinah got blackout drunk together, but he didn't seem so melancholy anymore and the two of them practically beamed at each other. It was nice to see another one of my teammates happy and in love. Who would have thought it would have been Aaron Riley, though? The KING of casual hookups. I guess that meant TJ was the king now, but a part of me wondered if he was ready to not be that guy anymore.

Other than whatever the hell happened with Rox and Benny, the party went off without a hitch. Once we said goodbye to everyone, Dinah and I started cleaning up the condo, even though we were both exhausted and could wait until morning.

"I'm really proud of you," I told her while I started clearing away the empty beer bottles from off the kitchen island and into the bin.

"For what?" she asked, closing the dishwasher and walking away into our bedroom. She changed out of the dress she wore for the party, and slid into comfy pajamas. She took off her earrings and threw her hair up in a bun.

I slipped on a pair of sleeping pants and tidied up my

side of the bed that had a pile of dirty clothes strewn about on the floor. "I'm proud of you for publishing your book and working on the next one. You amaze me sometimes."

"Aw. And thanks for picking up those clothes."

I smiled at her, because I knew that had been bugging her, but she didn't say anything. She washed her face in the bathroom and then we brushed our teeth together, before slipping into our bed together. Yeah, it might have been really soon to move in together after only dating for a couple months after getting back together, but it just felt right. I know the old cliché, 'when you know, you know' was trite, but with Dinah I had to believe it was true. When I looked at her, my heart flipped over in my chest and did a little jig. I felt warm all over at the fact that I got to have that with her.

"So why did Rox throw a drink on Benny?" she asked me from beneath the covers.

I laughed and slung an arm over her, snuggling down into her neck. "Is that what she did? I didn't really see it. You know TJ asked me to make sure they don't kill each other this summer?"

"Oh, geez. I tried to introduce her to Matt tonight, but she didn't seem interested."

"Really?" I whispered onto her neck. "She tends to go for the nerdy guys."

"Hmm, I thought so too. Although, she has been with Lisa the whole time I've know her. Maybe she doesn't like men anymore."

"Um, false."

"What?"

I sighed. "That's not how bisexuality works. Plus, she was basically eye-fucking Benny earlier, and he was doing the same thing."

She busted up laughing. "Oh my god! Her and Benny are so going to bone aren't they?"

I laughed. "That's what I was telling Riley, but he didn't seem convinced."

She laughed with me and stroked her hand across the arm I had around her. "I don't know, I've read a lot of romance books to see a setup. I've always suspected something between those two."

"Me too!"

"You're such a gossip!"

"Maybe just a little bit," I agreed. "When book three's done is there going to be a book four?"

She didn't even flinch at the change of topic. "Not sure yet. I think I might try my hand at sci-fi or fantasy."

"Really?" I asked surprised.

She shifted in the bed so we were facing each other. "Yeah, Fi and I talked about challenging each other to write in the other's genre. It would be really great to write something different."

"I'm glad you and Fi have writing to bond over. I know you have your writing group, but you two seem close."

She smiled. "Yeah, I like her a lot. I'm glad her and Riley figured things out."

"Me too. I'm glad we did too."

She smiled and kissed me goodnight. I kissed her back and flicked off the light, happy that I finally took the shot on Dinah and it paid off. My season might be over, and we had a lot of work to do to train for next season, but I was happy in this bed that was now mine and with my girl at my side.

ACKNOWLEDGMENTS

Honestly, I never thought this book was going to be a real tangible thing. This book started as a NANOWRIMO challenge to myself just to see if I could write romance. Then the couple from book two muscled their way into making an appearance in this book. So I said to myself, "Okay, I'll try to write a second romance book and that would be it. This is just for fun." Then while vacationing in Canada, I got the idea for a third book in this series. Um, and then I wrote a fourth book and had an idea for a fifth one? So somehow I had a romance series on my hands. So it felt like maybe I should just really try my hand at this thing.

I love hockey and romance books, so what a perfect way to marry my two loves. To be fair, my YA contemporary WIPs are also about hockey, so maybe this wasn't a stretch for me. And I always thought about writing a romance book about one of the brothers' from that book. (SPOILER ALERT: He might show up later in this series.)

I have to thank my partner Jordan for supporting me always, even when he had no clue what the heck I was talking about. When I got drunk on my birthday and starting spouting that I should just self-publish these books, he was nothing if not really supportive. Even more so when I threw myself full-in to researching how to really go about self-publishing my books. Thanks for hugging me when I worried that everything I wrote was just a pile of garbage and listening to me vent when I was really unsure about things in my books. Especially telling me to just "continue to write and get better" when I expressed worry that maybe I am actually terrible at everything I do.

To Jim Kenyon for being my first BETA reader and being able to look me in the eye at work after reading all my sex scenes. Thanks for reading this story and telling me I don't suck. Also shout out to my friends Phil and Megan for being so supportive of this book, even though you haven't read it yet.

Thanks also goes out to anyone who was intrigued by this book and bought it. You the real MVP! I can't wait for you guys to read Riley and Fiona's story next!

SNEAK PREVIEW OF SCORE HER HEART

FIONA

I bit my nails nervously, and this time my maid of honor, Katie, didn't slap my hand away. For the fifteenth time, I fixed the veil on my head, but I still thought it was crooked. Deep in my bones, I knew something was off. As soon as I woke up this morning, I knew something was going to go wrong. That's not exactly the feeling you want on your wedding day. Especially when the groom was missing.

What the fuckety fuck!

"Did he answer?" Katie asked and studied the bouquet of flowers that I was gripping a little too tightly. Her white face was tinted red with frustration, and her brown hair was starting to come undone while she raked her fingers through it in agony.

I looked down at my phone still in my hand. When I unlocked it, I saw a text from my best and oldest friend, Riley.

RILEY: *Girlllll!!! I can't believe you're getting married today. Can't wait to see you tonight!*

A smile curled up on my lips. I was afraid he wasn't going to make it. I knew that my fiancé was hoping he couldn't, which was why he insisted on a wedding during hockey season. Let's just say Eric didn't exactly love my best friend or want the two of us to see each other all that much.

"Well?" Ellen, my bridesmaid and one of my other childhood friends, asked. With her tanned skin and perfect blond hair, I was kind of annoyed that she wasn't as frazzled looking as I knew I was right now.

I shook my head and put my phone down. My fiancé was late for our wedding, and I couldn't help but have a bad feeling about this. Like Han Solo flying into the Death Star bad feeling.

I only had two people in my bridal party. Well, three if you counted my mom, who was the matron of honor. Eric didn't even want to get married, and I never pushed it because I had been happy with him, but his mom kept pushing the topic. After his dad died, he had finally asked. He hadn't even done it very romantically. He turned to me one night, sighed, and asked, "Hey, should we just get married already?"

So charming.

I wanted a courthouse wedding, but neither of our moms' would go for that. Somehow, by the grace of the hockey gods, we had managed to keep this wedding small, but Eric had insisted we do it in Vegas. I had never been a Vegas person or interested in gambling, so we fought a lot about it. Since he was the one who asked me to marry him, I eventually gave in.

Honestly, I would have had a better time if we had just eloped in Vegas, but we were basically told we would have been shunned if we did that. I didn't really care for weddings; they were fine for other people, but not for me. I felt like it was a pageant for my parents, and I was honestly pissed about it. Especially since they complained about how expensive it was. Even though I told them we would rather pay for it ourselves, but Dad insisted. Irish men were so stubborn; I guess that's where I got it from.

I chewed on my bottom lip and turned at the sound of the door opening. My mom stood there in her wine-colored dress, her dirty blond hair pulled smartly into a chignon at the nape of her neck. I was hoping for good news, but her mouth was a thin line.

FUCK.

"Anything?" I asked but couldn't help hearing the slight hitch in my voice.

She shook her head sadly, her brow furrowing in a worried expression.

"FUCK!" I screamed out loud this time and tore the veil off my head, taking some of my copper-colored strands with it.

Mom narrowed her eyes at me. "Fiona Marie Gallagher! Language!"

I rolled my eyes but wanted to yell, "Fuck you, Mom, this is my wedding!" Yeah, that would have gone over well.

This was turning into a fucking disaster. Where the hell was Eric?

Katie tapped away on her phone. Katie was Eric's older sister, but we had grown close over the five years I had been with her brother. I was bad at making friends. Ellen was one of the only people besides Riley who still put up with me. Scratch that; I was good at making friends but bad at keeping relationships intact. I assumed everyone would eventually abandon me, so what was the point?

Why put in the work when everyone would disappoint you in the end?

"The guys brought him back to the hotel early last night. So it's not like he's passed out drunk somewhere," Katie commented, but worry was still etched across her pale face.

A stone dropped down into the pit of my stomach. This was really bad.

Ellen put a hand on my shoulder. "Hey, it's going to be okay. Maybe he slept through his alarm," she tried to reassure me, but she didn't sound convinced.

Somehow, I knew that we both knew that line was complete and utter bullshit. Eric *never* slept through anything.

I pulled out my phone and texted him again while Katie tried to call him for the tenth time.

ME: *WTF!!!*

ME: *Where are you?*

ME: *Mother fucker, I know you aren't passed out drunk somewhere.*

ME: *Answer me!*

I saw Katie repeatedly saying the word "okay" into her phone, but she wasn't looking at me. Almost like she was too embarrassed to look me in the eyes right now.

I looked back at my phone and saw the three dots indicating typing, then they disappeared and immediately came back up. Finally, I was getting an answer on what the actual fuck was going on.

ERIC: *I'm sorry.*

ERIC: *I can't do this. I don't want to get married. Can't we go back to the way things were?*

ME: *Are you FUCKING kidding me?*

ERIC: *I don't want to marry you.*

ME: *Go fuck yourself. Get your shit, and get out of my apartment.*

ERIC: *It's our apartment.*

ME: *And everything's in my name. Kindly go fuck yourself gently with a chainsaw.*

I wanted to hurl my phone at the wall, but instead, I hurled myself out of the room.

"Fiona, where are you going?" Mom shrieked after me.

"The fucking bar!" I yelled back and hitched up the skirt of my ridiculous dress. I couldn't even think of the fiasco this would cause for my parents. I didn't care; I needed a drink.

I parked myself in front of the hotel bar in a huff. The bartender blinked at me in surprise. He glanced over my shoulder and then back at me. "I think you're early?" he asked in confusion.

"It's off," I seethed. "Give me a whiskey."

His face fell, and he nodded before getting to work behind the bar. He put a glass of whiskey down in front of me. "On the house, Miss."

I shook my head. "Oh, no, don't pity me."

He pushed the glass closer to me. "I insist."

I cocked my head at him. He was kind of cute with his spiky blond hair and five o'clock shadow. *Maybe I should fuck him just to get back at Eric.* Maybe it was the fact that my sex life had been lacking in the past couple months that I was entertaining the idea of sleeping with a stranger. I took the drink and downed it in one fell swoop. I looked at my phone and saw more texts from Eric.

ERIC: *I was happy before, but I don't see why we had to get married.*

ERIC: *Marriage is stupid. We don't want kids.*

ERIC: *Fi, don't be this way. I know you don't want this wedding either.*

I frowned but noticed my drink had been refilled. The cute bartender winked at me, and I nodded my head at him in thanks.

The truth was we hadn't decided that we didn't want kids; Eric had decided that and never gave me the chance to really think about it. I had been fine with that because I had loved him, but the fact that he didn't want to go through with the wedding either meant he didn't love me. How could I expect him to be committed to me if he didn't show up on our wedding day? PLUS! Canceling all of this shit was going to cost a shit ton of money. I didn't even want to think about it. My dad was going to be livid if he wasn't already. I might need to get him a whole bottle of whiskey to apologize. Maybe even a freaking case.

I maddeningly typed out my response into my phone.

ME: *AGAIN, how about you go fuck yourself, you fucking asshat? I can't believe you did this to me. We are DONE. Have a good life, Eric!*

My phone was blowing up with texts from guests wondering what was going on, but the only one I looked at was Riley's.

ME: *Don't come.*

RILEY: *What's going on?*

ME: *Wedding's off. Don't come. I'm sorry, I know it was hard for you to get here with your hockey schedule.*

RILEY: *Where are you?*

ME: *Bar.*

I put my head in my hands and finished off my second glass of whiskey. I put my phone down and decided answering all those texts was not what I was going to do right now. When I pulled my hands away, my eyeliner was smudged on my hand, along with some wetness. Great, I was the crying bride left at the altar drinking alone at the bar.

Way to be a cliche, Fiona!

A glass of water and another whiskey was placed in front of me. "You want to start a tab?" the bartender asked me.

Before I could answer, a deep voice from behind me said, "Yeah, put it on my card."

I turned to take in Riley in all his glory. He looked great in a suit, his broad shoulders and thick biceps filling it out nicely. His blond hair was tousled in that 'I couldn't care less' style that really meant he spent a long time on it. I'd only seen him a few times this year; with his professional hockey career and my writing career, we were both traveling a lot and rarely in the same city. But damn, he looked good today, filling out that suit tailored specifically for him. I felt heat pool in my lower belly, but maybe it was just from all the whiskey. I definitely wasn't remembering all those times in high school when Riley's mouth had been on mine. Definitely not.

Riley slid onto the stool next to me and ordered a beer. When the bartender handed him the bottle, that's when he turned to me and pulled me into a big bear hug. Maybe that's all I needed because I relaxed into his strong arms, leaning my face against his hard chest. But then I started crying again. To his credit, Riley was a good sport who let me cry on his shoulder as he rubbed my back soothingly.

It felt like an eternity had passed before I pulled away. "I'm sorry," I offered.

He placed his hands gently on my cheeks and wiped my face with the pads of his calloused thumbs. "Don't apologize. That dickweed should be the one apologizing. Fi, I'm so sorry. You want me to fight him?"

I slunk out of his arms and took a sip of my drink. "It's not your fault. And on that last part...maybe."

He eyed me cautiously and took a sip of his beer. The way he was looking at me sent shivers down my spine. Here's the thing. Riley was kind of a player, which was fine; he could do what he wanted. But we also lost our virginity to each other in high school. Then proceeded to experiment with each other.

Okay, we were fuck buddies. So sue me, Riley was hot back then and even more so now. Seeing him here looking sexy AF in that suit had me thinking a little too much about all those times in my parent's basement. Fuck. I shouldn't have drunk so much whiskey in such a short time. Whiskey makes me horny.

And it was no secret that my best friend was the hottest man I had ever seen. EVER. Which might have explained why Eric didn't exactly like him.

"So what happened?" he asked.

I sighed and took a huge gulp of my drink. "He said he couldn't do it but wanted to go back to the way things were."

Riley narrowed his blue eyes at me. They flashed in anger, but I knew it wasn't aimed at me. "What the fuck?"

I raised my arms in triumph. "Thank you!"

"What a fucking asshole," he spat out. "This douche can't show up to your wedding but expects everything to go back to normal?"

I hung my head. "I can't even imagine all the cancellations we have to do now. My poor parents."

He ran a hand down his clean-shaven jaw as if he was thinking really hard about something. He had this weird look in his eye, and it made me feel uncomfortable. "Well...do you still want to get married?" he asked.

I nearly spat out my drink. "To who?"

He smirked that signature crooked grin that I'm sure melted all the girls' panties. Mine included, but that might have been the whiskey talking.

He pointed a finger at me and then to him. "It's Vegas, right? So let's get married."

"What?!?"

ALSO BY DANICA FLYNN

PHILADELPHIA BULLDOGS

Score Her Heart

ABOUT THE AUTHOR

Danica Flynn is a marketer by day, and a writer by nights and weekends. AKA she doesn't sleep! She is a rabid hockey fan of both The Philadelphia Flyers and the Metropolitan Riveters. When not writing, she can be found hanging with her partner, playing video games, and reading a ton of books. *Take The Shot* is her first novel.

CPSIA information can be obtained
at www.ICGtesting.com
Printed in the USA
BVHW090105100222
628126BV00007B/24